WITH THE WILDFLOWERS

a novel

MARIA RIGOU

AUTHOR'S NOTE

With the Wildflowers is an open door romance. This means that it has on-page sexual content between two consenting adults. There is use of profanity and explicit language throughout the story. Mature readers only. **Please read with care.**

———

Thank you so much for taking the time to read ***With the Wildflowers***. It means the world to me that you are here. If you love this book, please review wherever you are able to, and tell your friends! Nothing helps indie authors like me more than a review and a recommendation.

Happy reading!

To the ones who stayed still
long enough to bloom 🪶

1

MARTINA

Two things were abundantly clear at that precise moment: I didn't belong there, and Manuela was hiding something.

The fire crackled, a slow, steady burn that sent embers spiraling into the dark sky. Someone had tossed in dry pine needles, and the scent of charred wood and leaves mixed with the crisp mountain air, thick with the lingering humidity from the afternoon's storm, despite the cold temperatures. Tres Fuegos always smelled like this in the winter—damp earth, firewood, something crisp in the distance. The kind of scent that clung to your clothes, your skin, the spaces between your fingers.

It was the last bonfire of the winter, a tradition that this town held on to even when it was too cold to handle, and even as the crowds dwindled and less and less locals attended year over year. But it was a way to mark the shifting of the seasons, albeit spring was weeks away. The days would grow longer, the evenings warmer, and life would settle into its usual, quiet rhythm right before the start of the summer. And it always meant something was ending, whether or not anyone said it out loud.

I shifted on the worn log I'd claimed as a seat, the rough bark catching against the back of my legs and making me extra uncomfortable. This wasn't my scene at all; it was loud and rowdy and something I would normally shy away from, preferring instead to stay home curled up with a book or a movie. I was used to quiet evenings at the coffee shop—closing out after a busy day and walking the narrow path between the shop and the house where I lived with my mother. I liked to settle in for the evening before doing it all over again the next day. The rough squeak of the iron gate that separated the café from our house had become a sort of nightly ritual, especially as I started taking on more of the business's responsibilities alongside my mother after I finished college a few years ago. I was preparing to take over ownership from her—finally giving her a break after decades of owning it.

Next to me, Manuela Torres, one of my closest friends since I could remember, sat with her elbows propped on her knees, staring into the flames. She had been quiet all night. Too quiet. The kind of quiet that made my stomach twist with unease.

The light from the fire flickered over her face, catching in the strands of blonde hair that had slipped from the loose bun at the nape of her neck. Normally, Manuela was the loud one between us. The storyteller, the sharp-tongued commentator on everything happening around us. Tonight, she was still. So, so still.

I nudged her knee with mine. "Spill."

She blinked, her gaze pulling from the fire to meet mine. "*¿Qué?*"

"You've been acting weird all night. You're barely even pretending to listen when Emiliano tells his ridiculous stories." I gestured to the other side of the fire, where another one of the locals was holding court, weaving some elaborate tale that had the people around him laughing loudly. "That's your favorite pastime."

She huffed out a small laugh, but it didn't reach her eyes. "I'm listening."

"*Mentirosa.*" I searched her face, the tightness in my chest growing. "Manuela."

She exhaled sharply, dragging a hand through her hair. "I was going to wait until later to tell you."

A slow, creeping sense of dread settled in my stomach. "Tell me what?"

"You're going to be mad, but I didn't know how to say it..." She hesitated, then said, "I'm moving."

I furrowed my brows as the words settled between us, heavy and absolute. My fingers curled against the bark beneath them, grounding me in place. "Apartments? I didn't know you didn't like the place you were at."

Manuela swallowed. She wasn't looking at me anymore. "Not apartments," she said with a slow shake of her head.

She shifted in her seat again, crossing her legs and then uncrossing them.

Something cold slid through my whole body, limbs included. "Then where?"

She licked her lips, like she was bracing herself for impact. "New York."

The night seemed to shift around me. The fire, the voices, the music—all of it faded into the background, muffled and distant. "New York," I repeated, like if I said it aloud, it would make more sense.

She nodded quickly. "I got a job offer. A promotion, actually. Remember the sister agency I told you about that works with nonprofits? With that girl, Elle? I wasn't even looking, but they—" She shook her head, her eyes lighting up with something I couldn't name. "I couldn't say no."

Of course she couldn't. Who would say no to New York? I wouldn't. Even if I knew nothing about the city and my aspirations didn't even get me as far as the capital city of our own country. But I nodded nonetheless, even as a knot formed in my throat, because this marked another one of my loved ones that would be leaving me.

I forced my mouth into a shape that I hoped resembled a smile. "That's...amazing." The words felt foreign in my throat, like something I had borrowed from someone else.

Her eyes flicked to mine, searching. "You mean that?"

I nodded again, too quickly. "Yeah. I mean, it's New York, Manu." My voice almost sounded convincing. Almost. "That's huge."

She exhaled, a small relieved laugh escaping her lips. "I know, right? It still doesn't feel real."

It didn't feel real to me either, but for entirely different reasons. I looked past her, at the group of people congregated across the flames. The town's golden boy, Jacinto Williams, threw his head back, laughing at something Emiliano had just said. He had that easy, effortless way about him, the kind of presence that pulled people in without even trying. It didn't help that, in addition to that charming personality, he was the youngest son of one of the most well-regarded families in town.

A group had formed around him, and I could hear the cadence of his voice, warm and teasing, though I couldn't make out the words. It didn't matter. I knew the rhythm by heart.

Manuela tucked her hair behind her ear. "I wanted to tell you sooner, but... I don't know. I guess I was nervous about how you'd react."

I swallowed the lump in my throat, the fire burning my skin everywhere. "Why?"

She gave me a look, one that told me she saw right through my very bad acting. "Martu."

I dropped my gaze to my hands, my nails digging into my palms. I didn't want to talk about this. I didn't want to admit that her leaving felt like another door slamming shut, another confirmation that the world was moving forward and I was standing still. And even though this was supposed to be a private moment—just us two sitting at the edge of the clearing, the fire roaring between us and everyone else, all eyes and ears were probably on us. It was evident that people had stopped talking and were eavesdropping on this conversation, the murmurs halting to a zero. I could feel someone's gaze on me, a whisper to my right from the group of younger girls sitting across the fire, right by the side of the road.

"You'll visit," I said instead, my voice steadier than I felt. It was the easier thing to do, a fail-safe at a moment when everything felt like it was crashing down. "Right?"

She nodded, but there was hesitation in the way she did it. "*Obvio*. It's only a little bit farther than Buenos Aires. A few cars and buses and airplanes away."

The kind of answer that meant *probably not as much as we both think.*

I tried to hold on to the words anyway, like they were something solid, something I could press into my palm and keep with me.

"We both know my grandmother would never let me stay away for long," she said with a scoff and a smile. "The woman will probably get herself admitted to the hospital if it means I come running."

Jacinto and a few others erupted into laughter after what felt like hours of deadly silence, the sound carrying across the night air. The world was still spinning around me, same as always. But everything had shifted. And there was nothing I could do to stop it. He looked comfortable. At ease. Completely in his element, while my body was trying to crawl out of its skin, heat settling into every corner of it.

I watched as Jacinto adjusted his body, turning slightly, his eyes sweeping the crowd before landing—unmistakably—on me. It was only a second, maybe two, but my stomach tightened anyway. His green eyes were shining brighter than usual, that sneaky smirk that followed him around plastered on his face—like he was up to something and everyone was in on it, except for me.

"Elisa is looking at him like he hung the moon." Manuela's voice cut through my thoughts, low and amused, as if absolutely nothing had just happened. I was trying to recover from what felt like the most earth-shattering news, and she was chuckling at the group of young girls fluttering around Jacinto and his buddies. She nudged my foot with the toe of her shoe, her body stretched out now on the blanket next to me. "Think Carmen will finally get her wish?"

I forced a breath, trying to ground myself in the moment, in the shifting glow of the fire and the weight of her words settling like a stone in my chest. Elisa was perched on the edge of a log, all soft smiles and shy glances, tucking a strand of dark hair behind her ear every time Jacinto so much as looked in her direction.

"Doubt it," I murmured, taking a slow sip of my drink.

Manuela hummed, unconvinced. "She's relentless, though. You have to give Carmen that."

I didn't answer. His eyes flicked to me again—this time

longer, less fleeting. And instead of looking away, I met his gaze and held it, unsure why, only that it felt…steadying somehow. The air between us shifted, barely, but enough to make me straighten without realizing it. Somewhere behind us, the laughter dipped, just slightly, as if someone had paused to look.

My best friend sighed dramatically. "You two are exhausting."

I shot her a look. "Nothing is happening."

"Exactly my point." I let out a small laugh, but it faded quickly. She frowned slightly, her expression softening after a few seconds. "I know it feels like I'm leaving you behind."

"Am I that obvious?"

"You've never been good at hiding things from me."

I looked down at my hands, tracing the rough edge of my thumbnail. "I just didn't see this coming at all."

She sighed, leaning back on her hands. "I didn't either. But Martu, you know this doesn't change anything, right?"

I turned to look at her then, really look at her. She believed that. She truly did. And maybe, for a little while, it would be true. But I knew better. I knew how distance stretched and pulled people apart, how calls grew fewer, how visits became postponed indefinitely. I'd seen it happen over and over again—first with my father over a decade ago, then with all my friends from high school choosing the more exciting, larger city life. Going to Buenos Aires for college, finding freedom outside the confines of this town, and then picking that over this.

I didn't blame them, really. How could I?

But I nodded anyway. "Yeah. I know."

The fire cracked, sending another spark into the sky. I followed it up, watching until it flickered out. Manuela smiled at me, and I smiled back, because that was what I was supposed to do. It was a little bit what the town had taught us—to smile and nod, despite the fact that we were in disagreement with what was being said or done.

I felt like that was partially the reason I ended up with the big, fat label that followed me around: just the coffee shop girl.

"Mirandaaaaaaaaaaaa." Jacinto's voice broke through the haze of my thoughts before I even saw him approaching. The shift in the air around me was almost tangible, a pull I felt before I turned my head. He was standing just a few feet away now, hands shoved into the pockets of his jeans, the glow of the fire outlining the sharp planes of his handsome face. His eyes flicked between me and Manuela, assessing, catching something unspoken between us as he walked in my direction, lowering his big body right next to mine.

"*¿Todo bien?*" he asked, his voice quieter now, just for me. Jacinto rifled through the cooler by the large tree, fishing a clear bottle from the melted ice.

I hesitated, fingers tightening around the log, the bark really pressing into my skin now. Was I? I wasn't sure what good even meant. But I knew how to deflect, how to give Jacinto the customer service *just-a-coffee-shop-girl* version of me that everyone in this town expected. I swallowed hard and forced a small smile. "Yeah. Just tired. And I should probably get going. I open tomorrow."

Jacinto didn't move, didn't look convinced. He lingered there, watching me in a way that made my stomach tighten, sifting through my answer for something real. I looked away first, and Manuela hummed in that infuriating way of hers.

"I'm going to go," my best friend announced as she stood, looking between Jacinto and me. "I should probably hurry to let my grandmother know about this whole New York thing before it gets to her before I get to it." I widened my eyes, and she shook her head in response. "I know, I know."

"I'll see you tomorrow?" I asked, hoping my innocent question would magically make the tension disappear.

"*Obvio*," she said again with a flick of her hand, then blew a kiss in our direction. "First thing, *amiga*."

She turned and melted into the crowd before I even had a chance to respond, swallowed by the persistent hum of conversation and bursts of laughter echoing from the other side of the fire. I watched her go, the warmth of her presence lingering for a moment before the cold night settled around me again—louder now, somehow blurrier.

"Miranda," Jacinto said again, with a hoarse voice that brought me back to the present. His voice was easy, familiar, like we hadn't spent the last few hours orbiting each other with careful distance. And that tone, it was almost a question, an *are you okay* buried under the surface somewhere and it was only a matter of reading between the lines. As if he knew, by just looking, that this was the beginning of the end for me, that something was shifting.

I turned my head in his direction, a small smile on my lips. I didn't remember when he started calling me everything but my actual name, but I didn't really hate it. "How many times do I have to tell you that's not my name?"

He smirked, titling his water bottle toward me like a toast before taking the last sip. "Need a ride?"

I looked around the bonfire for Valentina Martín, another one of my oldest friends, since we'd walked up the path and to the clearing together, but I couldn't find her among the growing crowd. "Are you offering or just being polite?"

That bright, devastating grin formed on his lips, perfectly straight teeth shining bright. "Would it kill you to think I might actually want to drive you home?"

I rolled my eyes but stood anyway, brushing a few pine needles from my jeans. "Fine. But we're not stopping for *empanadas.*"

"Not even if I ask really nicely?"

I shot him a look, and he just laughed, draping his arm around my shoulder and tucking me forcefully against his warm body. He dragged me around the fire, stopping every few seconds while we said goodbye to every single person in attendance. It made the departure process stretch for what seemed like hours, and the whole time, his arm was wrapped around me comfortably, like everything was going to be okay.

2

JACINTO

Martina hadn't said much since we left the bonfire, and I hadn't pushed. But I definitely felt the weight of her silence. It stretched between us, thick and heavy, like the air before one of our random winter storms, those that showed up unannounced and surprised everyone. We walked to my car, parked a few blocks down the mountain from the clearing where we had this annual town event.

I glanced at her out of the corner of my eye. There was something distant about her expression, like she was somewhere else entirely.

"What happened?"

"I don't want to talk about it," she replied instantly. She kept her gaze ahead, her arms crossed tightly over her chest. "At least not right now."

"Okay," I said slowly, focusing on how she kicked a loose

stone in the dirt path beneath our shoes and followed it with her eyes.

"She's my best friend."

"That's not what I asked."

She let out a sharp breath. "She's just… I know it's not personal, but it feels personal, you know?"

I did know. More than I cared to admit. But I wasn't about to make this about me.

I hummed in response, letting the silence between us settle again. The creek was close enough that I could hear the slow, steady current lapping at the shore, the sound mixing with the faint rustling of the wind through the trees.

"She'll visit," I said after a moment.

Manuela hadn't come out and said it directly to me, but I'd overheard fractions of their conversation by the fire earlier. And it was enough for me to see Martina's reaction to recognize what was happening.

Martina let out a short, humorless laugh. "That's what she said."

I stopped walking, just enough to make her do the same. When she turned to face me, I could see it clear now—the way her brows were drawn, the tightness at the corners of her mouth. She was bracing herself. Preparing for something inevitable.

"And you don't believe her," I said.

She hesitated. "Not really."

I studied her face, the flicker of doubt in her eyes, the way she held herself a little too still, like if she moved too much, she might break apart. And she had been this way since high school—she'd been good at pretending. But I'd learned, somewhere between high school and moving back to Tres Fuegos after law school, how to read the tilt of her shoulders. The way she looked up through her eyelashes, eyes focused on mine.

I opened the passenger door for her, but she didn't get in right away. Instead, she turned back toward me, the glow of the bonfire we left behind still catching faintly in the distance.

For a second, I thought she might yell at me, vent at the top of her lungs, tell me exactly how she felt in this exact moment. But she didn't. She nodded, swallowed hard, and climbed into my tiny yellow car, like her ever calm, cautious self.

I shut the door behind her, exhaling as I rounded the front of the vehicle and slid into the driver's seat. As I started the engine, I felt it again—the heaviness, that pull.

The short drive back to town was quiet, but not the easy kind of quiet. Not the kind where you let the silence fill the space because it was comfortable. This silence was thick. The kind that sat between two people like a third presence in the car.

Martina leaned her head against the window, her fingers absently toying with the hem of her shirt. I knew she wasn't asleep. She was thinking. Running something over and over in her mind, turning it inside out the way she did when she didn't have an answer she liked.

I knew the feeling.

I drummed my fingers against the steering wheel, eyes flicking between the road and her reflection in the glass. "You want to talk about it?"

She huffed out a quiet breath. "What's there to talk about?"

"You, standing at the bonfire looking like someone just took the ground out from under you," I said easily, keeping my voice light. "That seems like something worth talking about."

She let out a dry laugh, shaking her head. "You know what, Gato," she said matter-of-factly, using the nickname I'd had since middle school. "It's not just Manuela leaving. It's—" She hesitated, biting down on her bottom lip before exhaling sharply. "It's me. I'm just here. Doing the same thing. Watching everyone else move forward while I…"

She trailed off, staring out the windshield. I filled in the rest of the sentence in my head. *While I stay stuck.*

Something about the way she said it, about the way her voice had cracked just a little on the last few words, sent a strange, uneasy feeling through me. I gripped the wheel tighter. I knew what that felt like. But the difference was, I'd chosen it. I chose to come back to this small town. To work at my family's law firm with a shiny new law degree. To only commit to the things I knew I wouldn't run from.

Because running? Changing directions? I was excellent at that.

Hell, even in high school, I'd never finished a single side

project I started. Not the plan to start a garden behind my parents' house, not the volunteer reading nights at the library that eventually Charlie had to take over.

That last one… That one still stung.

Because I had promised Martina we would do it together. She had shown up with a pile of books and a hopeful expression, like she believed I'd actually follow through. When I didn't? She never brought it up again. She just looked at me slightly differently after that. Less bright-eyed. More… measured.

I never stopped thinking about it.

I cleared my throat, forcing something lighter into my voice. "Maybe it's not about being stuck. Maybe you're just… waiting?"

She turned her head slightly, watching me. "For what?"

I shrugged. "Something that makes everything worth it."

She scoffed, but there was something tired in the sound. "And if it never comes? I'll just die being the coffee shop girl."

I didn't have an answer for that. Because I hadn't found mine yet either.

The dark sign of the café came into view, the long branches of the old trees partially covering it. I kept driving, heading for my house instead. "I'll park at my house and I can walk you back."

"Okay," she whispered, leaning her head against the window again.

I pulled up in front of my small home, an unassuming white building that sat just barely on the edge of town, in a straight line from the pharmacy. It was close enough for me to walk everywhere and be at the center of the town's activity, but secluded enough that I could hide inside from time to time. Martina reached for the door handle but paused, her fingers resting against the metal.

She didn't look at me when she asked, "Do you ever feel like you're just waiting for something that's never going to happen?"

Something lodged itself in my throat. I swallowed around it. "All the time."

She turned then, her eyes meeting mine in the dim light of the dashboard. Whatever she was looking for, I wasn't sure if she found it. But after a long moment, she nodded once, pulled the door open, and stepped out into the night.

I watched her get out of the car, her shoulders curled slightly inward to protect her from the cold night. She didn't move and instead waited for me to get out and meet her on the sidewalk.

Martina looked tired. And not the kind of tired that would resolve with a good night's sleep, but instead something that lived in her bones.

"Martina." She turned, eyes catching the glow of the porch light across the small front yard. She didn't say anything, but I moved nonetheless, heading in the direction of my front door. "Come in for a bit," I said. "I have those lemon square things you like."

"How dare you?" she said with a gasp, and finally, a small smile formed on her lips. Martina looked back towards the town square and across from it, where her house and the café sat, and then at me again. Something passed through her face—a quiet acknowledgement or acceptance that she wasn't ready to go home. "You dick. You waited this long to tell me?"

Then she nodded and started walking towards me, her expression softening, the hint of a sly smile playing on her lips, as if the mere mention of the dessert I only baked occasionally and just for her had tipped the night in a new direction.

I unlocked my door and stepped aside to let her in. Martina paused at the threshold, like she was still deciding. But then she crossed into the hallway, and I closed the door behind her, the snick echoing in my bare-bones entryway. And the air shifted again.

3

JACINTO

Inside, the house was dim. I didn't bother with the overheads—just flicked on the old lamp in the corner that bathed the living room in soft, gold light. The fan above creaked faintly. My mom used to call it charming.

Somewhere, Beto got down from whatever surface he was lounging on, jumping to the floor with a loud *thud* and meowing faintly to remind me that he was still around.

Martina walked in slowly, fingers brushing the frame of the doorway between the living room and the hallway as she passed through it. She looked small in the space, even though we were almost the same height. She looked like she didn't know where to put herself, despite the fact that she'd been here hundreds of times before.

"I'll get you those lemon squares," I said, following Beto into the kitchen. He purred as he led the way directly to his food and water bowls and stared back at me with the most impatient look.

Martina sank onto the couch, tucking her long legs under her like she usually did. I returned with a piece of the dessert on a small plate, and she took it without a word. Beto, meanwhile, was still staring at me from his spot in the kitchen, right beside the door that led to my messy backyard.

She took a bite, then another one, before silently placing the plate on the coffee table.

"I don't want to go home yet," she said, eyes focused on the wall in front of her. The TV had been on all day, the sound muted but figures moving on the screen. I liked to leave it on for Beto, so he wouldn't get bored at home while I was gone.

"Then don't."

She looked up at me like she was still trying to gauge if I meant it. Her face—god, her face—looked wrecked. Not messy, not dramatic. Just exhausted.

"I'm tired of this, Gato." Her voice cracked on the last word. "I don't want to be alone tonight."

I sat beside her. Not too close at first. Just enough that I could feel the warmth of her shape next to me. I reached for her hand, slow and steady, and she let me. It was an automatic movement. We'd touched before, a lot. But this felt different, a little bit more intentional.

"You're not alone."

Her fingers curled around mine. She leaned into me like

her body was just waiting for permission. Forehead against my shoulder. Warm. Real.

I turned slightly and looked down at her. She looked up with a broken smile and her eyes searching for answers that I didn't have.

And then, I kissed her.

I was soft at first, like a question. But she answered by moving closer, her hand sliding up to my neck and pulling me deeper. The kind of kiss that hit every nerve I'd tried to ignore for years.

Her mouth parted under mine, and the second kiss wasn't soft at all. It was heat and tension, and something years in the making. Her hands slipped beneath the hem of my t-shirt like she knew exactly what she was doing—and she probably did. Martina didn't half-ass anything, not even this.

"Wait," I said against her mouth, pulling back a little, breathless. "Are we—?"

"Yes," she said, tugging at my shirt again, "unless you're going to make it weird."

I huffed a laugh, but my heart was hammering. "Me? You're the one undressing me in front of my cat."

"Beto's seen worse, I'm sure," she muttered, already yanking my shirt off. She tossed it somewhere behind the couch with alarming accuracy.

She leaned in again, kissed me harder this time, like this was a need she hadn't been allowed to admit until right now. And maybe it was. Maybe that was why it felt like we

were tipping over the edge of something without even realizing we'd been standing at the cliff.

I let my hands find the edge of her sweater, and she
raised her arms without hesitation. Off it went. She was
wearing a simple black bra underneath, nothing fancy or
planned. It made it hotter. Real.

Her legs were still tucked under her, but she shifted now,
swinging one over my lap so she was straddling me. Her
thighs pressed against my hips, and I let out a breath I didn't
know I'd been holding.

"Jesus, Martu."

"I told you," she whispered against my jaw. "I don't
want to be alone tonight."

She kissed me again before I could say anything else,
and whatever thoughts or doubts I'd had vanished. Her hips
rolled once against my erection, and I made a noise that
would absolutely get me roasted if any of my brothers ever
heard it.

I gripped her waist, trying to hold us still just long
enough to catch up to whatever the hell was happening. But
then her hands were in my hair and her mouth was on my
neck, and yeah, I gave up.

"You're driving," I muttered as she nipped at my
collarbone.

She pulled back just long enough to give me one of her
looks, almost like she was trying hard not to roll her eyes.
"What? Where are we going?"

I chuckled and licked up the column of her neck,

speaking against the soft skin. "You're very much in charge right now."

She grinned, and it was the first real smile I'd seen on her all night. "You're not complaining."

"*Ni un poquito.*" Not even a little.

She kissed me again, deeper this time, and I got my hands on her hips, thumbs brushing the softness right above the waistband of her jeans. Her skin was warm and familiar in a way that made my chest hurt a little. Her breath hitched when I slid the pants lower, and she reached down to help. Somehow we got tangled trying to get them off, and she nearly elbowed me in the face in the process.

"Okay, okay—wait—*tu rodilla*—ow." I laughed, grabbing her wrist.

"Stop moving," she said, breathless and laughing, too.

"You're the one crawling on me like I'm a jungle gym!"

She finally kicked her jeans free, and then we were both just... there. Skin to skin. The TV flickered behind her, casting faint light across the room. Her hair was falling into her face, and she looked down at me like she was trying to figure out how this wasn't a dream.

"You sure?" I asked again, one last time. This was definitely crossing the line of our friendship.

Her eyes locked on mine, clear and focused. "I've never been more sure of anything."

And just like that, we fell into each other.

It wasn't slow. It wasn't planned. It was heat and hands and breathless laughter, and her teeth grazing my shoulder as she tried not to make a sound when I hit just the right spot. Her nails dug into my back. I pulled her closer. There was no space left between us—physically or otherwise.

We moved together like we'd done this a hundred times. Like our bodies already knew what to do, what we needed. She kissed me hard, anchoring herself with my body. I couldn't tell where one of us ended and the other began. At some point, my jeans came partially off, and I sat on my couch in my boxer briefs, hard and waiting for more.

Her bra followed. Her hands guided mine to the clasp behind her back, and the second it hit the floor, I lost all coherent thought. She was soft everywhere, flushed and breathless, her skin warm under my hands. Her bare chest pressed against mine as she rolled her hips again over me, her pussy wet and hot and—

"Shit, Martu," I groaned. "You're—"

"Don't say wet," she whispered into my ear, voice shaky. "I will absolutely cringe."

I laughed, breathless, my hips moving involuntarily. "Noted."

I slid my hands down her thighs, gripping her tighter as she lifted just enough to give me space. We were messy and eager, and so far past the point of no return. I reached down between us to move her underwear to the side, just barely, my other hand holding on to her hip like I needed her to know I wasn't going anywhere.

And then—

A loud bang shattered the moment.

The back door slammed shut.

Hard.

We both froze.

Martina's breath caught mid-movement. Her body stiffened, her eyes wide as they flew to the sound behind her.

"What the hell was that?" she whispered, barely above a breath.

"Wind," I said quickly, automatically, though my heart had leapt into my throat. "The breeze sometimes pushes the back door if it's not properly latched. Happens all the time because Beto uses it to come in and out while I'm at work."

She blinked at me, her whole body suddenly still. Her hands were on my chest now, but not in the same way. Not hungry. Bracing. Like she was grounding herself.

"Shit," she whispered, eyes everywhere but on me.

"Hey." I reached for her face, but she was already shifting, already climbing off my lap. The sudden loss of her warmth made the whole room feel colder.

"I-I shouldn't have— I need a second," she said, gathering her clothes from the floor with shaking hands.

"Martina," I said, sitting up, trying to keep my voice calm. "You don't have to go."

"I'm not—I'm not going," she said too quickly. "I just— This wasn't supposed to happen."

I nodded slowly, heart still racing for entirely different reasons now. "Okay. Take your time."

She disappeared down the hallway without another word.

And I sat there, half-naked on my own couch, trying to ignore the way my hands were still trembling.

Trying not to think about how fast everything had just changed.

Trying not to wonder if I'd just ruined the one thing that I'd ever felt like I could stick to.

4

MARTINA

MY MOTHER's coffee shop always smelled like fresh bread and coffee first thing in the morning, the scent thick and familiar, curling into the air even before I opened the door to help her out for the morning rush. It was a scent I had grown up with, a scent that clung to me like a second skin. I could recognize it even if I were walking blocks away with my eyes closed. Some people associated their home with certain sounds or sights—mine was the smell of espresso and freshly baked *facturas*.

I moved through my routine automatically, unlocking the front door, flipping the sign to open, wiping down the already clean counters. My mother had done the setup earlier, leaving me to sleep in for a few extra hours while she prepped in silence, just like she preferred. The flow was familiar, muscle memory after more than a decade of working here. The café was small and cozy in a way that felt intentional rather than cramped, with wooden tables that had been worn smooth by thousands of elbows leaning against them, conversations unfolding over plates of pastries and a never-ending supply of coffee and tea.

The first customers trickled in slowly. Regulars, mostly. People who would normally stop by for a to-go cup before heading to their office jobs in the larger town nearby were still here in their casual clothes, enjoying the extra-long weekend. Older women settled into their favorite seats with small plates of *medialunas*, and the community center director and her wife sat at the counter flipping through an old magazine and commenting on the very outdated celebrity gossip. I moved between them with practiced ease, exchanging greetings, filling cups, offering the same polite, practiced smiles I had been giving for years.

But something felt off.

It wasn't the café itself—everything looked the same. The morning light filtered in through the wide windows, casting long golden streaks over the terrazzo floor, the three stools at the counter still wobbled if you didn't know how to sit on them just right, and the ceiling fan still groaned every third rotation, a sound I had long since learned to tune out.

But the air felt different. Heavy in a way that had been following me all morning, ever since I left Jacinto's house in a panic in the early hours after whatever had happened on his living room couch.

Then Emiliano smirked at me over the rim of his *café con leche* from his seat by the front window and said, "Didn't think you'd be working today."

I nearly dropped the tray of dirty dishes I had been carrying.

"Excuse me?" I managed, recovering just in time to slide the tray onto the display case for my mother to load into one of the dishwashers. "Why wouldn't I be?"

Jacinto's friend chuckled, dipping a piece of his *vigilante* into his coffee. Emiliano was one of those locals who had gone to high school with us, but he was never really my friend. Instead, we remained *friendly* and saw each other around town, mostly during shared social events. "Don't play coy," he said with an intimacy that was not what we shared. I would say we were acquaintances, friend-adjacent during the best of times.

"Everyone's talking about it." He took a slow sip, food still in his mouth, and watched me intently over the rim of his cup. "You and Gato, finally making it official."

The words landed with a dull thud in my chest, confusing and too sharp at the same time. I blinked at him. "*¿Qué?*"

Emiliano just shrugged, like I was the one being ridiculous. "Carmen was saying so this morning. Gladys confirmed it. Both of them seemed pretty convinced. Said it was about time, too. And you know how this town is once it decides something."

I stared, my fingers curling against the counter. He wasn't wrong. Tres Fuegos ran on stories, the kind that sparked from nothing and spread like fire on a dried-up wildflower field. One glance, one moment out of context, and suddenly it was fact. It didn't matter if it was true. It only mattered that people believed it.

That was why Manuela had practically sprinted out of the bonfire last night—because she knew that once a rumor started, whether it was true or not, it had a life of its own. It didn't matter what anyone said after the fact.

A strange, slow heat crawled up my spine. "I have no idea what you're talking about." I swallowed, pressing my hands flat against the counter. "And besides, Carmen and Gladys say a lot of things. Doesn't mean they are true."

Through the years, there had been a number of rumors that had me as their protagonist and they never really stuck. This would fade, right? It was a slight lapse in judgement on both of our parts that meant nothing, so there really were no grounds for it to stand...

"Mm," Emiliano hummed, unconvinced, and returned to dunking his pastry violently into his coffee.

"I think you need stronger coffee. You might still be a little drunk after last night."

The morning rush started to pick up, but I barely heard the usual chatter of customers, the hiss of the espresso machine, the clinking of cups against saucers. My mind was stuck on Emiliano's words, the way he'd said them so casually, like he was just confirming something so obvious to him and not spreading something completely ridiculous. And that was the worst part—not that it wasn't true and that the town was running with it. But that it almost could've been. That they'd look at me and think, *Of course she'd be the one pining after him all this time.*

I worked on autopilot, making elaborate coffee drinks, wiping down the counter, passing out pastries, until I heard my name spoken a little too loudly from across the room.

"Martina, *querida*," a voice called, honey-sweet and knowing.

I turned, barely suppressing my sigh as Estela, one of the older women who had been coming to the café for as long as I could remember, waved me over. She sat with her usual group of friends, a plate of barely touched pastries in front of them, their coffee cups refilled more times than I could count.

I grabbed the coffee pot and forced a smile as I approached. "*¿Necesitan más café?*"

"*No, gracias, mi amor,*" Estela said, waving a hand. "We were just talking about you."

That was never a good sign.

"Is that so?" I kept my voice neutral, but my pulse was already kicking up a notch.

The woman next to her, Delia, leaned in conspiratorially. "We were saying how glad we are that you and Jacinto finally stopped dancing around each other."

My stomach clenched. "Excuse me?"

Before Estela could respond, the front door chimed. Manuela walked in, sunglasses perched on her nose, her hair still damp from a shower, looking like she hadn't had nearly enough sleep. She scanned the café, her gaze landing on me immediately.

"Martu," she said, voice heavy with amusement. "What the fuck is happening right now?"

I exhaled sharply, setting the coffee pot down with a little more force than necessary. "*Por el amor de—*"

My traitor best friend smirked, pulling off her sunglasses and sliding into a seat at the counter. "Did you really think I wouldn't hear about this before I even had my first cup of coffee?"

Estela beamed at Manuela from her seat a few feet away, clearly thrilled at her arrival. "*¿Ves?* Even your best friend agrees. It was only a matter of time. You've been following him around for years, and it was about time he noticed our sweet coffee shop girl."

The words hit like a slap—loud, careless, and cruel in the way that this small town's gossip could be. My throat tightened, the burn behind my eyes arriving too fast to blink away. And Manuela saw it, her body tightening at those harsh words uttered by someone who spent way too much time minding other people's business.

My fingers clenched around the counter again, trembling slightly. I had to bite the inside of my cheek to ground myself.

Sweet coffee shop girl.

Like that was all I'd ever be.

Like being seen by Jacinto was some kind of reward after years of pitiful pining.

I turned sharply, keeping my face neutral, because if I didn't, I'd cry. Or scream. Or say something I couldn't take back.

I shot Manuela a look, but she just gave me an apologetic little smile, tearing open a sugar pack with careful fingers as she waited for her coffee. "I don't make the rules, *amiga*," she said gently, like she knew the comment stung more than I was letting on. "But you know this town. Give them the smallest breadcrumb and they'll spin a love story out of it."

I groaned, pressing my fingers to my temple while I made her coffee with my free hand. "What are you talking about? Everyone's been acting so weird all day, and I just don't understand. Emiliano said something about Carmen and Gladys confirming that Jacinto and I are together," I whisper-hissed in her direction.

I set the cup in front of her, and she adjusted it slowly, looking up at me with something between curiosity and concern.

"Mmm," she said as she stirred her coffee in slow motion. "What happened last night?"

"Nothing at all," I replied too quickly, and my best friend's smile widened, just a little. "You were there last night! Just tell me what's happening."

That made Manuela stop in her tracks. She set her spoon down, placed both palms flat on the counter, and leaned toward me like she was bracing for something serious. "What do you mean you don't know?"

I didn't answer. I just grabbed a rag and furiously wiped down the counter, trying to drown out the sound of Estela and Delia giggling like schoolgirls, as if they had just successfully orchestrated a soap opera plotline.

"Manu, you were there last night. There's absolutely nothing going on between us," I said, but even I could hear how flat it sounded. She could, too.

Her eyes softened. "Martu…"

"Yes, I left his house at the crack of dawn," I muttered. "But I've stayed late at his place before. It's not new. Nothing about that is new."

She was quiet for a second, her expression shifting from amused to something gentler. "But something is new," she said. "Because you're spiraling. And because you never lie well, especially not to yourself."

I winced. She wasn't wrong.

"Ay, *amiga.*" She sighed again, but it wasn't dramatic this time, it was fond. She leaned in a little closer, voice low. "You do know you're going to have to deal with this, right?"

I sighed, resisting the urge to drop my head onto the counter. "No shit."

She reached across the counter and squeezed my hand once, like a lifeline. "So, what's the plan?"

I pulled off my apron and tossed it onto the counter with a sigh. "I'm going to find Jacinto. *Mamá, ya vuelvo.*"

Manuela's smile returned, small and knowing. "Good. Tell him I say hi. And be nice. I'll keep your mom company."

I didn't look back as I walked out the door, but I could hear her chuckling softly behind me. Not mocking, just there. Like she always had been.

5

JACINTO

The walk to my parents' home from the small house I rented was often short, but today it felt longer than usual. The lingering gazes in the town square really confused me. I had slept like shit, tossing and turning all night thinking about Martina.

The sounds she made, the way her skin felt under my fingertips, what she tasted like.

Then a few cryptic text messages from my youngest cousin and Santiago, one of my older brothers, had me scratching my head.

Tres Fuegos was the kind of town where news traveled too fast, too easily. Every block held a new conversation, every open window another chance to overhear something you weren't supposed to. I usually didn't mind it. Hell, sometimes I loved it—being part of the noise, knowing I could walk into any store or restaurant and find someone I knew.

But today? Today I felt the town's eyes on me.

A woman outside the bakery, one of my mother's friends, watched me walk past, her lips quirking up like she had something to say. I nodded politely, keeping my stride even. An older man sitting on the plaza bench raised an eyebrow as I passed. I caught the tail end of his muttered conversation.

"—finally happened."

I pretended not to hear.

At the corner of my parents' street, a group of teenagers outside the greengrocer broke into hushed whispers. One of them, probably in high school, elbowed her friend before giving me a look.

I knew that look.

It was the same look people had given me my whole life whenever they had already decided something about me. Probably along the lines of how my attention drifted way too often, how I fluttered around from thing to thing without committing to anything seriously. Maybe something about how I had my job because my family owned a law firm, and I was just...*there*.

I clenched my jaw and kept walking towards my parents' house, the large, familiar structure getting closer with each step.

There were a few cars parked in the driveway, as expected on a weekend and especially so during the winter months, when things to do were few and far between. This house had always been the town's safe space, and people came and went almost as they pleased.

The kitchen was as familiar as breathing. My father sat at the table with the day's newspaper raised in front of him. The headlines were meaningless. The real news—the real stories—lived in town gossip. Which was why my much younger cousin, Ramiro, was practically vibrating with excitement.

Charlie, my oldest brother, sat across from him, more focused on his phone than anything else. He barely glanced up as I walked in, but the little snort he let out told me everything I needed to know.

I grabbed a mug from the counter and made myself some coffee, moving intentionally slow to avoid whatever Ramiro was doing from his lazy perch at the kitchen table, watching me like a cat ready to pounce.

"You and Martina?" he finally asked, stretching out the words like he was savoring them.

I sipped my coffee. Held his stare and said nothing.

Charlie let out a low laugh. "Should've seen this coming."

I finally set my mug down on the counter. "Okay. Someone tell me why the whole damn town has lost its mind overnight."

I felt a slight blush creep up my chest and neck, to the tips of my ears. Because how could it have gotten out?

Ramiro grinned. *"Ay, por favor."* He leaned forward, elbows on the table. "You really don't know?"

"Enlighten me, *te lo ruego*."

He was thrilled to do exactly that, rubbing his palms together like a villain in a movie finally executing his evil plot. "Word on the street is that you and Martina are finally official."

I blinked. "What are you talking about? We are not official. We're just friends."

Ramiro raised an eyebrow, his green eyes, so similar to mine, glinting in amusement. "That's not what everyone's saying."

My mother, who had remained blissfully uninvolved until now, turned from the kitchen island with a cheerful expression. "Jacin, I don't know why you are acting so surprised."

I looked at her, betrayed. "*¿Vos también?*"

She shrugged. "People have been waiting for this since you were teenagers. What did you expect?"

Charlie made a quiet noise of agreement around a mouthful of toast. I pointed at him. "Not helping."

He didn't even look up, his eyes glued to something that looked a lot like a legal paper on his phone. "Not trying to."

Ramiro, meanwhile, was fully enjoying himself. "It all started at the bonfire," he explained with a somber tone in his voice, as if he were either recounting old town lore or a scary story. There was no telling with him. "Someone saw you two looking cozy."

"Oh my god." I dragged a hand down my face. "I hate this town. And you weren't even allowed to be there, on account of the fact that you are, in fact, a child."

Charlie finally looked up, something akin to a smirk plastered on his normally serious face. "At least now we don't have to see Carmen trying to set you up with every single one of her granddaughters."

Ramiro burst out laughing, delighted. "You're right! Maybe now she'll give it a rest. Though... does this mean you're going to have to break it to Elisa gently?"

I groaned, rubbing my temples. "You're all ridiculous."

My father finally lowered his newspaper just enough to raise an eyebrow at me. Then, as if he hadn't been listening the whole time, said, "Are you going to the picnic together?"

I blinked. "What?"

He turned a page like this was just casual conversation, just a regular Saturday morning at the Williams' household. "The community picnic, next week. Gladys says the town is looking forward to seeing you two there. Together."

I stared. Ramiro beamed. My mother didn't deny it.

Charlie, the traitor, took another bite of toast and muttered, "You're screwed."

I sighed, leaning against the counter, gripping my coffee mug a little too tightly. "This is insane. It's not even like that."

My mother gave me a pointed look. "And yet, you're reacting like it is."

I opened my mouth to argue, but the words didn't come. Because maybe she wasn't entirely wrong.

I let out a slow breath, running a hand through my hair. The weight of it settled differently now. Maybe because Martina's words from last night still sat somewhere in my chest, despite what happened after. *Watching everyone move forward while I stay stuck.*

I set my coffee down carefully. "Did Granny hear?"

My mother shrugged, feigning innocence. "Why don't you ask her yourself?"

That meant yes, in Williams family speak.

I groaned again, standing up from the counter. "I need to go."

Ramiro grinned wider. "Going to see your *novia*?"

I flicked the back of his head on the way out.

"Hey!"

"Mind your business. It doesn't look pretty to be such a gossip, you know?"

He was still laughing as I stepped outside, slamming the large, heavy door behind me. The air out here was no better —it clung to my skin just as tightly as the tension I'd walked out of. Because no matter how many times I told myself we were just friends, no matter how many years I'd kept that line in place...

That line wasn't there anymore.

It had snapped last night, quietly and completely.

I told myself it was just the moment. That she needed

comfort, that I needed clarity. But now? Now everything felt tangled in a way I couldn't ignore.

As I walked away from the house, my mother's words echoed in my mind. *People have been waiting for this since you were teenagers.*

Had they?

Had I?

I exhaled sharply, rubbing a hand down my face. It wasn't that I had never thought about Martina that way—it was that I had. Over and over again. And I'd always known better than to let it mean anything.

Until now.

And now, thanks to Tres Fuegos and its insatiable need for a love story, half the town had already decided what came next.

And worse? I wasn't sure if I wanted to stop it.

6

My feet hit the sidewalk harder than necessary, each step punctuated by the dull echo of my frustration. The sun hung high in the sky now, the weight of the morning burning off, but the heaviness in my chest hadn't lifted. If anything, it had settled deeper, pressing down with each murmur and knowing glance thrown in my direction as I made my way toward Jacinto's house.

I hadn't even hesitated. The second I had torn off my apron at the café, I knew exactly where I was going. And exactly what I was going to say.

The problem was, I had no idea if he would actually listen. Not because Jacinto wasn't kind—he was. Infuriatingly so, sometimes, just like everyone in his family. But kindness wasn't the same as *taking something seriously*. And Jacinto... He had a way of laughing things off when they got a little too real. Or brushing past what mattered with a shrug and a joke, like if he didn't name it, it couldn't touch him.

The thing with Jacinto was that he made everyone feel seen without ever showing too much of himself. And maybe that worked with the town, with the clients at the family law firm, even with his family. But not with me.

And sure, this was just a rumor, and one we'd heard before, at that. Multiple times. The older ladies were always pairing us up with each other, year after year, to entertain themselves a little. This time it felt heavier, more pressing. Not just some misunderstanding we could joke around about, wink and weasel out of.

The familiar street came into view. The trees lining each side stood completely still—too still for my liking. As if they knew what was happening, and they were holding their breaths, waiting for the shitshow to start. Jacinto's house had always felt different from the Williams' big family home. Smaller, neater. A place that looked like it had been meant for someone passing through rather than settling down.

My stomach twisted at the thought.

We'd been good friends for a long time. And it had been the kind of friendship that formed when two people kept ending up in the same places consistently. He used to come to the café after school every day, when I was still just the girl behind the counter, and he was the kid who made everyone in the town square laugh about something or other. I didn't remember the first conversation we ever had, just that it felt like slipping into something easy.

He'd help me close up the shop on quiet winter nights, talking nonstop while I wiped down tables and got the place ready for my mother to open early the next day. Sometimes he'd drag all the outdoor furniture into the courtyard and stack the chairs, although it was unnecessary and a little bit extra. Just like him.

Then he left for law school and a bigger life than this town could offer.

A bigger life for a larger-than-life boy.

And I stayed. But somehow, every time he was in town visiting, it was like we hadn't missed a single beat. Like the space between us had just pressed pause and waited for him to hit play again.

That was probably why this all felt so disorienting. Because whatever we were—whatever we had always been—it worked. Quiet, easy, dependable. Something I didn't have to think too hard about.

I found him outside his house, standing near his car, keys dangling from one hand, his phone in the other. He looked up just as I stepped onto the curb, his brows lifting slightly as our gazes locked.

"Miranda," he greeted with a smile, leaning lazily against the side of his obnoxiously yellow car. His tone was easy, light—like we hadn't both woken up to find ourselves at the center of the town's latest obsession after a night that felt like a big mistake. "To what do I owe the pleasure?"

I didn't slow my stride, walking up to his front door and tapping my foot impatiently. "We need to talk."

Jacinto sighed, pushing off the car and slipping his phone into his back pocket. "That is never a good opener."

I stopped in front of him, arms crossed. "This isn't a joke, Gato."

He tilted his head slightly, studying me. "I didn't say it was."

My fingers tightened against my side. "Then maybe stop looking so damn smug."

He held up his hand in mock surrender. "Alright, alright." His grin softened, but there was still that unmistakable glint of amusement in his eyes. He started towards me, those damn keys jiggling with each even step he took. "What's on your mind?"

I exhaled sharply, dragging a hand through my long hair. "You know exactly what's on my mind, Jacinto." I looked out towards the street and saw an older man watering the grass at the end, across from the pharmacy. His eyes were locked on us, the spray of water falling directly onto his driveway instead of on the plants that probably didn't even need them. "Let's go inside."

He nodded and unlocked his house, opening the door for me and waiting until I had settled on the living room couch before closing the door softly behind him.

"Everyone thinks we're together," I blurted, standing up and pacing the length of his house, back and forth from the living room to the dining room, once, twice, three times.

Jacinto's lips pressed together, but he didn't look partic- ularly concerned. "So?"

I blinked at him, incredulous. "So? That doesn't bother you?"

He shrugged. "It's Tres Fuegos. They'll get bored eventually."

I let out a humorless laugh. "That's what you think? That they'll just, what? Wake up tomorrow and forget?"

Jacinto's silence stretched between us, and I knew that was his answer. He wasn't taking this seriously.

I shook my head, taking a step closer. "They aren't going to forget, Jacinto. Estela has been having a fucking field day at the shop. Your family has probably already accepted it as fact. People were talking about us like...Carmen and Glad—"

I cut myself off, biting down on the words before they could spill out.

Jacinto's expression finally shifted. Just slightly, but I saw it—the moment it finally clicked for him, too. His shoulders squared, his jaw tensing just a little as he glanced away, his gaze sweeping the clean house.

I took a slow breath. "This won't go away."

He didn't answer immediately. When he looked at me again, something unreadable flickered in his eyes. "So, what do we do?"

I opened my mouth, ready to snap back with something clever, something dismissive, but nothing came out.

Because in the quiet between us, all I could think about was the night before. The way he had touched me like it mattered. The way I had let him. Wanted him. Wanted all of it.

And for a few brief hours, it hadn't felt messy or complicated or wrong. It had just felt...good. Easy. Real.

But that didn't change the fact that it shouldn't have happened. That it couldn't happen again.

I had been so caught up in my frustration, in the inevitability of this whole thing, that I hadn't actually stopped to consider what came next.

What did we do?

I parted my lips, but no words came out.

Jacinto let out a slow exhale, shaking his head slightly, like he was just now realizing how deep this mess really went. He leaned back against the wall, tapping his fingers on his thigh, the sound a slow, thoughtful rhythm.

He finally met my gaze again, his voice quieter this time. "I think we both know there's only one way to handle this."

My stomach flipped.

Because in that moment, I knew exactly what he was about to say.

I folded my arms tighter across my chest. "If you're suggesting, and I hope to all that's good and holy that you aren't, that we just go along with it—"

Jacinto tilted his head, his gaze sharp on me. "Do you have a better idea?"

I opened my mouth, then snapped it shut. I hated that I didn't. My plan of action was to just say, over and over, that it wasn't true. Laugh it off. Eventually scream it at the top of my lungs, red-faced and exhausted. And he knew that.

He let out a breath, rubbing the back of his neck. His shirt lifted a tiny bit, and I swept my eyes down his body, the tanned color of his flat stomach distracting me for a fraction of a second. "Look," he said, pausing a second until my eyes were back on his, "we both know how this town works. The second they get something in their heads, it's impossible to shake."

"I know," I muttered, dragging my hands down my face. "Trust me, I know."

His voice softened, a rare thing for him. His fun, carefree, charming mask was completely gone. "Then why fight it?"

I dropped my hands, looking at him. "Because it's my life, Gato. My name, my choices. And none of them include being someone's pretend girlfriend."

His lips quirked, just a little. "Even if it means people finally stop pitying you?"

The words hit harder than I expected. I sucked in a sharp breath, my nails digging into my palms. "*Andá a cagar.*"

He didn't flinch. Just watched me with that same unreadable expression, waiting.

I wanted to argue, to say something sharp and cutting. But the truth was, he had a point. For as long as I could remember, I had been the girl who followed Jacinto Williams around like a lovesick puppy. The town's favorite little joke. My own mother had, very recently, started partaking in the teasing, too, saying that I would end up alone if I kept waiting for that *boy* to pay attention to me.

Now, for the first time, they thought he had chosen me back.

I hated that a small part of me liked how that felt.

Jacinto's voice pulled me back. "Think about it, Martu. If we go along with it, people will back off. Carmen will stop trying to set me up with her granddaughters. Your own mother will stop worrying about you ending up alone."

I scowled. "That's not—"

He raised an eyebrow. "Isn't it?"

I hated how easily he could see through me. Always had.

It had started all over again the summer Manuela told me she wasn't coming back from university—the same summer Jacinto moved home from Buenos Aires to work full-time at his family's law firm. I'd just closed the coffee shop for the night, standing behind the counter with the mop still in my hand, holding my tears back because life felt like it was moving too fast around me, without me. I hadn't even heard the door when he walked in.

"Hey," he'd said back then, like no time had passed at all. Like it was normal to show up at nine-thirty on a Tuesday after a few years away.

I had looked up, blinking through the sting in my eyes, and said the first thing that came to mind. "We're closed."

He had smiled, tilted his head like a confused puppy, then said, "That's okay. I'm not here for coffee."

Then he had walked behind the counter, took the mop

out of my hands without asking, and started cleaning like he'd been doing it every night. He hadn't said anything else, just mopped the floors while I stood there, feeling the sharp edge of heartbreak dull under the weight of his presence.

He hadn't even asked what was wrong. He never needed to.

And from that day forward, he just… quite literally inserted himself in my life and never left.

And now, the house was too quiet around us, the sun probably high up in the sky warming up the whole town, but I felt cold. The worst part of all of this wasn't the town's gossip or the way Jacinto was looking at me like he already knew my answer.

The worst part was that I was actually considering it.

The silence between us stretched, thick and suffocating, just like this town had the propensity to do to me on occasion. I shifted my weight from one foot to the other, arms still crossed tight over my chest, trying to keep my expression from giving me away. But Jacinto was watching me too closely, his gaze sharp and knowing, like he could already hear the thoughts running through my head.

I wasn't supposed to be considering this at all.

But alas, here we were.

Jacinto exhaled, running a hand down his face before looking at me again. His voice was even quieter now, more serious than before, like I'd never seen. "I'm tired of it, Martu. The town, the way they act like they have a say in our lives, *my* life. If we do this, at least we're in control of the story for once."

Something about the way he said it made my stomach twist. This wasn't just about the town or the rumors.

It was about him, too.

I swallowed hard. "And what happens when we're done pretending?"

Jacinto didn't answer right away. And for the first time since this conversation had started, I wasn't sure if he had an answer at all.

7

JACINTO

THE LIGHT in the living room was dim, despite the sun shining high up in the sky at midday. The scent of coffee lingered in the air, though neither of us had made any. The old ceiling fan hummed softly above, stirring the cold air that worked itself inside through the cracked windows and settling it between us.

A beat of silence passed.

Then quietly, I said, "About last night."

Martina sat stiffly on the far end of my couch, her arms still tightly crossed over her chest, like she was physically holding herself back from running out the door. The cushion barely dipped beneath her, like she refused to get comfortable.

"We should probably talk about it."

I sat across from her in the armchair usually reserved for my cat, Beto, watching her shift uncomfortably. She had come here ready to fight, but now that she was inside my house, the energy between us had shifted. She wasn't just angry anymore. She was uncertain.

"You think?" she said with a humorless laugh.

I met her gaze, serious. Steady. "Martu, I didn't mean for that to happen."

She winced. "Wow. That's comforting."

"That's not what I meant," I said quickly, leaning my body closer in her direction. "I just... I didn't plan it, obviously. I didn't think. I was trying to—"

"You weren't taking advantage," she said, cutting me off. "I know that."

The words came easily because they were true. It felt like we had just drifted closer, naturally.

God, I *wanted* her.

That was the part that scared me the most. That I had liked it. That it had felt good and familiar and so damn easy in a way nothing else ever did. That I could still feel the ghost of her hands on my chest, the weight of her body pressed against mine, the way her voice had sounded when I moved just right.

But that didn't mean it could happen again.

"I was just...in a weird place," she added, more to herself than to me. "I didn't think either."

"You don't have to explain it," I said softly, trying to comfort her.

I did, though. I had to explain it to myself and to her. To

the version of me that had kissed her like it meant something.

"We can't do it again," I said as I stretched my legs out, rolling my shoulders to ease the tension that had settled in them since she stormed up to me outside. I dragged a hand through my hair, letting out a slow breath.

Martina's jaw tightened, just a fraction. "I know."

"It would make everything more complicated than it already is."

"I know," she said again.

"And if we're going to do this fake dating thing, we need boundaries."

She scowled again, the move completely adorable on her face. "This isn't a joke."

I held up a hand and willed my smile to fade. "I know. I'm just saying, if we're actually going to do this, we need to be clear about what it means."

Her jaw clenched, but she nodded. "Rules."

I waited, letting her set the pace. She always needed to feel like she had control over things, and I wasn't about to push her more than necessary. But that didn't mean I wasn't enjoying this, just a little.

"We don't lie to each other," she finally said, voice steady.

I leaned forward, resting my elbows on my knees. "Agreed."

She inhaled deeply, like she was bracing herself. "And we don't let it get... messy."

I tilted my head. "Messy how?"

She shot me a glare. "You know what I mean. No… feelings."

A smirk pulled at my lips, but I swallowed it back. "Fine. No mess."

Martina hesitated, like she was debating whether or not to say something else. Her fingers drummed lightly against her arm, betraying the nervous energy beneath her frustration. Finally, she let out a sharp breath. "No sex."

I hummed.

"And only for a few months," she continued. "That's believable, right?"

"Sure," I said with a casual lift of my shoulder.

"Yeah, okay. This could work," she muttered to herself, nodding her head as she spoke. "Just until the town play at the end of the year. That's a clean end point."

And even though we had just said we couldn't do it again—even though we had drawn the line in sharp, clear ink—I couldn't stop thinking about how easy it had been to fall into her. How badly I'd wanted to stay in the moment.

"The play?" I raised an eyebrow.

"Everyone will be there. We show up, we break up, the end," she said, a little too matter-of-factly. "No extensions. No drawing it out."

Something about the finality of her voice made my chest tighten, but I ignored it. "Alright." I extended a hand toward her. "Deal?"

She stared at it like it was a snake, hesitation flickering

in her eyes. And for a second, I thought she might back out. But then, with a quiet exhale, she slid her palm against mine.

Her hand was warm. Smaller than mine. Her grip tightened just slightly before she pulled away, like she was reminding herself that this was nothing. That this wasn't real.

"Deal," she said.

I leaned back, rubbing a hand over my jaw, letting the weight of it settle in. "Well," I murmured, glancing at her with a smirk I couldn't quite suppress, "this should be fun."

She groaned, standing up so fast I barely had time to react before she was heading for the door. "*Te odio.*"

I grinned, stretching out in my chair. "No, you don't."

She muttered something under her breath—probably something sharp and cutting that she would never let anyone hear—but I didn't stop her as she yanked the door open and stepped out into the bright sunlight.

The door clicked shut behind her, and the house felt quieter than it had before. Like something important had just happened, something neither of us really understood yet.

I let out a slow breath, dragging a hand down my face.

Shit.

———————

I spotted Martina locking up the café just as the last traces of daylight faded later that evening. The deep indigo of the evening sky stretched overhead, stars barely flickering through the remnants of dusk. The streetlights buzzed faintly above, casting long shadows across the cobblestone street. A cold breeze stirred the scent of *asado* from some neighboring house, carrying it through the quiet night.

Tres Fuegos wasn't silent just yet. A few stragglers still lingered, voices drifting lazily through the street, laughter punctuating the occasional scrape of a chair against the pavement outside our lone bar down the block. Somewhere, a dog barked, the sound fading into the usual hum of small-town life winding down. Just enough people remained to make this worth it.

I grinned to myself, stretching my arms as if preparing for a grand performance. The best kind of audience—the kind that thrived on gossip. This would certainly keep them fed for days.

"Martina, my love!" I called, my voice carrying through the street like a bell ringing in an empty church.

The reaction was immediate. Conversations halted. A few heads turned. Someone paused in the middle of unloading groceries from a car. A woman near the greengrocer peered over a display of peaches, already whispering to the vendor beside her.

Martina froze, her keys still in the lock, her entire body going rigid, like she'd been caught mid-crime. Slowly, so very slowly, she turned her head toward me, her expression a mix of disbelief and barely restrained exasperation.

"Gato," she muttered, barely moving her lips. "What the hell are you doing?"

I ignored the warning in her tone, instead taking a few exaggerated steps forward, closing the distance between us with a swagger I knew would irritate her just enough.

"I am here to properly invite my stunning girlfriend on a date." I placed a hand over my heart as if the very thought had struck me with divine inspiration.

A delighted murmur spread through the gathered bystanders. Someone actually gasped. Gervasio, the chief of police, nudged his wife, his grin evident even in the dim light.

Martina's shoulders lifted as she inhaled sharply, then exhaled slowly, like she was summoning every ounce of patience she had. Her fingers tightened around her keys, and for a brief moment, I thought she might throw them at my head.

"You're insufferable," she hissed through clenched teeth, her eyes narrowing as she shot a quick glance at our growing audience.

I winked, undeterred. "And yet, here I am, and you love it."

I could see it then—the wheels turning in her head, weighing the consequences of fighting me on this versus playing along. She knew exactly what I was doing. And worse, she knew it was working.

I tilted my head. "Pick you up at twelve?" I knew she most likely would have the day off—usually, she did light work on Tuesdays at the coffee shop, only helping a few hours during rush and then using the rest of the time for herself. On a normal day, I could find her watching videos online on the most recent makeup trends or practicing said trends on her face. But since tomorrow was the last day of this extra-long *Carnaval* weekend, and technically the final few days of our busy season, she would be at the café.

Martina opened her mouth, likely to argue, but before she could, Carmen—the ever-watchful town gossip—strolled out of the bakery across the street, each of her hands holding her reusable bags full of things, eyes gleaming like she had just won the lottery.

"Ah, young love," she sighed dramatically, turning to the few women gathered outside. Her voice carried all the way from across the square, the slight rasp at the edges echoing behind us. "Didn't I say it? Didn't I tell you all it was only a matter of time?"

A chorus of agreement followed, and one of the women actually clapped her hands together like she was watching a romance unfold in real-time.

Martina's expression was unreadable, but I didn't miss the slight twitch in her jaw. If there had been any doubt before that the town had fully committed to this story, it was gone now.

I took a step closer, lowering my voice just enough for

only her to hear. "Come on, Martina. Make it easy on yourself."

Her gaze snapped to mine, the use of her full name catching her off guard. She searched my face for something, maybe sincerity, maybe an escape route. But I didn't give her either of those things.

I let my voice drop just a little more, barely a murmur between us. "Say yes."

She exhaled, barely audible, her eyes flicking toward the onlookers once more before landing back on me. Her lips parted slightly, then closed again, like she was debating every possible response in the universe before finally resigning herself to the inevitable.

A slow, careful nod.

It was barely anything, but it was enough.

The small crowd erupted in cheers. Someone actually whistled. Carmen looked like she was ready to start planning our wedding.

I grinned, lifting my hand to tuck an errant lock of hair behind Martina's ear, the movement slow and calculated, and intentionally meant for the crowd. Her eyes followed my hand, and she shut them slowly once my fingers made contact with the soft skin.

What I hadn't planned for—what I wasn't prepared for at all—was the jolt that shot through me at the touch. One night had definitely not been enough for me.

It was supposed to be part of the performance. Smooth

and harmless. The kind of move anyone would pull when they were trying to be charming. But the second my fingertips brushed her cheek, I felt something shift. Something tighten.

She leaned into it, just the slightest bit, and it wrecked me. Not because she meant it—I knew she was playing along—but because, for a fraction of a second, a part of me wanted to believe she wasn't.

I dropped my hand a second too late, the delay enough for me to catch the flutter of her lashes as she opened her eyes again. And for one breathless moment, I forgot we had an audience.

Martina swallowed thickly, tilting her head up at me, her voice level but edged with quiet threat. "You owe me."

"Anything for you, *mi reina*."

Her eyes narrowed dangerously, but she didn't argue.

I took another step back, then another, watching as she finally yanked the key from the lock and slipped inside the dark café, shutting the door with more force than necessary. It was a massive avoidance tactic—she was supposed to be heading out but instead was hiding inside the café again to avoid the crowd of nosy onlookers that had gathered everywhere.

The street was still buzzing when I turned back, Carmen already making a beeline toward a group of elderly men who sat outside the inn, clearly eager to deliver the latest update.

I let out a slow breath, rubbing a hand along the back of my neck.

It had worked.

The crowd was convinced, the rumor now fed and blossoming, but I didn't feel the surge of victory I thought I would from this ridiculous performance. Not really.

Not when the memory of her gaze still burned behind my eyes, that narrowed look of hers doing something to my insides that it shouldn't. Not when my palm still tingled from touching her. Not when the door had shut between us like a full stop I hadn't been ready for.

This was supposed to be easy. Just enough to get people off our backs and for the whispers to die down.

Instead, I was standing on an empty sidewalk, staring at a closed door, trying to figure out why I suddenly felt like the line had been crossed and then erased immediately. Whatever existed before it… didn't anymore.

And a part of me had no interest in going back.

8

MARTINA

THERE WAS a stillness to the café before opening, soft and steady, like a held breath. The kind of quiet I liked—familiar, predictable. That followed us home every night and woke up with us every single morning. The pattern in how my mother moved, how she hummed when she measured the coffee grains before dumping them into the large storage canister, how her fingers always tapped the same three mugs before the first customer came in.

When my sister, Belén, was here, she used to slip into that rhythm with us—half asleep, hair a mess, grumbling loudly about early mornings but still showing up. She'd man the register while I handled the espresso machine, tossing out sarcastic commentary that made our mother sigh and the customers laugh. We weren't always in sync, but when we were, it felt like a well-oiled machine ticking along—the three of us filling the space with the kind of noise that didn't disrupt the quiet that followed us but rather gave it life.

I was looking forward to her coming back this summer. It had always been the plan. She'd go to university, get it out of her system, and then come back so we could run this place together and give our mother a break.

I liked to think she missed it—the café, the routine, the nuances of the small-town life. Even if all these things were exhausting and oppressive at times.

Outside, the sun had just begun to stretch over my small mountain town, spilling warm light through the wide windows. The street was still empty, the town not quite awake yet. This was my favorite time of day, before the customers, before the noise, before I had to play my part in a town that had already decided who I was.

My mother worked quietly next to me, lifting a tray of pastries and setting them one by one on the cooling rack with practiced ease. Her movements were calculated, never in a rush, the rhythm of her muscles so ingrained that she hardly needed to think about them.

I wouldn't expect anything less from a person who had been doing the same thing seven days a week since before I was born twenty-eight years ago, when life looked so different for her.

"Are you going to tell me what's wrong or do I have to guess?" she asked, not looking up as she brushed syrup over the warm, golden *medialunas*.

I stilled, fingers tightening around the dish towel I'd been folding. "Nothing's wrong."

She hummed, unconvinced.

I should have known better than to try and lie to her. My mother, like all the people I stayed close with, had a way of seeing through me, of peeling back my layers with nothing more than a glance. She didn't push, though. She never did. She just waited, knowing that eventually, I would give myself away.

And the truth was I had almost told her. That first morning after the bonfire when I noticed the lingering looks, the smirks, the comments that didn't quite say anything but meant everything...I nearly opened my mouth. Just a heads up, a casual, *"You might hear something weird about me and Jacinto—it's nothing, and please ignore it, and I will refuse to answer any questions about it."*

But I didn't.

Saying it out loud would have made it real. And I didn't want it to be real. I didn't want her to ask follow-up questions or give me that quiet look that said she knew more than I wanted her to.

And now here we were. Me pretending everything was fine. Her pretending to believe me.

I knew she'd been watching. She always watched—not in the obvious way, but in the quiet, measured way that made it worse. Every time Jacinto stopped by the café, even before the rumors, she'd give me a look. Barely a lift of her eyes, a shift in her mouth. A silent warning of sorts.

As if to say, *Don't make yourself too easy to love.*

As if to say, *You're trying too hard.*

She never said the words. She didn't have to. I felt them every time she caught me smiling too wide when Jacinto came through the door, every time I moved just a little faster to refill his cup.

I exhaled slowly, turning to face her. "Everything feels loud."

She finally glanced up, arching an eyebrow. "Loud?"

I gestured vaguely. "The town. The people. The way everyone always has something to say."

Her expression didn't change, but something in her gaze softened. "Ah," she said simply. "The rumors."

I frowned. "So, you heard."

She let out a quiet laugh. "Martina, I think even the trees heard."

I sighed, dragging a hand through my hair. "It's ridiculous."

My mother went back to her task, plating the pastries with a precision that could only come from years of repetition. "It's not surprising, honey," she said after a moment. "You and Jacinto have always been"—she paused, searching for the right word that wouldn't say too much but just barely enough—"entwined."

I scoffed. "Entwined?"

She gave me a pointed look. "Oh, don't act like you don't know what I mean."

I crossed my arms, leaning against the counter. "We're friends."

My mother hummed again, this time in amusement.

I bristled. "What?"

She set down the pastry brush, wiping her hands on her apron. "I didn't say anything."

"You're thinking it. I can hear it."

She smiled, reaching for her coffee cup. "I simply think it's interesting."

I narrowed my eyes but turned to the dish towel, folding and unfolding it as I waited for her to continue. "*¿Qué es lo interesante?*"

She took a sip, watching me over the rim of the tiny cup in her hand. "That of all the people in this town, you've always been the one closest to him."

I rolled my eyes, turning to stack plates on the shelf. "I'm close to a lot of people. Manuela, for example. Valentina. Lucía, before she went back to Buenos Aires for her fellowship."

"But not like that."

I stilled, my back to her.

I shook my head. "You're reading into it too much."

"Maybe," she said lightly. "Or maybe you don't read into it enough."

I turned, leveling her with a glare. "*Mamá.*"

She chuckled, shaking her head. "Relax, *hija*. I'm just saying, you spend a lot of time on the sidelines of his nonsense."

I snorted despite myself. "That's one way to put it."

Her smile was small, knowing. "And yet, you never seem to mind."

I didn't have a response for that. Because she wasn't wrong.

Jacinto had always been chaos wrapped in charm, a whirlwind of bad ideas and good intentions, pulling people into his orbit with nothing more than a lopsided grin. And I —a cautious cat, wanting to be in control of everything— had always been the one watching from the edge, shaking my head, pretending to be unimpressed.

Pretending, because the truth was, Jacinto made everything fun.

Like the time he convinced half of our high school to paint a mural on the side of the community center without asking anyone for permission. He called it "community beautification." Townspeople called it vandalism.

Or the time he tried to run a movie night in the square using an old projector and a white bed sheet, only to blow a fuse in the municipal office where he'd plugged in an ancient extension cord and knocked out the power of three whole blocks. He apologized with empanadas and a charming smile, and somehow got invited to do it again the next month, with supervision from the community center staff.

Even when I wasn't directly involved, even when I rolled my eyes and swore I wanted no part in whatever trouble he was stirring up, I had always found myself there. On the periphery. Close enough to be pulled in but never close enough to fall completely. Standing just out of frame, arms crossed, lips twitching like I didn't find the whole thing wildly entertaining.

Until now.

Now, the whole town had decided that I wasn't just on the edge of his chaos—I was in the center of it.

I exhaled, rubbing at my temples. "This is going to get out of hand."

My mother just smiled, setting her coffee down. "It already has."

I groaned as she reached over, squeezing my hand gently before picking up the empty tray of pastries. "Just be careful, Martu," she said, her voice softer now, almost thoughtful.

I frowned. "Careful of what?"

She hesitated, then shrugged. "Of forgetting what's real and what isn't."

Something in my chest twisted. I wanted to tell her that there was no risk of that, that I knew exactly what this was —a game, a way to satisfy the town until they got bored and moved on to the next scandal.

But the words didn't come.

———

Jacinto's car was parked directly in front of the café, almost like he'd know I wouldn't have any way to avoid him. Bright yellow. And who even liked yellow cars anyway? He leaned against the passenger side door like he had nowhere else in the world to be, arms crossed, one ankle resting lazily over the other. The picture of ease. As though we hadn't upended our entire lives in the span of twenty-four hours.

He spotted me as I walked to the door, a slow, devastating grin pulling at his mouth.

"Miranda," he called, dragging out that ridiculous name in that ridiculous, theatrical way that told me this was about to be a disaster.

The bell over the café door jingled behind me as I stepped outside, the afternoon sun casting short, sharp shadows across the quiet street. I'd just finished my shift and was halfway through adjusting the strap of my bag when I heard his voice.

Murmurs rippled through the square across the street, the usual lunch crowd lingering outside Santiago's hotel, but I kept my gaze on Jacinto, smiling slowly at him. I had to sell this, too, if I wanted this whole thing to be over with.

Jacinto pushed off the car and opened the passenger door with an exaggerated flourish, bowing slightly like he was welcoming me into a five-star limousine. "Your chariot awaits, *mi vida.*"

A woman right outside the pharmacy actually fanned herself with her hand. I exhaled slowly, walking toward him, keeping the smile plastered on my face even as my ears burned.

"Why are you like this?" I muttered under my breath, low enough that only he could hear.

He smirked as he moved closer to me. He was tall, but I was tall, too, so I was almost eye to eye with him. "You love it," he said into my ear.

I scowled. "I really, really don't."

His grin only widened. "Sure."

I turned toward the gathered onlookers, pasting on my best unimpressed expression. "He's always been dramatic," I told them, loud enough for them to hear. "It's an unfortunate condition."

Carmen cackled. "We wouldn't love him any other way," she said loudly from across the street. "And Jacinto? Take good care of our coffee shop girl."

I froze for a fraction of a second. There it was again, the label that was so clearly used to define me in this town.

Logically, it was supposed to be harmless, right? Just the coffee shop girl. But it irked me to no end that that was the only thing I was to them. What if I wanted to be something else? Would they even take me seriously?

Jacinto stilled, too, and studied my face for a few seconds. He blinked slowly, as if to ask if I was okay. We'd been friends for long enough that he simply *knew,* and no words needed to be uttered. But I didn't think he'd ever witnessed, in first person, how the town talked about me, despite how I'd vent to him consistently about the things I heard at work.

Jacinto pressed a hand to his chest, turning to the onlookers for a final display of dramatic flair. "See? She gets me."

I rolled my eyes and stepped closer, hesitating just briefly before ducking into the passenger seat and trying to let the feeling melt away. The door shut behind me, and the world outside was immediately muffled, but the energy of the scene lingered on my skin.

He slid into the driver's seat, drumming his fingers against the steering wheel. "You ready?"

I exhaled, letting my head fall back against the seat. "I don't know."

He chuckled. "Too late to back out now, Miranda."

I turned my head toward him. He was grinning, but there was something softer beneath it, something almost unreadable. And for the first time since this whole thing had started, I let myself really look at him.

At the boy I had known forever, the boy who had been in my orbit for years. The one who never took anything too seriously, who never let anything weigh too heavily on his shoulders. The one who had always been larger than life, the town's golden boy who had been built for movement, for momentum.

And now, somehow, I was fully caught in his current.

I swallowed, looking away. "Let's just get this over with."

Jacinto laughed, starting the engine. "Ay, Miranda," he said, shaking his head as he pulled away from the curb. "This is only the beginning."

9

JACINTO

Martina hadn't said a word since I pulled away from the curb outside the coffee shop, just like the other night. She had always been cautious around people not in her inner circle, but now she felt farther away, like she was retreating, one step back at a time, even after everything that had happened between us.

The hum of the engine filled the car, the tires rolling smoothly over the uneven cobblestone roads of Tres Fuegos. Outside, the town stretched past in shades of sun-faded paint and tangled vines creeping up old brick walls. A few people milled about, and I caught the tail end of Carmen gesturing animatedly to someone near the grocer, no doubt already reciting the details of our little love scene.

I smirked to myself. That should keep them entertained for the rest of the day.

But Martina? She was stiff. Hands on her lap, her body

angled slightly toward the window, her fingers tapping an absent rhythm against her knee.

I knew that look. She was thinking—hard. Probably talking herself in and out of fifteen different things at once.

I tapped my fingers against the steering wheel, following the beat of the song that was playing on the radio. "You know, you could at least pretend to be excited. I did just pick you up for a date in front of half the town."

Her brown eyes cut toward me, sharp. "Exactly. In front of half the town."

I shrugged, keeping my voice easy. "It would've looked suspicious if I didn't."

She scoffed. "You enjoyed it."

I grinned. "Of course I did."

My fake girlfriend groaned, leaning her head back against the seat, her sigh exaggerated. "How do you sleep at night?"

I laughed loudly, accidentally swerving to the left.

"Jacinto!" she shrieked as she rolled her head to the side, leveling me with one of her looks, and for a second, I saw it. A tiny flicker of something behind the irritation—something I wasn't sure she had meant to show.

I shifted slightly in my seat.

The last thing I needed was to start noticing things like that.

The road curved as we left the town behind, heading toward the open countryside just beyond the main streets. The noise faded, replaced by the rhythmic crunch of tires against gravel, the occasional bird overhead. It was quieter out here, no one watching, no expectations pressing in.

And yet, the weight in my chest didn't lift.

"Where are we going?" she asked finally, breaking the silence.

I exhaled, adjusting my grip on the wheel. "Somewhere no one will bother us."

She frowned, turning more fully toward me now. "Isn't the whole point of this to be seen together?"

I let my lips tilt up, but it was smaller this time. Less for her, more for myself.

"I figured you'd appreciate one date where we don't have to put on a show."

Her expression shifted again. A flicker of something like relief. She hesitated, then quieter, "That's... unexpectedly considerate of you."

I smirked. "Don't sound so surprised, Martina."

She exhaled, shaking her head, but there was no real annoyance behind it this time. "Where, then?"

"You'll see."

She sighed again, but didn't press.

I let the silence stretch between us, longer this time. It wasn't exactly comfortable, like the long silences we let linger between us when we had nothing else going on, when she was curled up in my cat's armchair reading a book, the cat on her lap and a blanket covering her long legs. This silence wasn't sharp—it was as if we had settled into some-thing. Or maybe just given up and resigned ourselves to it.

A song echoed through the speakers, something soft and familiar. One of those songs that had been around forever, played at every town event, every family gathering. I didn't even think before reaching for the dial, turning it up just slightly.

Martina let out a quiet laugh.

I glanced at her. "What?"

She shook her head, a small, almost nostalgic smile tugging at her lips. "I haven't heard this in years."

Something in my chest shifted. "You used to love this song," I said before I could stop myself.

Her smile wavered, and she looked away, back out the window. "I used to love a lot of things."

I frowned, but before I could say anything else, she did it for me.

"Do you ever feel like you don't really know what you're doing?" she asked, voice quiet. "Like everyone else is moving forward, you're just... the same person, stuck in the same place?"

My fingers tightened around the wheel. I swallowed, keeping my eyes on the road. "Yeah," I said after a moment. "But where is this coming from?"

Martina didn't answer my question right away. She just exhaled slowly, eyes still fixed on the passing fields outside the window. The colors were changing ever so slightly, from dull yellows to a slow, bright green. Sun-drenched grasses stretched out in every direction, the occasional rustic wooden fence breaking up the rolling hills.

The road had narrowed now, the kind that didn't see much traffic, where the gravel kicked up in little dust clouds behind us.

Finally, she spoke. "It's just… Everything feels so predetermined sometimes. Like you're on a track, and no matter what you do, you end up in the same place."

Her voice was quiet, but something about the way she said it settled deep in my body. I tapped my fingers against the steering wheel again, thinking. "I mean… you don't have to tell me about that," I said with a laugh. "I'm as predetermined as it gets."

Only, that wasn't exactly true.

My family didn't expect me to become an attorney. Not really. That was mostly reserved for my two oldest brothers, who were more serious, much more talented. But they'd hoped. Quietly. Cautiously. I think they were relieved I stuck with something for once and that I didn't get bored and move on like I always had with every single project I started. Law school was supposed to be the thing that steadied me. And maybe it did.

I liked the work. Most days. But there were still moments, in the middle of depositions or when I was elbow-deep in contracts, where I'd catch myself wondering if I'd just fooled everyone. If this whole life was some long, unbroken streak of pretending. Charlie fit into responsibility like it was tailored to him.

And me? I was still the youngest. The wild one. The one who got away with things—who coasted on charm and good timing and the shine in my green eyes. The town's golden boy, whether I liked it or not.

I knew how to play the part. I just wasn't sure who I was when the performance ended.

She huffed out a laugh, but there was no humor in it. "At least you're fun, Gato. I'm just on the sidelines, leading a quiet life. Every day is literally the same. What if I never figure out what's next for me?"

I didn't know how to answer that. Instead, I cleared my throat and flicked on the turn signal, steering us onto a smaller dirt road that cut through a thick patch of trees. The sunlight filtering through the branches felt good against the chill in the air, even as it filtered inside the car through the windshield.

Martina sat up slightly. "Where are we?"

I smirked, keeping my eyes on the road. "Almost there."

A minute later, the trees thinned out again, opening up to a small clearing. Wildflowers spread across the field in dull bursts of color, swaying stiffly in the breeze. In the distance, a lone wooden picnic table that had seen better days sat beneath the shade of an old jacaranda tree, its branches lonely and boney, the purple blossoms waiting to make an appearance again as soon as the weather picked up.

I pulled the car to a stop, killing the engine.

Martina stared out the window, eyebrows furrowing. "You brought me to a field."

I unbuckled my seatbelt. "Not just any field."

She turned to look at me, unimpressed. "It's literally just a field, Jacinto. It's only thistles and, like... weeds."

I grinned. "Give it a chance."

She hesitated, then let out a long-suffering sigh, pushing open the door.

The cold hit immediately, thick and dry, but the wind carried the scent of grass and flowers, something fresh and clean. It was the kind of place that made me feel like the rest of the world didn't exist, and I hoped it could be for her, too.

I walked around to the back of the car, popping the trunk. Martina wandered toward the picnic table, trailing her fingers over the rough wooden surface.

"Why here?" she asked after a moment, glancing over her shoulder at me.

I pulled out the picnic basket and shrugged. "It's quiet."

She raised an eyebrow. "So why did you make such a big scene outside the café if you were planning for this to be completely private? And in the middle of nowhere no less?"

I grabbed the folded blanket and slammed the trunk shut with my elbow. "Because we'll say we had a very *private*, very romantic afternoon together, and no one will question it." I winked.

She snorted. "So, we're lying."

I grinned. "It's fake dating, Martu. The key word there is fake."

She shook her head but took the blanket when I handed it to her, shaking it open before spreading it out over the grass. I set the picnic basket down and sat, stretching my legs out. She sat more carefully, tucking her knees close, one of her hands resting on her ankle, the other one fiddling with a long leaf that had drifted from somewhere else.

For a while, neither of us spoke. The wind stirred through the remnant of the flowers, the distant hum of cars driving down the lone portion of highway nearby filling the space between us.

I exhaled, stretching my arms behind my head. "So, do I get points for at least picking a nice spot?"

She studied me for a second, then, to my surprise, she smiled. Small, but real. "Fine. A couple of points."

I grinned. "I'll take that."

We sat there a little longer, the silence shifting into one of those ones that I chased and craved when I was around her. Something easier. Natural, and *us*.

That's what it had always been with Martina—or at least what I wanted it to be. She didn't let me coast on charm. Didn't laugh when I deflected. She asked the kind of questions that stayed with me long after she walked away.

She didn't make things easy—and maybe that was why I kept coming back. Around her, I didn't have to perform. I didn't get to be *golden*. I had to be real, or at least try to be. And somehow, despite how much I hated that with everyone else, with her... it felt like relief.

10

A sʟow, lazy breeze rustled through the dried, winter grass, sending scattered leaves drifting through the air like something out of a movie. We had been sitting there for a while, long enough for the nervous energy from the drive and the whole scene outside my place of employment to settle into something more like we were used to. Quiet and comfortable and calm. The hum of town gossip felt far away, like it had loosened its grip on my chest the moment I stepped out of the car.

I reached into the basket at the same time Jacinto did, our hands brushing against each other. A small thing, electrifying. Something that had one hundred percent happened before. But this time, it sent a slow awareness creeping up my spine, a warmth that had nothing to do with the sun moving overhead and the shade of the trees inching farther and farther away from the spot where we sat.

I pulled back first, reaching instead for the bottle of water I'd been quietly drinking and taking a slow sip, like that had been my intention all along. Like I hadn't felt that moment of hesitation, that split second where neither of us moved.

Jacinto, of course, noticed.

He grinned, leaning back on his elbows in a stupidly unperturbed stance. Completely unaffected by anything. "Relax, Martu."

I shot him a flat look. "I'm relaxed, Gato. This is me being relaxed."

His chest rumbled with laughter, so contagious that I couldn't stop the smile forming on my lips. He made a dramatic show of stretching, long and lazy, before lacing his fingers behind his head and closing his eyes.

This was how we had always been between us—easy, playful. A contrast between the way we were outside of closed doors, when he was loud and funny and charming, and I just sat there watching him.

Something about this felt different, though. The silence made me increasingly aware of how much space he took beside me, both literally and metaphorically, and the way the golden light filtered through the tree above, casting shifting shadows over his face.

I cleared my throat, forcing my attention back to the grasses swaying in the breeze. The mountain was full of these little pockets of color, unexpected bursts of life where you least expected them, especially once spring turned into summer. It was such a welcome breath of fresh air when I came across one of these, sometimes when we were out just walking the trails in the spring, with nothing better to do. And these wonders were always there, growing even in the harsh conditions of the seasons.

Jacinto exhaled, tipping his head farther back and opening his eyes to look at the sky. "You know," he mused, "I've been thinking about what you said."

I glanced at him. "About what?"

He turned his head toward me, green eyes lazy but intent. "About feeling like you're on a track you can't get off of. Like everything is already decided for you, and how people are moving forward and you feel stuck."

I shifted, tucking my legs under me. "Okay."

His gaze lingered on me for a second before he looked away, staring at some distant point beyond the tree line. "I guess I just never thought about it like that before. But you're right. This town has a way of making up its mind about people."

My chest tightened, because I had never heard Jacinto talk like this before. He had always been the one who moved through life like it was an open road, like he could take any exit he wanted, change course at any moment. But here, now, there was something almost wistful in his voice.

I looked down at my hands. "Yeah. And once they decide, it sticks. It's...."

He let out a soft laugh, shaking his head. "I mean, look at

us. We're living proof. The town decided we should be together, and now it's fact."

I scoffed. "It's not fact."

He gave me a sideways look, smirking. "Tell that to Carmen."

I sighed. "I hate this town."

"No, you don't."

"Don't you feel like... like it's suffocating sometimes?" Jacinto turned to look at me, his eyes studying me intently, waiting patiently for the next words to come out of my mouth. "The town, I mean. The expectations, the labels, just..."

I shook my head, taking another slow sip of my drink. His smile weakened, not gone, per se, but it shifted— smaller, tighter.

"They think I'm the boy who doesn't take anything seriously," he said, voice light. "The town clown, the charmer. The youngest son who doesn't stick with things."

I stared at him, the words settling between us like a wildflower in the wrong season: unexpected and too pretty to make sense of.

I had always known this, of course. Had seen it in the way people laughed when he came up with one of his ridiculous schemes, the way they shook their heads fondly, like he was someone to be entertained by, not counted on.

I'd seen the way that sometimes, when no one was looking, he seemed just the slightest bit tired. His mask fell off, and instead silence and stillness were brought in.

He ran a hand through his dirty blonde hair, exhaling. "But hey, maybe they're right."

I didn't know why that bothered me so much. I studied him, trying to figure out what to say, but before I could, he suddenly grinned again, nudging me with his knee. "Anyway, enough existential crises for a lifetime. Are you ready to go back and pretend we're disgustingly in love for the town?"

I rolled my eyes and smiled. "You mean, are you ready to milk this for all it's worth?"

His grin turned wicked. "Oh, Miranda, you know me so well."

I sighed, standing and dusting off my jeans. "Let's get this over with, then."

Jacinto stood, too, stretching his arms overhead. "I think we should be extra affectionate when we get back. Maybe a little caress on the cheek? A dramatic forehead kiss?"

I shoved the blanket at him. "Get in the car, Gato."

He laughed, tossing it in the back seat before getting into the driver's seat with the biggest smile on his face.

———

Jacinto let out a low whistle. "Damn, they really are invested."

I sighed. "I told you."

He smirked. "Should we give them something to talk about?"

I glared back at him. "They already have plenty to go around. Please, no, *te lo pido*."

But he was already grinning, fully committed to his role.

The center of town was alive with its usual weekend buzz. It was Tuesday, yes, but it felt more like a Sunday than anything else. Tables spilled onto the sidewalk outside of Santiago's inn, filled with locals sipping cold drinks and nibbling on *picada*, pretending not to stare. Carmen was standing at her usual spot on the other corner, one hand fluttering as she leaned in close to deliver whatever version of the story she'd spun this morning.

I caught the eye of Delia across the street. She smiled a little too knowingly before turning her head down back to her crossword puzzle. Two young children zipped past us on bikes and immediately doubled back, a grin plastered on both their faces. Even the older man that sat in the square every day and barely looked up from his newspaper most days glanced up as we rolled past, tracking the car with vague curiosity.

Eyes were everywhere. I felt them crawling over my skin, making something low in my stomach twist. But Jacinto, of course, looked unbothered—like he lived for this, for playing the part and dialing it up just enough to keep them watching.

As he pulled up in front of the café, he reached over, sliding his warm hand down my thigh and placing it on my knee.

"Might as well sell it properly," he murmured, voice low and gravelly and soothing. Just for me.

I stiffened, but forced myself to stay calm. Because this was the whole point, right? To sell this massive lie to this town of curious grownups who had nothing better to do than lurk and root for two people in a relationship.

Jacinto got out of the car and jogged to my side, opening the door with a dramatic flourish. He let out a contented sigh, leaning his weight into the open space. "Ah, what a perfect date with my beautiful girlfriend," he said, loud enough for anyone lingering around to hear.

I resisted the urge to elbow him and got out of the car. "I'm going inside," I said as I walked in the direction of the café.

I barely made it two steps before Carmen called out. "How was your afternoon, dear?" she asked, too sweetly, her voice carrying once more through the town square. She liked to pretend that we were always in close proximity, even if we had a large space between us.

Jacinto, the traitor, answered before I could. "Absolutely wonderful, Carmen, thank you for asking," he called back, grinning. "My girl is just a dream."

Carmen beamed. I wanted to sink into the ground.

I spun, shooting him a murderous look. He just winked, his eyes set on me, unwavering.

I exhaled through my nose, then, before I could over-think it, I reached out and grabbed his hand, lacing my fingers through his and pulling him towards me. If we were really doing this, I might as well commit, too.

Jacinto stilled, just for a second, long enough for me to notice. Then, smoothly, he curled his fingers around mine. And for some reason, that felt like something real.

Once we were inside, away from all the curious eyes, I dropped his hand and turned to face him.

"Gato," I said with a sigh, and Jacinto laughed quietly, his shoulders moving up and down and his face full of guilt. The same exact expression he had the day he blew the fuse in the community center that left half the town without power.

"What?" he asked, all wide-eyed innocence. But his eyes sparkled with that infuriating mix of charm and mischief, like he knew exactly what he was doing and couldn't help himself.

"Stop with the gestures," I said, but my voice didn't come out as sharp as I intended. It landed somewhere between annoyed and almost charmed, against my better judgement. Like part of me didn't totally hate it.

"No more public declarations of love," I started, using my fingers to enumerate. "No dipping me in the middle of the town square, no serenading me at the café, and for the love of god, no calling me corny nicknames loud enough for half of Tres Fuegos to hear."

He looked scandalized. "You wound me."

"I'm serious."

Jacinto nodded solemnly. "You got it. No grand romantic

gestures that might make you look like you actually enjoy my company," he added with a giant smile on his face.

I narrowed my eyes. "Don't twist this."

"I wouldn't dream of it, *girlfriend.*" He took a step closer, eyes dancing. "Any other rules I should be aware of?"

I crossed my arms, trying to look like I wasn't already five seconds from smiling. "I'll think of more and send them over in writing."

He was close now. Not too close, but enough to make my heart beat a little faster. He tilted his head, gaze dropping briefly to my mouth before flicking back up again.

"Just give me one I *can* break," he said, voice low.

I rolled my eyes, but my cheeks burned.

This was definitely going to be a problem.

11

JACINTO

"We go away for a week and come back to a completely different town," my sister-in-law Victoria announced the moment I stepped into my parents' house and into the dining room. "Didn't realize we'd be returning to a full-blown *novela*."

"That's on you for leaving for such a long time," I retorted as I walked up to her to say hi. They'd returned earlier that morning from visiting family in Buenos Aires for a few days while the courts were closed for winter break.

"Ignore her," Santiago, my brother and her husband, said. "She's been catching up on gossip all day."

I narrowed my eyes at her, panning around the room to see who was still missing. "How the hell did you hear about this already? You literally just got back today."

Victoria grinned, completely unbothered. "I have my sources."

I scowled. "Of course you do."

Santiago and Victoria had been married less than a year, and already, she had seamlessly settled into the wild Williams family, like she had always been there. Their wedding—a large, loud but beautiful affair in the backyard of this very house—had been the last big family event before things settled down again. Before everyone slipped back into their roles, into the places the town had decided for them.

Apparently, the next big event was my fake relationship.

I sighed, knowing there was no escape. I grabbed the seat next to Lucía, my only sister, who was in town for the long weekend and to help her previous practice hire a new doctor since she had recently started an oncology fellowship in Buenos Aires. She barely glanced up from her phone as I dropped into the seat beside her, but the smirk on her face told me she was absolutely listening. "Get it out of your system."

Silence.

For a brief, shining second, I hoped maybe they'd let it go.

But Lucía just smiled and nodded before getting back to her text conversation with her boyfriend, Francisco.

"How's Valentina, by the way? I haven't seen her around much this summer."

Charlie, the oldest of the siblings, snapped his head in my direction, stopping mid-sentence to stare. Lucía returned the stare with a knowing smirk, shaking her head slightly before replying to me. "She just came back from Buenos Aires a few days ago, right before the long weekend. She's been busy interviewing for the clinic, and I'm supposed to vet the final candidates tomorrow."

Charlie hummed, like whatever was said was the most important conversation to ever be had. I blinked, because his reaction wasn't normal at all, but I had never been able to figure him out fully. He was ten years older than me and we'd never been close, especially because by the time I was in high school, he had already been away in law school for a few years.

"Is Dr. Martin going back to the practice, then?"

"Yes," Lucía replied with a smile, "for a few weeks. There's a doctor that looks quite promising from San Clemente. I think we might try to convince him to move his practice here."

"That's good," I replied, absentmindedly. My sister had been living in Tres Fuegos for three years before finally deciding to move back to Buenos Aires to pursue a specialization. During the time she was here, she'd been the town's only pediatrician—and doctor, really—until she finally burnt out and took the leap. It was a surprise to everyone, especially our parents, because she seemed happy and content in her new role in town.

And our parents were ecstatic, all four of their children living in town at the same time, something that hadn't happened in a decade.

Hence the newly appointed weekly dinners and really

every single excuse to get us all in the same place, even if the occasion was to celebrate the full moon or the new moon or the wildflowers blooming.

After a moment, everything returned to normal—the dining room was full, the long table set with mismatched dishes and a spread big enough to feed the entire block. My mother was fussing over something in the kitchen, half-listening to what had been said, and my father flipped through the evening paper at the head of the table.

Charlie and Santiago sat side by side, deep in conversation about something legal and boring, while Victoria sipped from a glass of wine, watching them intently and waiting to give her point of view.

My mother emerged from the kitchen with a smile on her face. She took her seat beside my father, setting down her glass of wine and placing the fabric napkin on her lap. The moment she had settled, everyone started at the food, filling their plates and moving the conversation along. Charlie, Victoria and my father naturally migrated to talk about the firm's clients, discussing details of some of the cases we were preparing for in the next few months. Santiago and Lucía talked about my brother's upcoming busy season, with occasional comments from his very attentive wife.

"How is Martina?" my mother asked, her gaze set on me with a soft, caring smile. It was the smile always reserved for us, when she was asking about our lives, what we had done in school, what we were up to.

I swallowed a bite of food before answering. "She's fine."

Something about the way she studied me made my stomach twist. "And you're treating her well?"

The question landed heavier than I expected, because of course I was treating her well. We were friends, always had been, and I wouldn't dare disrespect her.

I blinked, taken off guard. "Of course I am."

I grabbed a serving spoon and piled more rice onto my plate, even though I wasn't done with my first serving, but I was determined to pretend this conversation wasn't happening.

That lasted all of ten seconds.

"So," Lucía started, reaching for a piece of bread, "you're telling me that, *de repente*, you and Martina just, what? Decided you were in love?"

I groaned. "*Dios.*"

Victoria let out a soft hum. "See, that's what I don't get either. Because if you ask anyone in this town, they'll say it was inevitable."

I glanced around the table, looking for an ally, but they were all in on this. Charlie was smirking, probably enjoying my pain. Santiago looked unbothered, but I could tell he was listening and paying attention in between bites of our mother's cooking. Even my father, who was usually more invested in his newspaper than our conversations, was eyeing me with mild amusement.

"Can you blame them?" my mother asked, another soft smile aimed at me. "They've been dancing around each other for years."

I choked on my food, but that spurred them on.

"Yeah, well, the town also thinks Gustavo Laprida faked his own death and moved to Spain. Doesn't mean we should trust their theories."

Lucía grinned at that, knowing quite well that the old man had just moved to Buenos Aires to be closer to his daughter so she could help care for him. But the town loved to theorize and romanticize every single thing that happened here. "No, but you have to admit, it does explain why his wife never seemed all that sad."

I shot her a glare. "Not helping."

She shrugged, popping a piece of bread into her mouth. "Not trying to."

"Stop hanging out with Charlie, you're starting to sound like him." I sighed, pushing the food around my plate. "Look, I don't know what you want me to say. We're just"—I gestured vaguely—"taking it one day at a time."

Victoria arched an eyebrow. "One day at a time?"

Charlie snorted. "That's a new one. Most people call it dating."

Something in my stomach twisted as they all stared at me. Yes, sure, we were dating for all intents and purposes. And I could guess what they were thinking. That this was something I was committing to with no intention of following through. Just like the podcast I'd sworn I'd launch to capture the oral history of Tres Fuegos. Or the time I tried to start a side hustle selling local honey, even though I knew absolutely nothing about bees or beekeeping. I designed the labels, came up with a name, and promptly forgot to actually talk to a beekeeper. There was still a box of empty jars somewhere in this house.

And countless other things I had started but never finished.

They weren't wrong. Not really. I *had* a habit of dropping things the moment they lost their shine, the second something else caught my attention. It wasn't intentional—it was just how my brain worked. I was always looking for the next thing, always craving a spark.

This felt different. This wasn't a garden or a side project. It wasn't something I had picked up on a whim.

This was Martina.

She had been part of my life for as long as I could remember. Slowly growing on me since the eighth grade, when I walked into the café for the first time by myself and basically never left. I wasn't about to ruin that just because the town had decided to stick us in a fucking romance novel.

I let out a slow breath and forced a smirk. "You are obsessed with my love life."

Victoria grinned. "It's a slow news week."

I rolled my eyes, but the tension in my chest hadn't gone away.

My mother, who had been mostly quiet save for those pointed questions, finally spoke up. "I think it's nice," she said simply, cutting through the chaos in a way only she could.

I glanced at her, half-expecting another teasing remark. But her expression was softer than the others, unreadable.

"Martina's a wonderful girl," she continued, dabbing the corner of her mouth with her napkin. "She's always brought out the best in you."

I hesitated because I knew she meant well. I knew that in her mind, this wasn't a joke or some fleeting town gossip. Was this something she had always seen as inevitable? And she was just waiting for me to catch up?

That was what unsettled me the most.

Should I have told them the truth? Quickly blurt out that this wasn't real? That Martina and I had only agreed to play along to make things easier on both of us. That none of this was supposed to *mean* anything.

The words got caught somewhere between my chest and the back of my throat, because this did mean something, albeit not exactly what my family and the town had in mind. And the more people talked about it and said it out loud, the harder it was to convince myself that this was just a passing thing.

Santiago finally broke the tension with a sigh, shaking his head. "Whatever it is, just don't mess it up."

I looked at him. "Why does everyone assume I'm the one who's going to mess it up?"

He raised an eyebrow. "I'm not. Just saying, from experience"—he looked over at his wife, who had a soft look on her face—"make sure you do everything in your power to make her happy."

I nodded, acknowledging his words, but the ever-present knot settled in my throat. I sighed again, pushing back my chair. "I have to go."

Lucía looked up at me, her blue eyes shining with amusement. "But we were just getting started."

I muttered something under my breath and grabbed my plate, heading toward the kitchen to clean up. The whole conversation had felt like a punch to the gut, unsettling and confusing me even more.

12

I shouldn't have come here.

It was the thought I had every single time I found myself itching to go to Jacinto's house. To escape the comfort I'd always found at the café that was now smothering me.

Normally, I would have hidden in the back room, a corner where there were stacked boxes high up enough that I could crouch against a wall and text Manuela or my sister, or walked to the medical practice to yap away with Lucía and Valentina until I felt the air loosen around me. But today, without thinking, my feet brought me here instead. To Jacinto's. And that was the problem, wasn't it?

It had been exactly one week since our first "date" in the wildflower fields, and I had just barely seen him around Tres Fuegos. He came in for his morning coffee, lingered for a little while I worked, then winked and said goodbye in a dramatic exit just for the benefit of the locals.

It was great. If this was what fake dating meant, then I was all for it.

I hesitated outside the door, my fingers hovering over the doorbell. The porch light that was permanently on was attracting an absurd amount of insects. Jacinto's house was only a fraction of what the Williams' family home was, but it had a kind of effortless charm that suited him. A porch chair that was screaming for a new coat of paint, a rough blanket tossed over the back, and a small, forgotten plant in the corner that was barely hanging on, dry soil cracked like it had been overlooked for months.

The door swung open before I could knock, and Jacinto, in all his boyish charm, leaned against the doorframe, his sharp green eyes flicking over me in quiet assessment. He wasn't smiling, but the warmth in his gaze was unmistakable.

"Miranda," he greeted, his voice low, familiar.

I rolled my eyes. "Are you ever going to call me by my actual name?"

He grinned, stepping aside to let me in. "Not if I can help it."

I stalled for half a second before stepping inside, the scent of him immediately wrapping around me. The mix of coffee, something woodsy, and the faintest trace of citrus from his soap. It was ridiculous that I even noticed.

He was wearing his work clothes, tailored dark gray slacks that did wonders for those long, muscular legs, and a white button-down that had the sleeves rolled up to his forearms. I didn't think I'd ever seen those sleeves in their correct place since he came back from law school, choosing instead a more casual approach to the dress code his family's firm followed.

I set my bag down on the kitchen island. "I needed a break."

Jacinto shut the door behind me, stretching his arms above his head, the hem of his shirt lifting ever so slightly. I looked away quickly, annoyed at myself for even noticing how toned he was everywhere.

"From what?" he asked, taking a few steps in my direction and leaning against the counter.

"From being Tres Fuegos' favorite new gossip topic."

He chuckled, shaking his head. "You act like this town hasn't been waiting for this moment for years."

"Oh my god, you're just like one of them!" I groaned. "And you're not helping."

"Come on, Martu," he said, nudging my hip as he passed on the way to the refrigerator. "You have to admit, it's a little funny. A lot of fun, too."

I shot him a glare. "Oh, hilarious. I fear my mother might be already planning our wedding. I don't even want to ask, I'm too scared to know."

He smirked, but there was something else in his expression. Something a little too unreadable.

I exhaled, dragging a hand through my messy hair. I needed a haircut, but everywhere I went, all this gossip followed me and... "I just needed some peace and quiet. And before you say anything—yes, I realize the irony of coming here for that."

Jacinto placed a hand over his heart. "I am deeply offended. I *can* be peaceful. Give me a chance."

For all his theatrics, Jacinto had a way of making things feel lighter, easier. I hadn't even been here five minutes, and already, the weight in my chest had begun to loosen.

He moved toward the living room, tossing himself onto his couch, his long legs sprawled out. He patted the empty space beside him.

"Come on," he said, stretching his arms behind his head. "Tell me about how the town has ruined your life today."

Without thinking too much about it, I crossed the room and sank into the seat next to him. And the second I did, Jacinto exhaled like he had been waiting for me to do exactly that.

I shifted in my seat, tucking my legs under me, stretching an arm along the back of the couch. I wasn't touching him, not exactly, but the heat of him was close, warm, like something I could reach out and sink into.

"Manuela is leaving," I blurted, just to keep my mind busy, otherwise I would be too tempted to touch him.

Jacinto turned his head slightly, eyes flicking toward me. "You told me that already."

I exhaled slowly, pressing my thumbnail against the pad of my pinky finger. "Yeah, well. Now it's real. She went to Buenos Aires and packed up everything, and is using the next few weeks to sort through all her stuff and see exactly what she's taking with her. I'm assuming that whatever she's not bringing will just end up in storage or jam-packed into her childhood bedroom."

He didn't say anything right away. I could feel him watching me, though, waiting, letting me sit with the realization that, even though one of my best friends already lived a few hours away, this was heavier than ever. It felt permanent. He'd been through this, too, only a few weeks ago after his sister—who coincidentally was part of my group of friends—moved back to Buenos Aires for a new job at a hospital.

And I didn't know if he wasn't talking because he had nothing to say or maybe because what he had to say would be too much for me. It felt selfish, too, that I was taking Manuela's move so hard. I wanted to be screaming for joy for her, but it just felt slightly on the side of miserable with a tinge of jealousy. *Why her and not me* bounced around in my head over and over. And I knew the answer, but I was refusing to acknowledge it to anyone, especially myself.

I never even tried, to be honest with myself. Every time I thought about doing something else, really something else outside of the coffee shop, I talked myself out of it.

What kind of career was makeup, anyway? That's what I'd always told myself. But the truth was, it made me feel alive in a way nothing else did. And I was good at it. I'd done dozens of girls for their *quinces*, helped with weddings here and there. Yet I'd never let myself believe it could be more than a side thing.

The living room was dim, the last of the afternoon light filtering in through his thin curtains, casting soft golden streaks over the worn floor. The only sound was the faint hum of the old fridge in the kitchen and the occasional rustling of fabric when one of us moved.

"I guess I just thought eventually she would move back to town," I admitted, my voice quieter now.

Jacinto let out a low hum. "I don't think you actually thought that, though."

I stilled. Something about that statement—the way he said it so simply, like it was obvious—pressed too deep. I let out a slow, measured breath, staring at the uneven stitching on the couch's fabric. "No, I guess I didn't. I hoped. So much hope."

There was another pause. Then, soft and thoughtful, he asked, "That's what's really bothering you?"

I blinked, my throat tightening. "What do you mean?"

Jacinto titled his head against the cushion, looking at me fully now. "That she's leaving? And moving forward and growing in her career and her aspirations? Or that you're staying?"

I shifted my gaze to look around the room. There were framed photos on the wall. Books stacked messily on the coffee table. And a floor lamp in the corner was on, despite me not having recollection whatsoever of ever seeing that lamp lit once.

I had spent so much time here over the years, but I had never let myself think about what it meant. What it meant that Jacinto had always been part of my life, no matter how many people left. What it meant that I was still here.

I cleared my throat, forcing a small, humorless laugh. "You're really going to analyze me right now?"

Jacinto smirked, but there was something softer beneath it. "You came to my house. I feel like that gives me permission."

I sighed, rubbing a hand that smelled too much like coffee over my face.

"I don't know," I said finally, sinking back against the couch. "Maybe it's both."

I looked at my hands. The same hands that had blended foundation over Manuela's high cheekbones last month while practicing a new technique, the ones that had painted tiny flowers on a flower girl's temples just because she asked. The same hands that now served coffee six days a week like none of that ever mattered.

Jacinto nodded, as if that answer made perfect sense to him.

I bit the inside of my cheek, letting the quiet stretch again. I was so good at pretending, at making things seem like they didn't bother me, like I wasn't falling into some slow, aching grief for a life that kept shifting without me.

I turned my head toward him, the glow from the lamp catching in his eyes. His gaze was steady on me, studying me closely to see if he could finally crack the code inside my head.

I sighed dramatically, reaching for a pillow and shoving

it against his face. "Enough emotional depth for one day. You're ruining your reputation."

He laughed against the fabric, grabbing my wrist and pulling it down just enough to grin at me. "I don't have a reputation."

I smirked. "You have exactly one reputation, Gato."

He rolled his eyes, but the tension had partially dissolved. It was still there, humming beneath the surface, but lighter now, softer. Diluted into this comfortable space we'd built over decades of friendship.

Jacinto kept my wrist in his grip a second too long before letting go. I let my hand drop onto the pillow beneath us, watching as he exhaled, running a hand through his dirty blonde locks. He looked at me for a long moment, something unreadable in his expression.

Then, quieter, more careful than before: "You want to get empanadas?"

I swallowed my smile. "Yeah."

I was thankful for the words he didn't end up saying or didn't make *me* say, after all.

13

BETO WAS BEING DRAMATIC. The little traitor had been winding himself around my ankles for the past five minutes, meowing like I hadn't just fed him dinner the moment I stepped into the house after work.

"*Esperá un poquito*," I muttered, shaking the bag of cat food over his dish. "You eat better than I do, you know that?"

Beto meowed in response.

Martina's voice floated in from the couch. "That's because you spoil him."

I rolled my eyes, crouching to scratch behind my cat's ear before setting down his dish. "He's an old man. He's earned it."

"He's not even a year old, Gato," Martina replied, just as a sharp knock rattled the door.

I straightened, tossing the almost empty bag of cat food

onto the counter. "Food," I announced, rubbing my hands together. "Can you get that? My wallet is on the little shelf with the keys."

Martina made a noise of protest. "Why me?"

I smirked. "Because you're closer to the door."

She groaned but got up anyway, muttering something under her breath as she padded toward the entrance on bare feet. I bent to refill Beto's water dish, only half-listening. Until I heard an excited squeal from the threshold.

"Oh my god." The voice practically vibrated through the entryway. I froze, lifting my head slightly.

Martina sighed again. "Hi, Kari."

Oh, no. I *knew* that voice.

Karina was one of the delivery girls from the bakery— young, chatty, and a direct pipeline to Tres Fuegos' gossip network. She was Gladys' great niece or something like that and had been living with her for the past few years.

"This is so exciting," she gushed. "I *knew* you two were together! Even before Gladys confirmed it."

Martina let out a tired sigh. "Yep. Guilty as charged."

Karina giggled. "But finally seeing it in person is so much better." A beat. "I was visiting my grandmother in San Clemente this weekend and hadn't had the chance to witness this in all its glory. Are you living together now?"

I choked on my own saliva. Martina whipped her head towards me, eyes wide and a slight flush on her cheeks.

I barked out a laugh, striding in the direction of the door

as I plucked the bag of empanadas right out of Karina's hand.

"Not yet," I said, flashing her my most charming grin.

Martina elbowed me in the ribs, and the girl's eyes practically shone with excitement. "Oh my god, yet? So, you're thinking about it?"

I bit back a smirk. "I never said that."

Martina slapped a few bills into Karina's hand, desperate to end the conversation. "Thank you, Kari. We're going to eat now."

"Oh, yeah, of course." She turned abruptly on her heels and headed in the direction of the town square, her long ponytail bouncing behind her.

Martina shut the door a little too forcefully, pressing her forehead against the wood with a deep inhale. I balanced the bag of empanadas in one hand, propping my other against the frame beside her. "Martu," I said innocently.

She lifted her head just enough to glare at me. "This is never going to end, is it?" She snatched the bag from my hand and marched back towards the couch, dropping onto the spot she'd had before and setting the bag with our food on the messy coffee table. Beto was still at his dishes in the kitchen, but followed our movements with his eyes.

I flopped onto the cushion beside her, close enough that our knees almost knocked together. I smirked, reaching into the bag and pulling out one empanada.

"You're unbelievable," she muttered.

"I know," I said around a mouthful of food.

A few minutes passed in comfortable silence as we ate. The couch was too soft, too easy to sink into, and at some point, Martina had tucked one foot beneath her, turning slightly towards me as she chewed.

The cat kept us entertained, going from her lap to mine and back to his chair in a rhythmic sequence. I flicked a glance at her between bites, and it hit me suddenly, how normal this felt.

Like this wasn't some *fake* thing we were entertaining for the town's sake. Like we'd been doing this for years and the expiration date we had discussed was merely a formality, just for the sake of the unconventional pact we had made.

My fingers tightened around my food. I had always known how easy it was to be around Martina. That wasn't new. The feeling of my brain shutting down and everything quieting wasn't new either.

She was here, in my home, curled up on my couch, stealing bites of empanadas from my plate without asking, petting my cat like he was hers, too. She was barefoot, makeup-free and relaxed.

And I was entirely too aware of her.

Too aware of the way her body angled towards me naturally, the way the soft glow of the lamp highlighted the curve of her cheek, the way she flicked a crumb off her thigh without thinking.

I shouldn't have been looking. And yet... I couldn't stop.

Martina let out a slow exhale, resting her head against the couch cushion. "I wish it could always be like this."

I froze. It was her voice—soft, quiet, vulnerable in a way she rarely let herself be—that sent a slow, creeping warmth through my chest.

I swallowed. "Like what?"

She shrugged, staring at the ceiling. "Quiet. Simple. Like the rest of the world doesn't exist for a little while."

I watched her, my throat suddenly dry. It was the same reason I had always loved this little corner I'd carved out. A place that felt like a breath of fresh air when I didn't even know I was holding it in.

I turned my head towards the ceiling, mirroring her. The thoughts I was having were dangerous. The idea of adding her into my space and keeping her there forever.

"You know, Miranda, if you wanted to spend more time alone with me, you could've just asked."

She laughed loudly, shaking her head. "I take it back. I hate it here." She let out a soft sigh, stretching her legs over the couch, her heel brushing lightly against my shin.

Neither of us moved away. The lamp in the corner flickered slightly, casting a warm golden hue over the room. The smell of our food lingered in the air, mixing with the faintest trace of her—vanilla, coffee, something slightly floral. It wasn't strong, but it was there, familiar.

I should have said something stupid to break the moment, something obnoxious to make her roll her eyes at me. That was what I did, my role.

Instead, I just watched her. Watched the way her fingers traced absent patterns against the couch cushion. Watched the slow, steady rise and fall of her chest.

"You ever think about leaving?"

I exhaled, tipping my head back as I let it settle.

"All the time," I admitted.

Her eyes opened, watching me now. "Why don't you?"

Martina's lips parted slightly, almost as if she wanted to add more, say more, question more. But instead, she let her head rest against the couch once more, her gaze flicking toward the ceiling and following the lazy movement of the fan.

I didn't answer, just dragged my hand down my face and stared up at the ceiling, like the answer might be hiding somewhere between the messy strokes of old paint above us.

My fingers brushed absently against the hem of my shirt, my body suddenly too aware of hers beside me. I reached for the last empanada, broke it in half, and handed her a piece without a word. Martina blinked, looking down at it before taking it from my fingers.

She didn't say thank you. She didn't need to. We ate in silence, and for that stretch of time, the whole fucking world felt like it had shrunk to this.

A couch, a quiet room, a cat. And her.

14

JACINTO

"You just might be the luckiest man alive," Martina said, in a calm, almost pleasant voice as she stepped out of the café and onto the cobblestone street a few days later. "Because I haven't murdered you."

I chuckled, shutting the door behind me. "Nah, you'd miss me too much."

She hummed, noncommittal, tugging the long sleeves of her shirt down over her wrists as we neared the town square. "*Lo dudo.*"

I grinned, stretching my arms over my head. "And yet, here you are, showing up to this lovely date with your devoted, handsome boyfriend."

Martina shot me a look. "Handsome is doing a lot of heavy lifting over there."

I clutched my chest, feigning deep, personal injury. "That hurts, Miranda. Really."

She rolled her eyes, but I caught the small tug at the corner of her lips. The barely-there amusement she was trying to suppress.

It had only been a couple of days since we sat on my couch talking about leaving—or not leaving—and things had felt... quieter between us since. Still easy, still familiar. But like we were both waiting for the other to make the next move in this fake relationship.

"Why are you like this?"

"Like what?" I replied, lifting one shoulder casually. "So handsome?"

"Oh my god," she retorted, turning on her heel, back in the direction of the café. "Jacinto."

"Okay, okay, I'll tone it down."

"Or else," she said, walking back in my direction. Her hair was frizzy and rowdy, way longer than I'd ever seen her wear it. Sometimes, when the humidity was out of control, it got so wild and cute—

Keep it together, man.

I focused my attention back to the town square, buzzing with energy. The air was thick with the scent of food. This was another one of those events the town put together to signal the end of the winter, except that this time, everyone was present. Whereas the bonfire was mostly for the younger people, attendance to this picnic was strongly suggested.

Some *mandatory fun*, if you will.

Every table was packed, plates balanced on laps, conversations overlapping, and laughter filled the air.

And, of course, people were watching us.

Martina must have felt it, too, because she laced her hand with mine and tugged me tighter against her body. Her long locks of hair brushed against my arm and gave me goosebumps.

I stilled. Not because it was part of the act, but because she did it so naturally. Effortlessly. Like it wasn't even a thing to think about.

It shouldn't have meant anything.

We wove through the crowd, and I became painfully aware of every small touch, every shift in her body against mine.

Her fingers briefly curled against my forearm when we stopped to greet someone.

My hand brushed the small of her back, guiding her past a crowded table.

She leaned, just slightly, into my side when someone bumped her from behind while we were getting drinks under the shade of a London plane tree.

I didn't want to move away.

We stopped at one of the main tables where my grandparents sat with a few of the other town elders. Granny wiped her hands on a napkin, peering up at us with something between longing and quiet hope.

"*Ay, miralos,*" my grandmother mused, reaching for her drink. "Practically inseparable."

Granny's words hung between us for a moment,

anchored in the air as if she had just stated a simple fact instead of unknowingly tossing gasoline into a fire neither of us had been prepared to light. I could feel the small shift in Martina's breathing, the way her shoulders had barely tensed under my arm before she forced herself to relax.

If the past few days had been any indication, she would roll her eyes. Or huff or scoff or mumble some half-hearted denial. But this was my grandmother we were talking about, and I never in a million years thought she would dare to reply back to her with anything but a smile.

Everyone in this town had a soft spot for Granny Williams.

Instead, Martina picked up the drink I'd been carrying. Her plump lips closed around the plastic straw and she took a long sip, swallowing down slowly while listening to my grandparents speak.

I stared while the conversation moved around us, but my brain had short-circuited.

She didn't hesitate. Didn't make a big deal out of it. She just set the cup back down, as if she did it all the time. She had done it so casually, so easily, like she'd been doing it for years.

Granted, we'd shared food before. An occasional drink on our hikes in the summer.

But this felt slightly different. Like it wasn't just pretend, but normal, natural. Not an act for the sake of the town and our reputations.

I should have let it go. Really.

I still wasn't sure what had thrown me more in that instant—Martina playing along so effortlessly, when she'd fought me every step of the way since the town went up in flames over this so-called relationship, or the fact that I didn't mind it at all.

Martina laughed at something my grandfather said, and she reached out for me, lacing those fingers through mine again. I grabbed my drink and took a sip, feeling the weight of her small, subtle touches lingering against every nerve ending of my skin.

"You know, Jacin," my grandfather started. His ankle was set on top of his opposite knee in a classic stance. I couldn't remember if I'd ever seen him sitting any other way. "This reminds me of when your parents first got together."

I sighed, dragging a hand down my face. "*Tata.*"

Martina turned to me with a soft smile on her face and said, "Ohhh, I want to know more."

Granny ignored me, settling into her seat and leaning towards my grandfather, completely at ease. "It was the same back then," she said. "Everyone already knew. Your father tried to act like he had a choice in the matter, but we all knew it was just a matter of time with those two. And look at them now." She turned her head slightly, looking into the distance where my parents were... swaying to the music being played? My father whispered something in my mother's ear that made her laugh out loud.

Martina's thumb rubbed absentmindedly against my

hand, something small and calm that she probably didn't realize she was doing. "And he… didn't mind that? That everyone had decided for him?"

My grandfather chuckled. "Did it matter? Some things just *are*, honey." He gestured between us, his mischievous grin widening. "Like this."

Martina didn't look at me, but instead her gaze lingered on my parents. They'd always been so in love, it was some-times disgusting to see. And something about the way she'd framed the question, like she wasn't talking about my parents at all, made me stop.

"They just needed a little push," Granny said, turning to my grandfather with a soft smile. The conversation moved on quickly, and they kept talking like nothing had changed, like this was the most done deal to ever deal, a matter of fact, just like it had been for my parents. And probably for them before that.

"They're all in," I said under my breath, gesturing toward my grandparents as they chatted with someone else at the table.

Martina didn't answer right away. She took another sip from the drink we were still sort of sharing, then shrugged.

"Everyone likes a good story," she said. "We are giving them one."

Her tone wasn't sharp, exactly. But it landed heavier than I expected.

I leaned back a little, studying her profile. "So, that's all this is to you? A story?"

She turned to me, brows raised, her voice even. "Isn't that what it was supposed to be? Just temporary, to get the town off of our backs and..." She gestured vaguely with her hands, almost like she was presenting the town to me.

I didn't have a good answer to that. She was right, of course. It *was* a story.

Before I could say anything else, Manuela called her name across the square. Martina pulled her hand from mine, waving quickly before slipping away toward her best friend.

I sat down beside my grandparents. My plastic cup was still warm from where her hand had been.

15

"I could use a little nap just about now," Martina said an hour later, once she'd made her rounds of the picnic, yawning like I'd never seen her yawn before. The adrenaline of the past few days had finally caught up to her, the weight of them probably settling in her limbs. The picnic, the stares, the way the town just spoke about us... And on top of it all, she had spent the morning at the café, making up for the hours she'd lost when I had dragged her to our date.

She looked bone-deep exhausted.

By the time we left the square, the sun had started to dip low over the rooftops, casting long shadows across the cobblestones. The town's picnic had finally wound down, and everyone was slowly making their way to their homes, worn out from the final event of the season.

"Okay," I replied, grabbing her wrist in a gentle way and tugging her towards me. Martina had been walking back to the café. They were closed, of course, but it was almost auto-matic, muscle memory at this point for her. Her body just knew where to go, even though the doors were locked and the day was over.

But that wasn't where she needed to go.

I pulled a little harder, making sure she understood what I meant by that.

"Let's go home."

Martina stilled for a few seconds. Then, her body swayed slightly toward mine, and for a brief second, she was close enough for me to catch the scent of sugar still clinging to her skin, something soft and warm beneath it, something that smelled so clearly like the end of winter.

She blinked up at me, her brows furrowing slightly, opening and closing her mouth like she was trying to make sense of me.

I wasn't ready to call it a day. I needed more time. More uninterrupted time that was just ours, and not something we performed for the town. More quiet conversations that I could roll over in my head later, picking apart the way she looked at me, the way she hesitated just before speaking.

More days to figure out what the hell was happening here. Why there was a flutter in my chest every time she was near me. A knot in my throat every time she even looked in my direction.

She shook her head, slow and deliberate.

"No," she finally said, voice softer than I expected. "I'm just going to go take a nap. I think I'm done for today."

But she didn't move. Not right away. She just stood there, in the middle of our small town's sidewalk, still caught in whatever this was between us.

I leaned in just enough to make sure she had no choice but to hear what I had to say. "Come take a nap at my place," I murmured.

There was a small shift in her shoulders, fingers curling against her side like she was gripping onto something invisible.

"That's not a date," she murmured back, not meeting my gaze.

I grinned. "I disagree," I said, keeping my voice low, even. "Sleeping next to someone? That's pretty intimate, Martina."

She finally looked up then, her brown eyes searching mine, and I could see it, the way she was running through excuses in her head. The reasons she should say no. The reasons she shouldn't let this—whatever it was becoming— keep happening.

And then, finally—

She sighed.

Not dramatically. Not annoyed. But like she was giving in to something that was inevitable. As if, finally, acknowledging this town was right.

"Fine," she said, shoving her hand in the back pocket of her jeans. "But if you steal the blanket, I'm leaving."

I laughed, stepping back to let her fall into place beside me. "That's fair."

She didn't argue. Didn't even complain when I nudged her gently with my shoulder, guiding her through the narrow streets of our town in the direction of my house.

We walked in silence most of the way back to my corner of Tres Fuegos. I glanced occasionally out of the corner of my eye. She still looked tired, her steps slightly slower than usual, her hands covered by the cuffs of her long sleeves like she was trying to hold on to whatever warmth she had left from the day.

The front door creaked slightly as I pushed it open, stepping aside to let Martina in first.

She didn't hesitate or pause. She just walked in like she'd done it a hundred times before and took off her sneakers by the door, leaving them in the exact spot where she removed them.

"I can't promise Beto won't try to nap on your face."

Martina let out a soft huff of laughter, dropping her phone on my entry table. I watched as she walked farther inside, her hands brushing absently over the back of my couch, the edge of my bookshelf. "That's okay. You know I can't say no to him."

I walked into the kitchen, needing a second to reset, to pretend like this wasn't doing something to my insides.

"Want something to drink?" I called over my shoulder, opening the fridge.

"*No, gracias,*" she replied, voice quieter and muffled slightly. When I turned, she had already curled up in the corner of the couch, tucking a blanket around her legs, completely at ease. I leaned against the counter, watching her for just a second too long.

She let out a slow breath, her head dropping back slightly against the armrest. Her eyes fluttered shut.

I should have walked away and let her sleep. Probably should have used the moment to find my cat and lock him in my room so that he wouldn't wake my girl up.

But instead, I stood there, hovering like an idiot, watching as she shifted on my couch, tucking her hands beneath her cheek.

Her breathing slowed, deep and steady, the kind that only came when you let yourself feel safe. I sighed, running a hand through my hair before giving in and grabbing the spare blanket from the armchair. I was probably going to end up covered in Beto's fur, but at that precise moment, I didn't give a shit.

I sat on the couch and leaned back, letting my arm settle on the backrest behind her head.

That was all. That was fine. I could turn the TV on and watch something with no sound on. Maybe read a book or doom scroll on my phone. Just keep her company until she wakes up and then take her back to her house.

Martina shifted, the blanket slipping from her shoulder. I didn't think. Didn't let myself. I simply reached over, pulling it back to where it was.

And then her fingers brushed mine, a small, barely-there touch, and for a second, neither of us moved.

Then, she shifted. Not much.

Just enough that the weight of her foot pressed against my thigh, her toes resting against it like they had always belonged there.

I stayed absolutely stock-still, because if I moved, I'd have to acknowledge it. Martina let out a quiet exhale, the kind that wasn't a sigh but wasn't a hum either. Her fingers twitched slightly, curling against the blanket.

The weight of her breathing, the way it hitched for just a fraction of a second before settling again, it was too much.

I let my eyes drift over her face, her lashes resting against her cheeks, her lips slightly parted. She looked so soft like this. Not just physically, but entirely.

Like the parts of her that held everything together—the sharp edges, the quiet deliberation, the exhaustion she carried around her like armor—had finally let go.

Her hand shifted again, this time peeking out of the blanket and settling on her thigh as if she were searching for something. My fingers, traitorous and reckless, itched to move.

Not much. Just enough to close the distance and to trace the back of her hand, to feel something real in a moment—a situation—that wasn't supposed to be. God, I was so tempted to touch her.

I exhaled slowly, staring at the ceiling, willing myself to ignore the way my entire body felt too aware of her. Too awake.

This wasn't like those other moments. The shoulder

bumps, the linked arms, the fake doting meant for an audience. This wasn't for the town.

A hundred tiny decisions brought us here. A lie told once. A town that kept repeating it. A girl who said yes for reasons she didn't fully explain and maybe didn't fully understand.

And me.

The one who said it wouldn't mean anything.

I let my eyes close, not because I was tired, but because I couldn't keep looking at her without wanting more.

The room was quiet. Her breath was steady again. And for now, at least, that had to be enough for me.

16

MARTINA

I woke up slowly, like surfacing from somewhere deep. The air was warm, heavy, filled with the familiar scent of clean laundry and something undeniably Jacinto. It was dark, like the sun had set and the world had slowed down to a halt.

For a moment, I didn't remember where I was. All I knew was that I was so, so comfortable. It wrapped around me, solid and steady, seeping into my skin like sunlight after a long stretch of cold. My body felt heavy, that delicious kind of drowsy where I wasn't fully awake but not quite asleep either.

I blinked groggily. The dim light of the porch sconce filtered through the front window. The couch. The ceiling fan turned lazily overhead. The scratchy texture of Jacinto's blanket beneath my fingertips.

And then, I felt him.

The realization settled slowly, creeping in through the

fog of sleep until it was impossible to ignore. There was an arm draped across my waist, fingers curled slightly against my stomach. A broad chest at my back, the deep, even rhythm of someone else's breathing.

Sometime during the nap, we had shifted.

Or maybe I had. Or maybe he had.

The heat of his body seeped through my clothes, through my skin, right down to my bones. Every nerve seemed to wake up before I did. My legs buzzed with something electric. My chest felt too tight, like my lungs couldn't fully expand.

And I felt all of Jacinto. Including the part of him that wasn't exactly asleep anymore.

Oh.

Oh.

My entire body went still, but it was the wrong kind of stillness—every muscle locked tight, my pulse pounding in my throat so loud I was sure he could hear it. My stomach swooped, heat blooming low and fast and out of my control. There was a strange, terrifying ache between my legs, sharp and insistent, like my body had made a decision before I had a chance to even talk myself into anything.

Jacinto let out a deep, sleepy exhale, the warmth of it ghosting against the back of my neck, and my whole body shuddered. I tried to stay still, to pretend that I was still asleep, but I was a terrible liar. My skin was giving me away.

Then came that tiny groan from him. Low. Content. And I nearly whimpered with need. It was the kind of sound that felt like a secret—intimate and half-aware, like it came from a place in him that didn't know how to pretend.

For one reckless, oxygen-starved second, I wanted to press back into him. To feel him wake up the rest of the way. To see what he'd do.

Jacinto stirred, and the arm across my waist tensed and pulled, his breathing changing just enough to tell me he was waking up.

Then, slowly, carefully, he adjusted. A small shift of his hips, an almost imperceptible movement, but I felt all of it. His thigh against the back of mine, the way our hips lined up too neatly, the slide of his barely-there fingertips over the hem of my shirt.

Oh, *shit.*

Heat coiled low in my belly, sharp and all-consuming. My skin tingled, hyper-aware, my mouth dry and jaw tight with effort. I couldn't even breathe right. I was scared to.

Slowly, carefully, he started to pull back. He was moving in such a way that made me feel like he didn't want to startle me or acknowledge it either. His hips shifted first, putting the necessary space between us, his arm loosening its hold on me but not quite letting go.

I squeezed my eyes shut, hoping he would think I was still asleep, that we could pretend, even for just a minute longer, that this hadn't just happened. That it was nothing.

But then, in the quiet of his home, he exhaled.

A deep, slow breath followed by his fingers brushing ever so slightly over my ribs.

"Martina." His voice was rough with sleep, right at my ear.

All right. Okay, yeah.

Nope.

I cleared my throat, sitting up way too fast and immediately regretting it.

The room was dark in the late evening, and I could faintly hear the sound of crickets and some laughter that came from the town square just a few blocks away.

Jacinto was beside me, his body half-stretched against the back of the couch, his shirt rumpled and hair slightly mussed from sleep. The blanket we had shared was a mess of tangled fabric between us, evidence that we had, in fact, shifted into something we shouldn't have.

I cleared my throat again, louder this time. Forced my limbs to move, to function, to do literally anything other than remember how it had felt to wake up like that, with one of my best friends draped around my body.

"Great nap. Amazing," I said, and my voice sounded foreign to me. "Excellent job there."

I shot him finger guns as I stood. Por el amor de dios, *get it together. What is wrong with you?*

Jacinto blinked at me, still sluggish from sleep, his green eyes half-lidded and too fucking soft, like he wasn't in the present yet, instead lingering somewhere in between.

I needed to get out.

"Uh," I said, taking a step back quickly and nearly tripping over another blanket that was on the floor by the sofa. "I'm going to... I'm going to head out."

I nodded to myself, as if that made it less of a freak-out.

Jacinto sat up slowly, stretching slightly, his movements lazy and comfortable. As if he hadn't just woken up with my whole body pressed against him. As if he couldn't read my thoughts right now.

"Hmm," he murmured, scratching the back of his head, watching me with that too observant expression he always had on when I tried too hard to act like something hadn't rattled me. "You probably have to go to work, right?"

"Yes," I said too quickly, looking at my watchless wrist, even when I knew the coffee shop was closed because of the town-wide event earlier today. "Yes! Exactly. Work. My mother is probably—probably looking for me. Worried sick."

Jacinto nodded slowly, one of the corners of his mouth lifting ever so slightly with amusement.

I could feel his gaze on me as I whipped around, scanning the room for my things, because at that moment it felt like I'd left behind an entire life's worth of belongings strewn about instead of just my shoes and my phone. I found everything near the door, and shoved my feet into my shoes with unnecessary force, the tongue crumpling inside and making it impossible to put on as I tried to hurry.

"I'll—" I stumbled over my words, still avoiding his gaze and the couch or the blanket, or the way the room felt different now. "I'll see you this week? At the coffee shop."

A pause.

And then—his smirk.

"I'll be sure to make a big scene when I walk in."

I groaned. "Yes, yes. Make it loud. Embarrassing. Maybe even get on one knee, throw some wildflowers around. I think we could use some confetti, really sell the whole thing."

Jacinto grinned, leaning against the armrest of the couch, watching me with way too much amusement, like he knew exactly what I was doing.

"Anything for my girlfriend."

Fake girlfriend. "Don't push it."

He laughed. Deep, easy, natural.

And I had to get out of there before my body spontaneously combusted from the heat between us.

"Okay, bye," I blurted out, reaching for the door.

I didn't wait for his response or give him time to say anything that would slow me down. We didn't need to make this harder, heavier, even more dangerous than it already felt. It was supposed to be easy, just a few fake dates and to be seen around with him so people would stop pitying me. Attraction? That wasn't on my bingo card, and it should stay the fuck away from it, too.

The moment I stepped out and closed the door behind me, I ran like my life depended on it. Like the walls of his house were closing in on me, because if I stayed even a second longer, something irreversible would happen. *Again.*

The cool evening air hit my face, but it wasn't enough to

cool the heat still trapped under my skin, making everything bubble underneath the surface. Everything. And I meant *everything* was beating.

Tres Fuegos had begun to quiet down for the night, but there were still people out and voices spilling from the square. A few shopkeepers were back inside their stores, probably taking advantage of the fact that food and drink from the picnic was long gone to make a few extra sales. The streetlights flickered to life above me as I hurried down the dark sidewalk, my breath coming too fast, my pulse still racing.

I prayed—actually prayed—that no one saw me. That the people still lingering near the square were too busy, too tired, too drunk to remember the sight of me fleeing Jacinto's house like something—someone—was on fire.

Me. I was on fire.

17

"Wildflowers."

"Yes," I said impatiently. I wanted to roll my eyes and shake someone. I had spent all morning on my phone trying —and failing—to get people to understand what I was looking for.

"Like the flowers that grow in the fields?"

"Yes, Charlie," I said with a groan. My oldest brother was mocking me, I was sure, but I couldn't quite see his expression from where I stood. After last night, and Martina's not-so-subtle freakout after the nap date we had, I had racked my brain to try and figure out where the hell in this town I could find wildflowers this time of year. Just for her.

Yes, we had winter flowers—snowdrops and hellebores and thistles—but none of those were beautiful enough for her. She needed the biggest, wildest bunch of flowers I could find.

I took a step in the direction of Charlie's office, and Victoria followed me with her eyes. She was pretending to be clicking away on her computer, but her desktop reflected slightly on the window behind her, and there wasn't a single document open on there.

"What do you need wildflowers for, Gato?" she asked, crossing and uncrossing her legs. Finally, she gave up clicking on her mouse and shifted her body slightly so that she could see better out her door and into the open space in our office where I stood.

"None of your business," I said with a smile and a wink. "Respectfully, you're worse than some of the older ladies in town."

"Pft," she said with a nonchalant hand gesture. "I'm honored."

"So, wildflowers?"

"Why would you assume that I would know where to find wildflowers in the middle of winter?" my brother called from his office tucked in the back of the building. He had the biggest and messiest one yet, but it suited him completely.

"First of all," I replied, taking a step forward and leaning against his door frame. His desk was covered in piles of paperwork—legal briefs, some in folders, some in envelopes, text books, small notebooks everywhere. There was a precarious pile of no less than three coffee mugs in a corner of the tabletop, one quick move away from falling off and crashing against the floor. "How dare you? And second of all, you're always going on walks around town. One could easily assume you know exactly where all the secrets live in Tres Fuegos."

Charlie scoffed just as Victoria joined me, walking straight into Charlie's office and taking a seat across from him.

"Yes, Charlie, tell us all your secrets."

Charlie leaned back in his chair with a groan, like the very idea of sharing anything mildly helpful was exhausting. "There's a reason they're called wildflowers, Jacinto. They're wild. Seasonal. They don't just... show up on command."

I ignored him and turned to Victoria, who was clearly enjoying this too much. "You're more resourceful. Where would you go?"

She grinned, lacing her fingers behind her head and carefully avoiding messing with her perfectly styled hair. "Well, I'd probably start with Simona's farm. Sometimes she lets the back pasture grow out a bit and it gets full of weeds and color. But even that's a gamble right now."

"Nope. She was my first call this morning," I said, dragging a hand through my hair. "She laughed at me. Told me to check with the universe."

Charlie snorted. "Sounds about right."

"I tried the trails near our parents' house, too," I added, counting it off on my fingers. "Nothing but stiff thistles. I even walked down that abandoned access road behind the doctor's office. *Nada.*"

Victoria raised her eyebrows. "That's commitment."

"Commitment?" I let out a breathless laugh. "You don't

even know. I've got a list, Vee. A literal list. This is stop four of nine." I pulled out my phone, scrolling through a hastily compiled note. "I'm thinking the hills behind the cemetery next. Or maybe the big ditch near the soccer fields? I know that sounds insane, but—"

Charlie chuckled, a slow grin spreading across his face.

"Forget it," I muttered, pocketing my phone with a frustrated sigh. "You're both useless."

I turned to go, already mentally mapping the fastest way to get to the hills behind the cemetery before the sun dipped too low.

"Gato," Victoria called after me, her voice teasing but not unkind. "At this rate, you're going to end up in San Clemente bribing a florist for daisies that grew last week."

———

By the time I reached the next town over, I'd already crossed off three locations from my list, picked a dozen half-frozen weeds, and questioned all of my life choices.

I hadn't worked a single minute today, completely derailed by this ridiculous, desperate side quest like my life depended on it. And the result was a closed florist shop, sign flipped. But the lights were still on. *Why would someone close their business so early in the morning?*

I jogged to the door and knocked like someone who didn't care that his pride was already in shambles. Approximately one hundred percent of Tres Fuegos—minus

Martina—had witnessed my panicked mission. They were probably having a field day right now, sitting by a fire and exchanging jokes about me.

Inside, a woman—late twenties, headphones in, very much done with her work day at nine in the morning—looked up from the register and immediately narrowed her eyes. She shook her head slowly and pointed to the CLOSED sign.

I knocked again, more insistently.

She hesitated, then finally walked over and cracked the door open just an inch. "Jacinto Williams," she said, one brow raised. "What in the world are you doing here?"

I blinked. "Wait, *¿te conozco?*"

She rolled her eyes. "You argued with me for ten minutes about the best ice cream shop in the *sierras* at Valentina's birthday party two years ago. She's my first cousin, twice removed."

"Right. Right." I nodded my head dramatically. Even though I had absolutely no recollection of that conversation ever happening, and I had absolutely no idea what *first cousin, twice removed* even meant. "Nice to see you again."

She crossed her arms. "This better be good."

I nodded quickly. "I need wildflowers."

She stared. "You came all this way for...wildflowers?"

"It's for a girl," I said, and immediately wanted to punch myself in the face for sounding like I was in the middle of a teen drama. "And before you say anything... Yes, I know it's winter. No, I don't care. I'll pay whatever you want. Just—

please. Do you have anything that looks remotely like they grew in the wild?"

She exhaled, her face caught somewhere between exasperated and intrigued. "God, you really are as dramatic as everyone says."

"That's a yes?"

A long beat. Then she pulled the door open wider and stepped aside. "Come in," she finally said.

I stepped inside, instantly hit with the humid warmth of a flower shop.

"Sorry to disappoint," she said as she walked in the direction of a back door, tossing her long braid over her shoulder. "But if you were expecting some sort of magical meadow in here, you're out of luck. Winter is brutal on us."

She paused to unlock a sliding door at the very back of the shop. A wave of warm, earthy air escaped before she opened it fully and motioned for me to follow.

"What's this?"

"My secret stash," she said over her shoulder. "Where I keep the good stuff."

I stepped into the greenhouse behind the shop and stopped breathing for a second. It wasn't huge, but it was packed. There were two rows of pots and vertical stands, flowers blooming from every corner, tiny irrigation lines weaving through like vines. Pinks, purples, oranges. Wild, untamed color against the pale walls of the greenhouse. It looked like something out of a dream.

"You're kidding me," I whispered.

"Grew most of these from seed that I've been collecting for years from the mountain. Takes a lot of work. And heat. And pure stubbornness."

"I need all of this," I said, eyes scanning the chaos of petals. "Like, every single day."

She raised an eyebrow. "You want to hire me?"

"Yes."

"Daily bouquets? That's not cheap."

"No, just a daily bloom. So that her bouquet always looks fresh. I'll pay whatever."

She chuckled, soft and knowing. "*Pobrecito.*"

The florist moved past me, plucking a few stems here and there, humming as she worked, occasionally glancing at me like I was a particularly entertaining stray dog.

"First one's on the house." She turned, handed me a loose bunch of brightly mismatched blooms—sunbursts, sprigs of chamomile, a few orange and dark red things I couldn't name—and shooed me away with her hand and a smirk on her face. "Good luck."

18

MARTINA

The door swung shut behind an older man as I handed him his change and smiled politely.

"Tell Mariana I said *feliz cumpleaños,*" I added as my hand returned to the register drawer and pushed it shut.

"Only if you promise to come do her makeup again next year," he said, waving his free hand and heading to the door.

I laughed, but it came out uneven. "We'll see. I might be too busy running the shop."

He smiled again and exited, the bell above the door jingling again.

Just like that, I was alone.

The morning rush had thinned, leaving the café bathed in warm light and quiet. I wiped my hands on a towel and leaned against the counter, staring at nothing in particular. Outside, Tres Fuegos was slowly waking up after the weekend. The early risers had already passed through, grabbing their morning drinks and pastries for the road before heading to the bigger towns just outside ours for their jobs. The pace had started to slow, settling into the comfortable lull that always came after the morning rush, a brief pocket of quiet before the day stretched on and the afternoon crowd arrived.

Now that school was back in session after the winter break, afternoons were chaotic and unpredictable, sometimes seeing upwards of thirty or forty kids after their day was over.

I usually found comfort in my calm routine. That was the moment where I could catch my breath for a minute, look at some makeup videos on the Internet and daydream about how I would apply them to possible clients. But today, it only left me feeling adrift.

I had tossed and turned the night before, barely closing my eyes before I had to wake up to open the store. Every time I forced my mind to relax, my body remembered the press of Jacinto behind me, the warmth of his body, the way my name had sounded in that deep, groggy voice, like it had slipped out before he could stop it. Even now, standing behind the counter, I felt restless. Almost as if waiting for something.

My mother came back to the front from the storeroom, balancing a large pile of napkins in one hand and a bag of sugar packets in the other.

"You look tired," she said, her tone more observant than concerned.

I didn't bother looking up from the counter. "Didn't sleep much."

Her gaze flickered, just slightly, like she was considering whether or not to press further. Instead, she grabbed a damp cloth and started wiping down the espresso machine, falling into the pace of the work alongside me.

"Your sister called this morning."

My stomach tightened, just slightly, and I reached for a dish, drying it carefully before stacking it in its place. "Yeah?"

"She's finalizing everything for December," my mother continued, still focused on her cleaning, as if this wasn't something that sent a strange, unfamiliar tightness curling around my ribs. "She says she's excited to come back. To be home."

My stomach clenched.

Home. Sure. For her.

For me? It suddenly felt like the walls were shifting again, like I was standing in the wrong room entirely, just waiting to be told to make space.

I should have been relieved. I should have felt something other than this strange, pressing tightness in my chest.

But all I could think of at this precise moment was: what would happen to me?

I hadn't made a plan. I hadn't looked beyond next week, really. My only deadline was the end of my fake relationship with Jacinto, something that would mean a before and after for me. At the café, I'd just filled in the space she left behind.

And now that she was coming back to claim that space, I wasn't sure what was left for me at all. Yes, I would definitely have my job here and running the books like I'd been doing with my business degree since I'd graduated, but what else? Where was I going to go after?

My mother must have seen something in my face, because she gave me a look, soft but firm. "It'll be good for you, too, Martu," she said, her voice quieter now, as to avoid any lurking neighbors. "You'll finally have more time to figure out what's next and do more of that makeup thing."

Next.

"That's just a thing I do for my friends," I replied instantly, diminishing the hope that I could make it something else. Nothing had really happened, anyway. Even if I had done Victoria's makeup for her wedding, it didn't mean that the town would take to it and start hiring me out of the blue for that purpose. It was wishful thinking, really, but tons of fun to dream.

I forced a small smile, nodding as if it made sense.

The door swung open, startling me. Marta Romero, director of the Tres Fuegos community center, walked in, clipboard in hand and hair frizzing from the fine rain outside.

She smiled at me and my mom. "Perfect, you're both here. I meant to catch you yesterday."

I stepped away from the espresso machine slowly. "Hi, *buen día.* Everything okay?

She beamed. "More than okay. We just finalized the

casting for the town play, and I remembered the makeup you did for that girls' dance show in San Clemente last year." She turned to my mother. "She has a real gift, you know? I was wondering if you'd be up for handling stage makeup for our play in a few months?"

I stood frozen. My mother's eyebrows shot up, but she didn't say a word.

"Oh," I said finally. "That's... Thank you. I hadn't really thought about it."

"Well, think about it. And name your price," Marta said warmly. "We'll need someone who can work with the kids and the adults, and I'd rather go with someone local than outsource it to anyone from the other towns since we all know how that turned out last year."

She shook her head and blinked at me, then tapped her clipboard once and left as quickly as she had come in.

My mother studied me for a long moment before moving on, disappearing back toward the kitchen.

"I just want you to be happy," she said with her back turned to me.

She said it like it was simple—but nothing about wanting more had ever felt simple to me.

———

I didn't turn around the moment I heard the door open, instead focusing on the coffee cup in my hands, the drying cloth moving over the rim in slow, deliberate circles. But even without looking, I could feel Jacinto's energy—easy, confident, a little too smug for this early in the day.

I sighed, bracing myself before finally glancing up.

And that's when I saw them.

A bouquet of wildflowers: bright, messy, untamed, held loosely in one of my fake boyfriend's hands.

The stems were uneven, some of the petals already slightly wilted at the edges, like they'd been plucked by hand in a hurry or maybe with too much enthusiasm. They weren't perfectly arranged, weren't something ordered from a florist or wrapped neatly in cellophane with a huge ribbon to complete it.

They were real, gathered, thought of.

They were him.

My heart lurched before I could stop it.

Jacinto stood in front of me like he had all the time in the world, one hand tucked into the pocket of his slacks, the other holding out the bouquet like it was the most natural thing in the world.

"Good morning, *mi sol*," he said, his voice smooth and just loud enough to make sure everyone in the café heard.

I groaned, barely resisting the urge to roll my eyes. "Gato—"

But he just tilted his head slightly, cutting me off as he lifted the flowers a fraction higher. "You mentioned them the other night," he said, casually, like it was nothing. "Sorry it took me so long to get them for you. It was a busy week."

A flush crept up my neck and into my face, unbidden and

entirely unwelcome. I wasn't even sure he meant to remind me of the last time we'd spent time alone together or the way I had left his house in such a hurry that I barely remembered what I had said in my panicked haste. But there he was, right in front of me, proof that he had remembered anyway.

I wiped my hands against my apron, hesitating before reaching for the bouquet, my fingers brushing against the rough stems. I expected the flowers to be cold, but they weren't. They were warm, as if they had just been relaxing in the sun before being handpicked by this handsome man that stood in front of me with a lopsided smile and the softest eyes.

"You—" I cleared my throat, struggling for words. "Where did you get these?"

Jacinto smirked, shifting his weight against the counter. "You know, around."

A hush had fallen over the coffee shop, subtle but unmistakable. The group of older women in the corner had stopped pretending to mind their own business. Someone near the door whispered something, muffled giggles breaking through the silence. The young man who sometimes helped at the register-—who I knew for a fact had no real interest in town gossip—was now leaning slightly closer, watching.

Jacinto didn't seem to care. If anything, he was relishing in the spotlight and playing his part beautifully. But his eyes

—those sharp green eyes that held so much mischief—his eyes were watching me.

Waiting.

I cleared my throat and forced a small, skeptical smile onto my lips, trying to drag this back to where it was supposed to be—an act. A joke. A performance for this town. "Dramatic gestures much?" I asked, lifting the bouquet slightly. "You are enjoying this way too much."

His smirk didn't fade. If anything, it softened into something more genuine, a smile just for me to understand.

"Of course I am."

My fingers curled around the stems as I studied his face.

"See you tonight?"

"Sure," I croaked, and watched him walk away, both hands tucked into his pockets, right to his office across the town square.

19

AT THIS HOUR, no one should have been coming in. Not unless it was my mother returning for something she forgot or Jacinto showing up unannounced just to get on my nerves.

I turned, expecting either of those things, but I found Manuela instead, standing just inside the door and shaking off the evening chill like she belonged there.

I blinked. "You're back."

Her lips twitched in amusement as she dropped her purse on the first chair she saw. "Wow. What a warm welcome. So glad to be home."

I huffed out a laugh, rolling my eyes as I tossed the cleaning rag into the small prep sink we had right by the coffee machine. "Didn't you just text me last night to say that you were staying two more weeks?"

She shrugged, stepping farther inside, her shoes clicking softly against the floor as she moved toward the counter. "I was supposed to, but everything is packed and ready to go, and there is no point in paying more rent if I can work from my parents' home until I leave. And I have to go to New York in a few weeks to house hunt and all that so…"

"Yeah," I said, the realization that this was real hitting me right in the middle of the chest.

Again.

"And besides, you looked like you were dying for an excuse to stay open late."

I didn't argue. Didn't tell her that, for once, I actually hadn't been desperate for an excuse to linger there. I'd already lingered too much today, avoiding the man that suddenly made my heart beat faster than normal.

My gaze flickered, without meaning to, towards the bouquet of wildflowers still sitting near the register. The bright purple and deep red petals stood out against the wood of the counter.

Manuela noticed immediately, and I could feel her watching me as she slipped onto one of the barstools and folded her arms on the counter. She didn't say anything right away, which was worse.

She tilted her head toward the flowers. "So."

"Nope," I said with a sigh. "Manuela—"

"A grand gesture."

I pressed my palms against the counter and leaned

forward, lowering my voice as if someone could still be listening, despite the fact that the place was deserted. "It's not like that, I swear."

She hummed under her breath, tapping her fingers against the surface. "Could've fooled me."

I exhaled sharply, feeling something tighten in my chest that I wasn't ready to name. I couldn't lie to my friend, especially because she had the unnatural ability to suss me out. I pulled my apron over my head and hung it up on the hook by the kitchen door, trying to ignore the weight of her gaze following me.

"That's the whole point."

"Okay," she said, grinning as she propped her chin on her hand. "I'm still trying to wrap my head around this." She let out a laugh, sinking back into the chair with a dramatic sigh. "You two have been dancing around each other for years. And now you're... Fake dating?" Manuela gestured with her hands, resting her body slowly against the back of the chair. "Except you're clearly having the time of your life, and he's out here picking you wildflowers like a boy with a crush."

I turned back around, my arms crossing automatically over my chest. "We're just playing along until people get bored."

Manuela smiled softly, the movement reaching her eyes in a way that made everything feel lighter. "Martu."

"*¿Qué?*"

Her expression softened. "You're allowed to like it."

I let out a long breath, pressing my thumb into the wood of the counter.

"And what would that even look like?" I asked finally, quieter this time. "What does that even mean—us?" I looked at her. "We've been friends forever. I know how he thinks. He's always been... Jacinto. This isn't supposed to feel like anything."

Manuela blinked. "But it does."

I looked away again, the truth too sharp in my chest. "Yeah. It does. And that scares the shit out of me."

The words settled around my heart and stayed there, a mix between uncomfortable and validating. But how would I admit to everyone that this was the most fun I had had in a long time? Sometimes, it made me feel like I was living the most boring life, just standing on the sideline of this town, chuckling along with everyone's shenanigans.

But with Jacinto...it was brighter, sunnier, much more fun. Like living life in technicolor consistently.

She must have sensed that she had pushed enough, because she didn't press any further. Instead, she hopped off from the stool and walked behind the counter, crouching low to grab the bottle of wine we kept hidden in the small fridge for nights just like these.

Manuela stood and grabbed two of the big mugs, pouring a generous amount in each one before heading off to sit at one of the tables by the windows. "January. After the holidays," she said with an exhale as she sat, stretching her long legs and setting her feet on the seat of the chair next to her.

I frowned. "What?"

She looked at me now, really looked at me. "That's how much time I have left here."

"You make it sound like it's a death sentence." I tried to joke, but it suddenly felt real. Of course it had felt real when she dropped the bomb on me at the bonfire and then disappeared to Buenos Aires, and all hell broke loose with Jacinto.

But this was normal. Manuela lived in Buenos Aires full-time, and visited—a lot—so her absence was barely noticeable. We spoke almost every day. And this felt...

She was leaving Tres Fuegos entirely, moving across the world to the city of dreams, a place that felt more like an illusion than something real.

I sat down across from her, suddenly needing the support of the chair beneath me.

Manuela had been my person for as long as I could remember. Through every boy-crush disaster, every "should we leave this town?" daydream, every closing shift where we plotted futures bigger and brighter than Tres Fuegos while wiping down tables.

She was the one who knew what kind of silence meant I was spiraling. The one who never asked if I was okay—just showed up with wine and a plan.

We used to make lists. Of cities we'd visit. Of jobs we'd have. We used to send each other apartments we'd never afford and pictures of subway stations we'd never set foot in, and somehow all of that felt more solid than this conversation.

Because now she was actually doing it. And I wasn't.

She exhaled, dragging her hands through her hair before shaking her head. "It's weird, right? I keep thinking about how long we've talked about leaving, how we always said we'd do it together, and now..." She let out a soft laugh, but there was something hollow beneath it. "Now I'm actually fucking doing it."

I stared at my hands and felt the weight of what she wasn't saying. *Now you are not.*

I forced a small smile, but it felt wrong on my lips. "You're going to love it."

Manuela smiled, too, but it didn't reach her blue eyes. "Yeah." She hesitated, then nudged my leg under the table. "You know you don't have to stay, right?"

"And go where?" I asked with a laugh, shaking my head.

"Anywhere." A small lift of her shoulder, like it was no big deal. Easy peasy. *Just grab your things and go.*

I swallowed, suddenly feeling that suffocation that came and went, when the walls of the café that had been in my family for decades were too tight, like my skin didn't belong to me and it was itching to melt away.

"I just don't want you to wake up one day and realize you never even tried." She nudged me again, lighter this time.

I took a sip of the wine in my obscenely large coffee mug,

the cold doing nothing to relieve the pressure and the fact that Manuela was leaving.

Not just in theory, not in some distant, far-off way that we could laugh about over late-night drinks and call a pipedream. She was actually packing her things, getting on a plane, and starting over.

I had never felt so stuck in my life.

I opened my mouth to say something, anything, but no words came out.

She smiled, soft and knowing, before she chugged her wine and stood.

"Come on," she said, her voice gentle. "I'll walk you home."

I laughed at her joke—the fact that my house, the home where I lived with my mother and, soon enough, my sister too, was attached to this café. A walking, talking metaphor for my entire existence. Might as well have had my name on it.

"Meh," I replied, grabbing my phone from under the counter and turning off the lights while Manuela waited at the door. "I might go for a walk, actually."

Outside, the last of the evening light was folding over the street in golds and grays. I caught a glimpse of Valentina heading left at her street, her hair loose, her jacket a little too thick for the weather. She was heading away from her house, into a random dead-end street tucked right at the edge of town.

I blinked, the moment slipping past like a quiet evening at home.

My eyes drifted back toward the bouquet of wildflowers, sitting by the register, their petals still and open and waiting. I thought about what I'd said to Manuela. That it wasn't supposed to feel like anything. And yet there I was, looking at that stupid bouquet like it had something to say back.

20

MARTINA

There was this thing with Tres Fuegos that, I thought, was what made it so unique. Besides the fact that everyone was up in everyone's business and all of that…The town knew how to put on an event.

Our small—dare I say, tiny—mountain town was mostly busy in the summer, when the tourist season was in full bloom. There were so many things to do here: the hiking trails and the river beds and the paragliding from the top of the mountain. But it was so temporary that the rest of the year felt almost paused. Like we were all holding our breaths until the summer came back around and we could collectively breathe again.

So, a few years ago, some of the older people got together with a few towns down the mountain and they came up with a series of events to encourage some activity. I secretly thought that they did it to keep the gossip mill alive and well, especially once the weather turned and the locals weren't as keen to spend so much time outside.

A weekend market, in the middle of September. A town play, put on by some of the more talented folks in the area in either November or December, depending on how good the actors were each year. An extended weekend to observe the National Festival of the Peanut with no intention to actually honor the fatty legume. A service day to clean up the roads before the tourists came back up in early December, and the heat wasn't as brutal.

And this year, we were hosting the two main activities.

The market pulsed with life, a familiar rhythm of voice, footsteps, and the occasional burst of laughter cutting through the crisp afternoon air. The scent of fresh bread curled from the bakery booth, mixing with the sharp tang of citrus from the fruit vendors. Sunlight filtered through the stalls' colorful awnings, dappling the cobblestone streets with shifting patterns of light and shadow.

I picked up a tomato, turning it over in my hand, pretending to inspect its ripeness while really giving myself something to do. Jacinto's presence loomed beside me, easy and unbothered. He reached for a piece of fruit from another crate, tossing it lightly in his palm like we weren't under intense surveillance.

"You'd think we were celebrities," he murmured, voice low and edged with amusement.

I exhaled sharply, forcing my focus on the produce.

"You've always been a celebrity. This shouldn't feel any different, Gato."

He hummed, shifting his stance slightly. The movement brought him closer, just enough that I felt the brush of his arm against mine.

"Somehow it does," he said, so close to my ear that my body reacted with goosebumps up my arm.

"They're just waiting to see what we'll do next."

He chuckled, mumbling something under his breath as we moved along to the next stall. It all felt so performative, so much like him, that I was surprised by the fact that he had even noticed.

"Stop thinking. I can hear you from all the way over here." I narrowed my eyes at him, shaking my head before moving toward the next vendor. He followed, falling into step with me effortlessly, as if we'd done this a thousand times before. "Don't get any ideas."

"You just make it so easy."

We'd walked through this market—in its many iterations across the years—side by side countless times, weaving through vendors, sharing casual conversations over tiny samples of cheese or fruit.

But this August afternoon felt different.

The sun was warm, but the breeze still carried a hint of mountain cold, and the stalls overflowed with autumn colors—golden pears, deep red peppers, honey in glass jars that caught the light just right.

And maybe Jacinto was right. The weight of the town's gaze had shifted.

Or maybe it was just me.

Because somewhere in the last few weeks, between the first fake date and the way he'd stopped at the coffee shop every single morning with a knowing smile and a wink, something had cracked open.

Enough to make this feel like new ground instead of something we'd walked a hundred times before.

I reached for a plum, fingers brushing against his as he did the same. It was barely a touch and yet the moment stretched, suspended between us like a thin thread pulled tight.

Neither of us moved or said a word. Or reacted, for that matter.

The sounds of the market faded into the background, but I could feel the warmth of his skin, just for a second too long, before I finally jerked my hand back.

Jacinto didn't step away immediately. His eyes flicked to me, searching, measuring. For a moment, they were intent on my mouth, something I—

I swallowed, heart beating in a way that made absolutely no sense at all. So I tried to ignore it and turned, moving toward the bread stall to force some air between us.

Jacinto followed and reached for a small piece among the samples right in the middle of the table, popping it into his mouth like he belonged there. Which, to be fair, he did.

This was Jacinto's town and everyone knew it.

I, on the other hand, felt like I was standing in wet cement, sinking slowly and unable to do a thing about it.

"Are we still pretending this isn't fun?" he asked, voice smooth, mouth still full of bread as he leaned against the wooden post propping up the tent.

I shot him a glare. "Buying tomatoes is serious business, Jacinto."

He grinned. "That's not what I meant."

I exhaled, shifting my weight and avoiding his gaze. "I know."

Another beat passed, another moment that felt bigger than it should have.

And then—

I looked up.

He was already watching me, and something in his expression knocked the breath out of my lungs.

The teasing was still there, but underneath it, something else smoldered. A quiet intensity, a flicker of that same thing I had seen at his house weeks ago, the day we fell asleep on the couch.

My stomach fluttered, and the urge to look away was strong.

Jacinto tilted his head slightly, voice lower now. "You ever think maybe the town got this right?"

"The market? I mean, it's—"

Before I could even think what was happening, he kissed me. Or maybe I kissed him.

I wasn't sure.

One second, we were standing in front of the bread lady, sunlight cutting across the cobblestones, the sound of vendors having conversations with the locals ringing in the air.

And the next, his mouth was on mine, firm, searching, overwhelming.

Whatever I had been holding in my hand slipped from my fingers and tumbled to the ground, rolling between our feet.

Jacinto's hand moved fast, gripping my waist, pulling me in towards his warm body, grounding me.

And I let it happen, because for the first time in a long time, I wasn't thinking. I wasn't worrying about the town, about what this meant, about what would happen next.

It was pure ecstasy and euphoria, all put into one big, delicious feeling.

I stepped back first. Or maybe he did. Who even knew at this point, really.

The one thing I was certain about was that one second, his lips were on mine, his hands firm at my waist, his body solid and warm against me. And the next, there was air between us, and my heart was beating so hard I could feel it in my fingertips.

The world rushed back in.

The noise of the market, the chatter and the shuffling of feet and the playing kids, all came back into focus.

"—great," I finished.

"See? About time!" I heard from behind me, a voice I

couldn't place, but definitely someone who had been invested in this. Maybe the woman from the bakery or the man with the plump, juicy tomatoes.

Heat flamed up my neck. Jacinto still hadn't moved. He was watching me, lips slightly parted, his breathing just a little too uneven. The sun caught the green of his eyes, and for the first time in my life, I didn't know what the hell he could possibly be thinking.

Because he wasn't grinning or brushing this off like nothing had happened.

Neither of us were.

I swallowed hard, but my throat felt tight. My hands flexed, as if trying to remember what they were supposed to do, but all I could feel was the ghost of his touch still on my skin, scorching hot and leaving a permanent mark.

Jacinto exhaled first, shifting his weight and running a hand through his hair in a way that looked almost restless. The familiar glint of amusement flickered back into his expression, but it wasn't the same as before.

"Well," he said, voice hoarse, rough around the edges. "That's one way to keep them entertained."

I let out a sharp breath that wasn't quite a laugh but so desperately wanted to be. My fingers curled into my palms. "You really think that's what that was?"

His gaze flicked to my mouth just for a second.

I sucked in a breath, but he was already stepping back. Already shifting, stretching his arms above his head like he was shaking something off, like he was resetting.

"Martina." His voice was lighter now, forced casual. "If I answer that question honestly, you might have to admit you kissed me back."

My stomach somersaulted. And this traitor of a body betrayed me—heat curled at the base of my spine, something twisted deep in my chest, making me feel off-balance and unsteady.

"We should go," I said, looking around at the prying eyes.

Jacinto watched me a second longer, long enough that I thought he might say something else. Laugh it off and pull me into his body to walk beside him like nothing. Instead, he nodded once, sharp and easy.

"Yeah."

I cleared my throat. "Okay, let's go."

21

JACINTO

THE HEAT of Martina's mouth was still on mine.

Even as we walked away from the market, away from the watchful eyes and the murmured gossip, I still felt it. I felt the shape of her lips, the way she had melted against my body like she had wanted it, too.

But it was more than just a kiss. It had felt like an aggregate of all the small moments we had spent together over the past few weeks—me stopping by at the café every morning with a flower to add to her collection and the soft smile that preceded that, the moment she felt me coming.

It was the way she stared out the window around lunchtime and smiled the moment she saw me leave the office to head to lunch with my brother or my sister-in-law, or sometimes my grandparents.

It was more than just a kiss.

And now, we were walking—silently, side by side,

through the market and away from the town square towards my house.

We moved, drawn together like something inevitable.

Martina didn't say anything, and didn't need to, really. Her arm brushed mine once, then again, and instead of stepping away like she normally would have, she stayed close. The warmth of her skin seeped into me like it had every right to be there.

And maybe it did, didn't it? Maybe it belonged.

My pulse was hammering, blood rushing so hot and fast it felt impossible to slow down. Every step built the sentiment higher, every unspoken word, every stolen glance.

I wasn't sure what we were doing. Or what this meant. All I knew was that it wasn't fake anymore. Not for me, at least. I couldn't fake the way my hand had ached, for weeks, to touch her again or the way her silence somehow said everything.

This was thick. Pressing. Alive.

Martina's hand brushed mine, and I had the clarity to lace my fingers through hers, holding on to it like I was afraid she'd pull away and start running in the opposite direction.

The town was very much alive behind us—the faint music coming from the square, the chirping of birds. But all I could hear was her breath, quick and uneven, matching my own.

All I felt was this sharp, consuming need that I knew I wouldn't be able to ignore for much longer.

Not after knowing what she tasted like, and that she wanted it, too.

My house loomed ahead, quiet and still under the canopy of yellowing leaves and the early fall sun.

She'd been in my home a hundred times before, sat on my couch, drank my beer, thrown a ball for my cat. She was familiar with the way the late afternoon light slanted through the kitchen window, the way the old wooden floors creaked in the same two spots, and how my bed was never properly made.

Back then, those little moments didn't mean much.

Now, they meant everything.

I reached for the door, and Martina hesitated. For half a second, I thought she might say something. Maybe break the silence and stop this before it went too far.

My chest rose and fell, slow and deliberate, trying to settle my body. My jaw was tight, fingers curled around the knob to keep me steady.

Martina and I stood there for a second, possibly longer. Long enough that I could count every breath between us and for the tension to pulse between our bodies like a live wire.

But instead, she let out a slow, shaky breath and followed me inside.

The door shut behind us, sealing the outside world away. The inside was dim and hushed, the air thick with the smell of the wildflowers I'd been collecting day after day for her and whatever candle I had burned the night before, trying to erase Martina's scent from my space that seemed to linger even if it had been weeks since she was there last. Of course it had proven to be impossible, because it was imprinted on my walls, stuck to my nose and right there when I closed my eyes.

The chair was occupied by a lazy cat, tail flicking high up in the air because we were interrupting his sacred nap.

It was familiar.

But nothing *felt* familiar.

Not the silence. Not the low thrum building beneath my ribs, burning hotter with every second that passed, sizzling and impossible to ignore. Not the way Martina was standing in front of me, close enough that I could feel her but not touching, breathing measured and controlled.

The lock of the door felt final. Felt like crossing a line neither of us could—*would*—uncross.

Martina turned towards me, and I met her eyes.

And fuck if it hit me all over again. The kiss, the way her body responded to mine, the way she hung on to me like she wasn't sure she could ever let go.

For a fraction of a moment, I thought to myself that I'd wasted so many years, just hovering around her and being friends.

Something cracked wide open inside my chest, and Martina swallowed, her throat working around words she didn't have to say.

I took a step closer. She didn't move, didn't step back or stop me.

I lifted my hands, brushing my fingers just barely against her arm. Testing, feeling, needing, and finally setting them on her waist.

Warm and soft and like she was mine.

I exhaled, a slow, deliberate sound against the side of my friend-turned-fake-maybe-not-so-much-girlfriend's neck, and she flushed, a slow-motion movement that dragged heat from her chest to her face, making her eyes close in a decadent way.

Her breath hitched, and then she moved. Her fingers fisted into my shirt, and before I could dare to think, she was pulling me towards her. Or maybe I was the one moving, dragging her against my body so that every inch of it was touching her.

The second our mouths met again, there was no hesitation. Our lips collided in a kiss that had nothing to do with keeping up appearances and everything to do with what we wanted.

Martina's lips were urgent and demanding, her body pressing against mine like she was chasing something she had already decided she was going to get. So I kissed her like I'd never kissed anyone before. Like I was trying to memorize the shape of her mouth, the way she gasped when my hands slid over her back, the way she arched into me when I pressed her against the wall, things falling and crashing all over the place.

It wasn't slow or soft. It was needy and messy, and

entirely too much and not enough at the same time, and I didn't care if it destroyed me.

I let my hands roam, grip, claim—

Yes, this is real. Yes, this is happening, Yes, I want this. I want you.

Her fingers dragged through my hair, nails scraping against my scalp, sending heat rushing through me down to my aching cock.

I was so fucking gone.

My hands slid up her back, fists curling into the fabric of her shirt as I pulled her against me, chest to chest, like the space between us was the problem I hadn't been able to solve until now.

She gasped into my mouth, and I swallowed the sound like it belonged to me. Tilted my head. Took the kiss deeper. Wilder. Because if I didn't, I would go insane.

It was rough. Unfiltered. The kind of kiss that had all the weight of the past few weeks behind it—weeks of waiting, denying, pretending. I didn't even realize how far gone I was until I had her in my arms like this, and suddenly every part of me needed more.

Her hands were everywhere—my jaw, my hair, holding me like she wasn't sure all of this was real. Like she was checking to make sure I hadn't disappeared.

I kissed her harder.

We'd been heading towards exactly that the whole time. I saw that now, with perfect clarity. Every look, every fake date, every almost-touch and lingering gaze and soft smile across the town square. We were never going to be just friends again.

I walked her backward without thinking, our mouths locked, her body hot and responsive under mine. Her hip bumped something—a chair, maybe, or the doorframe—and she made a sound I'd never heard before. A broken little noise that hit me square in the chest.

I groaned in response as I pushed into her, one thigh sliding between hers and hands under her shirt, dragging my fingers over bare skin.

Warm.

Soft.

Unreal.

She tipped her head back, and I didn't think—I just followed. My mouth landed on her neck, finding the erratic beat of her pulse. I dragged my teeth over it, tongue soothing the spot after, her characteristic taste settling on my tongue like a damn addiction.

Her hands weren't still either. They slid up beneath my shirt, over my stomach, fingers skimming my ribs. Her touch was firm, needy, like she wanted all of me at once. Like she wasn't scared to take what she needed at that moment.

I had no idea how we made it to the hallway, but suddenly we were there, moving in sync, her hands in my hair, my palms on her waist. I couldn't—wouldn't—stop kissing her.

She stumbled slightly, her nails digging into my shoulder, and I caught her instantly, letting out a breathless laugh as I steadied us both.

Then I stopped.

Mid-hallway. Her face flushed. Her chest rising and falling with every shallow breath. Her eyes—*fuck*. Looking at me like I was something worth unraveling.

I wanted to say something, but I didn't trust my voice. So instead, I bent down, grabbed her by the thighs and lifted.

She let out a sound, half surprised, half amused, as I threw her over my shoulder like it was the most natural thing in the world.

"You're ridiculous," she muttered, laughing into the back of my neck.

"Completely," I said, and meant every word. "But you love it."

22

MARTINA

"Jacin!" I yelped again, my hands flying to his back, legs kicking uselessly against his front in protest.

"You were moving too slow," he said, voice wrecked but smug, and hands gripping the back of my thighs. "I'm helping out."

And then, before I could snap back at him, I was on his bed. Flat on my back, blinking up at him as he stood over me, breathing hard, eyes dark. His hair was much wilder than usual and his shirt was hanging off one shoulder, where I had tugged too hard in the desperation of the moment.

He looked, simply put, spectacular.

Jacinto's tongue darted out, wetting his lips, and my stomach clenched.

I had never seen him look like this. Like he was about to devour me whole and enjoy every second of it.

I braced myself, chest rising and falling fast, my pulse stuttering as my body strained to keep pace with it.

"You—" I started to say, but I didn't get any further.

Jacinto climbed over me, fit his body against mine, his weight solid, grounding, exactly where I needed him. He paused for a second, watching me struggle to breathe, and then he kissed me.

Deep. Unraveled. Nothing careful about it.

His hands dragged down my body, fingertips pressing every inch of my heated skin. He moved against me, and I gasped into his mouth, my fingers tangling in his hair and pulling him toward me.

"*Ropa*," he mumbled against my neck, a lick following those words that were more an order than anything else.

He sat back just enough to yank my shirt over my head, tossing it somewhere behind him in the slight mess of his room, his hands immediately returning to my skin—bare now, exposed, burning beneath his touch.

My own hands went for his belt, fumbling, but he caught my wrists, stopping me.

I opened my mouth to argue, but then he was kissing down my neck again, across my collarbone, my stomach. His lips tracing fire against every inch of skin he could reach.

I forgot how to think. I didn't know words.

All I knew was this—Jacinto's body against mine, his breath hot against my skin, the need in my core coiling tighter.

And the realization that this was happening. *Finally*.

I arched up into him, chasing his heat. And Jacinto—one of my closest friends, my fake boyfriend, the boy I had known practically my entire life—let me.

"*No me alcanzan los ojos,*" he said, blinking up at me as his palms dragged over my stomach and past the curve of my ribs, like he was memorizing me and discovering those places neither of us knew were sensitive until his fingertips brushed over them and made me gasp.

He groaned in response, a seizing, bruising sound that sent a sharp jolt of heat between my legs.

We weren't holding back. There was no teasing, no playing with the moment, no slowing down.

Just desperation. Pure, unadulterated need. A hunger too long ignored, finally breaking free.

My hands slipped under his shirt, pushing it up again, while my fingers explored the warm and solid expanse of his back. I could feel the winter fading on his skin, taste the first hints of the sunshine that marked the slow return of warmth to Tres Fuegos.

"Off," I breathed, and he obeyed immediately, yanking it over his head and tossing it aside before his mouth crashed back into mine.

My bare skin met his, and it was like a spark catching flame.

His body was hot, his weight pressing into me just enough to make my head spin. I tilted my hips up, chasing friction, chasing him.

"Needy girl," he whispered, pressing his hard cock against my stomach. His grip on my waist tightened, and a barely restrained growl escaped his throat as he rolled his hips with mine, pressing right where I needed it.

I gasped.

Jacinto cursed under his breath, his head dropping to my shoulder and his breaths coming hard and uneven.

I moved again, deliberately this time.

"Fuck," he muttered, his voice low and gravelly, holding on to my hips like his life depended on it.

The thought sent a fresh wave of heat through me, making my thighs tighten around his hips in an attempt to get some release. I reached between us again, finally snapping his belt open. His hands covered mine for a second, guiding me through it, fingers brushing against my skin as he pushed the fabric of his jeans down his legs.

Then his hands were back on me, undoing my button, sliding my pants down my thighs, and finally spreading me open for him to see.

I dragged in air like it could steady me.

This was happening.

As if he had read my mind, his forehead pressed against mine for a brief second, lips barely grazing as he whispered, "*¿Segura?*"

I answered with my body, lifting my hips up, sliding my hands down his arms, nails digging into his muscular frame.

I didn't just want this. I needed it.

And Jacinto—

I shivered at the thought, at the reality of this, my breath hitching as his teeth bit the skin of my neck, trailing down, his tongue smoothing over the bite.

"Jacinto," I breathed, my hands curling against his back instinctively.

I lifted my hips, letting him, this, everything, happen.

I parted my legs, and the moment he noticed, his mouth was on my stomach, moving lower, then jumping to my inner thigh, teasing, exploring, learning.

It felt urgent, but at the same time, like time should stay still so that we could both enjoy this, consequences be damned.

Even as his breath ghosted over the one place I needed him most, he took his time. He kissed the inside of my thigh. Then higher.

My heart slammed wildly against my ribs.

"Please," I whispered, and I didn't even know what I was asking for.

Release, maybe.

Anything, most likely.

The first flick of his tongue against my clit sent a jolt of pleasure through me so sharp, my hips lifted of their own volition. My fingers tangled in his hair, pushing his face until he groaned.

"Fuck, *perdón*," I whispered, a sudden flush of embarrassment coursing through my entire body. His grip on my hips tightened as he held me down and open, exactly where he wanted me.

And then he devoured me.

I lost myself in it.

In the way he tasted me, in the way his mouth moved against my body with expert movements, in the way his hands refused to let me shy away from the pleasure he was dragging from me.

I came fast and hard, my body arching, my breath breaking, his name spilling from my lips in a shattered moan. By the time his lips found mine again, I was already reaching for him.

Tugging at his waistband, pushing it down, needing him as desperately as he had needed me.

His breath shuddered against my mouth as he kicked his boxer briefs away, his body settling between my thighs.

Shit, this was happening.

The realization hit us both at the same time, heavy, undeniable, and Jacinto paused for a fraction of a second.

His forehead pressed against mine, his breath ragged.

"Martina," he murmured, like he needed to say my name, like he needed me to understand exactly what we were doing.

I cupped his face, ran my thumb over his jaw, his lips.

"I know," I whispered. "Condom?"

His breath hitched, moving fast to grab something out of his nightstand. It took him what felt like hours to cover himself. And finally, after all this, he slid inside me.

I gasped against his lips, my nails sliding down his back as he filled me completely. The most wonderful feeling in the world as he stretched me.

A feral groan ripped from his throat, his arms tightening around me, and he stilled, letting me adjust, letting me feel all of him.

Jacinto pulled back, just enough to make this the most pleasure I'd ever felt in my life. I'd had sex before, many times, but it'd never been like this. All-consuming and like all of my nerve endings were focused on one single synapse, pulsing pleasure straight to where I needed it the most. He thrust back in, slow, deliberate, his mouth pressing against my shoulder in what I interpreted as an attempt to calm himself down.

I moaned, my body responding instantly, meeting him thrust for thrust as his pace quickened, and his movements got rougher and more desperate.

"Martina," he rasped as I clung to him, letting him take me apart again.

The tension built again, fast and reckless, coiling in my stomach, in my spine, in the place where our bodies were joined.

"I'm coming," he said, and his breath grew ragged, body shuddering against mine as I came again, my orgasm white and blinding like the brightest summer morning.

Jacinto followed, a groan breaking from his throat as he buried himself deep, his body trembling and arms locked tight around me.

For a moment, neither of us moved.

Our breathing was the only sound in the room, heavy, spent, tangled together.

Jacinto pressed a soft, lingering kiss to my temple.

And everything was different now.

23

MARTINA

THE FIRST THING I noticed was warmth, again.

Soft sheets beneath me, heavy blankets tangled around my legs, and a slow, steady heat pressed against my back.

The second thing I noticed was him.

A breath—not mine, slow and even, so close it sent a shiver down my spine.

It felt like the couch incident all over again.

My body went stiff, my heart slamming against my ribs and my mind scrambling to put together the pieces before I dared to open my eyes.

This was going to be fine. We were both two extremely logical and consenting adults that could manage a few more weeks of being seen together around town, and then we could do a clean breakup. No harm.

Except it wasn't.

Because his arm was still draped over my waist, and I

felt the rise and fall of his chest against my back. The slow and steady warmth of his breath near my shoulder. Every inch of my skin still hummed with the memory of him—the way his body felt between my thighs, the sound of his voice in my ear, the way he had looked at me in the intimacy of his bedroom.

I had to leave, run back to my safe corner in town where I could pretend this wasn't happening. *Again.*

Sometime during the night, I must have dozed off.

The room was dim, the early morning light slipping through the curtains and casting bright lines across the floor. The scent of him lingered, and it hit me right there, that I was in his bed, in his house, with him.

My breath hitched, and the arm around me shifted slightly enough to make me panic. Slowly, carefully, I started to move. Inches at a time, barely breathing and peeling myself away from him like an escape artist picking the lock on her own cuffs.

The moment I lifted the blanket, Jacinto shifted and his arm tightened around me, body pressed closer to mine. And his breath was slower now, deeper against my shoulder.

A sound rumbled low in his throat—not quite a word, not quite a sigh. But enough to make my stomach flip and enough to remind me exactly how we had ended up here in the first place.

"Gato," I whispered, shimmying slightly to see if his arm would loosen its hold on me. "I have to go to work."

One last, slow pull set me free. The moment my feet hit

the floor, the cold air rushed over me, a sharp contrast to the heat I had just left behind.

I grabbed the first piece of clothing I could find and pulled it over my head, slipping out of the room and leaving behind the man still fast asleep in his bed.

Spring had hit hard, and the streets of Tres Fuegos were quickly waking up, faster than during the slow winter months and bathed in the kind of amber morning light that made everything look softer, hazier—like the world hadn't settled into focus yet.

It was dangerous to walk out like this for the second time since the whole dating setup erupted, like someone was chasing me.

I wasn't afraid of being seen—I lived here after all. It was as much my town as it was Jacinto's. But I was definitely afraid of what they'd see. That it was written all over my face, *I had sex and it was amazing* carved on my forehead.

This had been exactly how the rumor started—someone saw me creeping out of his house in the early morning hours and all hell broke loose. What would they say now?

I didn't even know what to call it, this thing that had cracked open inside me last night, but it didn't feel fake.

And that was the problem.

Jacinto's house sat on the opposite end of town, just three or four blocks away from mine, tucked in a quiet street, which meant that I had at least five minutes before I crossed into dangerous territory. The cobblestone streets would lead me straight to the café, through the center of town, straight past every single person who would take one look at me and know.

I stopped short at the corner before crossing towards the town square, breathing hard. The breeze carried the scent of the season, and the sounds of early morning settled into place. Somewhere in the distance, I heard the scrape of chairs being pulled across a patio, the low hum of voices warming up for the day, someone cleaning a sidewalk with a garden hose.

I couldn't walk into the café like this. Not when my skin still smelled like him and my lips were probably swollen from kissing him all night.

The house behind the café was dark when I slipped inside, the wooden stairs creaking beneath my hurried steps. My mother was at the coffee shop already; the lights inside were dimmed but on, and I saw her moving about inside when I slipped into the passageway that connected both properties.

I had minutes, maybe less, before my Sunday shift officially started.

I yanked off my top, shoving it into the back of my closet like it was some kind of damning evidence and I was just a mere teenager walking into my house after curfew. My jeans followed, kicked off and replaced by a long, knitted dress just as quickly. The water in the bathroom was shockingly cold as I splashed it against my face in between frantic swipes of my toothbrush.

When I caught my reflection in the mirror, I barely

recognized myself.

Hair a mess. Lips swollen. A flush still clinging to my cheeks.

I pressed my hands flat against the counter, exhaling slowly.

"Get it the fuck together, girl."

Manuela saw me immediately.

Her eyes flicked up from the pastry case, locking into me with laser precision. One second. Two seconds. Three.

Then slowly, so infuriatingly slow, her lips curled into a knowing smirk.

I barely made it behind the counter before she was speaking. Low, amused, devastatingly perceptive.

"Well, well, well," she murmured, carefully stacking the sugar packets and building a precarious tower with them. "If it isn't our missing person of the morning."

I rolled my eyes, determined to keep my face neutral. "*Buen día,* Manuela."

She put the sugar packets back into their holder before turning fully toward me, crossing her arms. "You look well-rested."

"I slept fine," I croaked, desperately wanting to clear my throat, but she would know. That would be all the confirmation she needed.

"Did you?"

I grabbed a rag and started wiping down the espresso machine, pretending like my entire body didn't just heat with the memories of last night. "Don't you have work to do?"

Manuela hummed. "How's Jacinto?"

I blinked and paused. Too long. Too knowing. And my friend grinned.

I wanted to die.

"I don't know, probably heading to work?" I said, turning toward the grinder, pretending like this coffee suddenly required all of my attention. I was slipping, tremendously, because it was Sunday and neither Manuela nor Jacinto worked on the weekends. My attempts to distract her were turning on me.

She leaned against the counter, tilting her head. "Martu."

"No."

"I didn't say anything!" she shrieked playfully.

"I know what you're thinking, and no."

She laughed, shaking her head. "You're too easy."

I groaned, rubbing my temples. "Manuela, *te juro por dio—*"

"*Ay, tranquilizate.* It's me." She lifted one shoulder in that casual way of hers, but her voice dropped, softer now, something close to understanding creeping in. "I'm not going to say anything. I just..."

I risked a glance at her.

She studied me carefully. "You okay?"

The question hit harder than I expected. Was I okay?

I didn't know how to answer that. So, I just nodded, too fast, and turned back to the espresso machine. "Of course. Why wouldn't I be?"

I refused to say anything to Manuela, not because I didn't trust her—god, she probably knew me better than anyone—but because the second I gave voice to what was happening, the second I let it live outside my head, it would become real in a way I wasn't prepared for. As long as I kept it to myself, it could still be fake, a fun little passing fling. A story I'd one day tell without cringing. But telling her meant admitting that something had shifted, that this thing between Jacinto and me had changed, and I wasn't ready to face that yet.

Not when I didn't know what any of this was becoming.

She didn't push or press and rather let the silence settle between us, as if she already knew.

24

I WASN'T LOOKING for an excuse to see her.

The night had been messy and raw and everything I never knew I needed.

But this morning I woke up to a cold bed and an empty house, and the only evidence that Martina had been there was the smell that still lingered in the air.

That's what I told myself as I walked straight past my office, through the middle of the town square, and into the café instead of literally anywhere else.

I had a legitimate reason. Martina had been summoned.

The Williams family weekly Sunday dinner was practically a town event, and my mother had specifically requested her presence. Ever since Victoria had moved to town, these dinners had become more and more sacred—a space for my parents to have us all in one place and enjoy the family they had built that kept growing year after year.

Lucía had moved back to Buenos Aires after a few years in town, but even she took a moment from her busy life to call and participate in these moments.

I pushed open the café door, immediately hit by the warmth of the place, the exact combination of stimuli that reminded me of the many afternoons we'd spent here when we were growing up, just the two of us moving about in the space. The morning rush had long since ended, leaving only a few lingering customers scattered at the tables.

And Martina, standing behind the counter, deep in conversation with Manuela.

She hadn't noticed me yet, which gave me five precious seconds to enjoy the view.

Martina always looked good. That was just a fact. But something about seeing her like this—working, moving, existing in her element—made my chest tighten in a way I didn't care to examine too closely any longer. Her hair pulled up, sleeves rolled to her elbows, and furrowed brows as she discussed something with her friend.

"Miranda, Miranda, Miranda," I called as I pretended to rush into the space, bumping a few chairs along the way. "*Mi cielo*," I said, projecting my voice just enough for a few heads to turn.

She froze.

Manuela smirked, and several of the old ladies sitting in the corner perked up immediately.

My girlfriend exhaled slowly, turning to face me.

Flat. Unimpressed. Irritated.

A perfect reaction, really.

"Why do you always have to be so dramatic, Gato?" she asked, her body turning in my direction from behind the counter. Manuela's eyes ping-ponged between us, watching our interaction with bated breath. She really represented the town, as I was sure the older ladies in the back were mimicking her, holding their breaths for the next crumb we would throw their way.

"*Mi cielo*," I repeated, the obnoxious nickname making her roll her eyes, but the corner of her mouth tipped up. "I forgot to tell you something."

"Okay." Her drawl was something out of a movie, slow and impatient and so irritated that I could only grin. It was like nothing had happened the night before—like it wasn't the hiccup I'd made in my brain, turning it over and over to see if I could figure out where we went from there.

"Don't forget we have Sunday dinner at my parents' place tonight, my love." It was a blurt, such a quick succession of words that it bunched them up together and made it sound like a mumbo jumbo of letters, nonsensical at its best. But her eyes widened regardless, and she rubbed her hands on the front of her apron, like they were already sweating from the nerves.

"Okay," she replied. A simple statement. She didn't fight it. Didn't grumble or try to sneak out of it. Even though it would be the first time since we'd made it *official* that she attended one of these, despite being a semi-regular in the past. "You'll pick me up later?"

"Yeah, at seven," I said, blinking at her. Because *how easy*.

———

She didn't look up when I walked into the café later that evening, right around closing time, so that we could go to dinner at my parents' house. She simply kept her back to me, wiping down the counter with slow, deliberate strokes like it was the most important task in the world.

I leaned on the edge of the register, careful not to get too close, but close enough that I could smell the floral scent and the undertones of sugar and coffee on her.

"Hey," I said. Quiet. Careful.

I was sure she'd left my house that morning in a panicked state—to be expected, of course, especially given her reaction when we had woken up together after that glorious nap on the couch.. We'd crossed a line and made things messy again. But it was so good... So different to anything I'd ever experienced so far...

She didn't answer right away.

"Are you almost ready to leave?"

"For what?" she asked, voice flat.

I blinked, thrown for a second. "Dinner at the big house." How could she have forgotten? I had been there to discuss it mere hours ago, making a big deal so that the older ladies that had sat in the corner were apprised of what was happening.

"I'll meet you outside," she said, undoing the knot at the back and pulling off her apron.

The town was alive with chatter, the early evening scent from people's houses mixing with the crisp evening air. The sun was already dipping lower, streaking the sky in warm oranges and soft purples, and a long line of pink clouds decorated the view, almost as if it were pointing us to where we had to go.

I stood near the curb, hands tucked in my pockets, waiting for her to close up the café. She slipped outside and made quick work of locking up, her gaze fixed on the sidewalk like she wanted it to open and swallow her whole.

"You okay?" I asked quietly, glancing at her after a while. We were walking in the direction of the dead-end street where my parents lived, and the big house was looming in the distance. Warm, welcoming, and every bit a Wiliams if you'd ever known one.

Martina crossed the street next to me, arms wrapped around herself, steps even. She wasn't in a hurry, but she also wasn't looking at me.

She smirked. "Why wouldn't I be?"

"You're mad," I said, keeping my voice low.

My gaze flickered over her, reading between the lines.

"I'm not."

She didn't even look at me when she said it, which was the only confirmation I needed.

"Martina, you've said two words to me since you left this

morning. You snuck out like…" I trailed off, then sighed. "Like I was a mistake."

She turned then. Fast. "Because you were a mistake."

I felt that in my gut. A mistake. Not enough.

Her eyes widened like she hadn't meant to say it like that—but she didn't take it back.

"What I mean is—" She tried again, voice cracking slightly. "I mean that this complicates things. That night… Last night shouldn't have happened."

"So, you regret it?" I asked. Straight to the point, because I had to know if I needed to add this to my never-ending list of things I didn't follow through with.

She winced. "That's not—"

"No, just tell me." I was trying to keep my voice steady, but it was getting harder by the second. "Because it didn't feel like regret when you were holding on to me like—" I stopped myself, biting down hard before the rest came out.

"Jacinto," she said with a sigh. "We said no feelings."

"I'm not asking you to be in love with me, Martina. I'm simply asking you to not pretend it meant nothing."

She looked both ways, making sure there were no listening ears close by. This was Tres Fuegos, after all, and we could never, ever, be safe from eavesdroppers—it was the town's favorite pastime. "Now the whole town is going to know we had sex!" she said in a whisper-hiss, then buried her face in her hands. "I don't know how to do this, okay? The whole town already thinks I'm in love with you. That you finally noticed me. That I'm pathetic for waiting for you for so many years. And now I just gave them fucking confirmation that that's who I am. How sad is that?"

"Is that what you think?"

"It's what I know! You should hear the things they say at the coffee shop. It's exhausting on a good day. This was supposed to get people off my back, and guess what?"

"Martina."

"No, Gato. We said we wouldn't let it get messy."

"And here we are."

We stood there for a beat, and I could feel the distance between us getting heavier. I wanted to fix it. Say something clever and funny and witty. Make her laugh and forget and pull her back into me.

But I couldn't. Not this time.

So, I shoved my hands into my pockets and nodded toward the street.

"Come on," I said, my voice low. "Let's just get through tonight."

She didn't say anything. Just started walking next to me, eyes straight ahead.

The weight of last night was still sitting between us, wrapped up in unspoken words, in the way her body shifted just slightly when a group of teenagers passed by, in the way I could still feel her touch like a phantom against my skin.

"Do you think they're going to ask about last night?" she asked finally. Her voice was so low, so insecure.

I turned my head, watching her. "Who? My family?"

She hummed.

"Oh yeah, for sure."

She groaned, rubbing her hands over her face. "Oh my god."

By the time we reached my parents' house, the scent of *asado* filled the air. The house was alive with the usual sound of my family—laughing, bickering, dishes clanking.

Martina hesitated at the bottom of the steps, tightening the hold she had on the strap of her purse.

I offered my hand. "Ready?"

She exhaled, then nodded and placed her hand in mine.

Too easy. Too familiar. Yet undeniably new.

"Let's do this," she muttered.

And if she was nervous, I didn't think anyone noticed. Because it was exactly as I expected—loud, chaotic, full of laughter.

My mother made casual but pointed comments about how lovely it was to have Martina over, finally. *As your girlfriend*, she didn't say, but that's what she meant.

Charlie pretended not to care, but definitely noticed when I pulled Martina's chair closer to mine.

"Martu," my father said, clearing his throat with an almost finality to his words. "When is your sister coming back? Your mother mentioned that she is graduating soon."

Martina stiffened next to me, and she snapped her eyes in my direction. I wasn't sure what she needed, if for me to intervene or to deflect. My specialty, really.

Instead, she placed her hand on my knee and squeezed, as if the touch anchored her to the present. "The plan is

December," she said politely. "She's coming in for peanut weekend. It's going to be fun."

My father hummed, and Martina smiled.

The problem wasn't going to be my family.

The problem was us.

The way Martina's hand stayed on my knee just a little too long.

The way I leaned in when she laughed, like I was drawn to her without thinking.

The way she fit into my family like she had always belonged there.

25

MARTINA

You would think the question they just asked me would be easy to answer. I had an answer, yes, but it didn't feel final.

Belén and I hadn't talked in a long time. Mostly since the winter months had been unexpectedly crazy here, and she had been working her office job and now was busy with her last semester of school. But I had slowly felt like she was withdrawing from this—from the town, the coffee shop, the expectation of her life after what she was doing in the city.

It was easy for me to think about her next steps, since I'd done the same. Go to college, come back and work at the coffee shop like our mother had built for us decades earlier.

"Oh, you must be so excited," Jacinto's mother, Gabriela, said. "Finally to get some help around in the coffee shop so you don't work yourself to the bone."

"She'll have more time for me," Jacinto replied, wiggling his eyebrows at me with a sneaky smirk on his lips. His hand tightened around my knee, and he pulled my chair closer to him, placing that arm at the back of my chair. He reached for my hand with the other one and laced our fingers together.

Everything happened so fast. Jacinto moving naturally so that we were always touching, grounding me like he knew exactly what this conversation was doing to me.

"Right, *corazón*?" he said, another knowing smile on his gorgeous face.

"Mhm," I was able to reply, attempting to roll my eyes at him. I felt everyone's gaze on me, waiting for whatever I was going to say next, even though I had no more words to share.

"And how's the makeup going?" Victoria asked from her side of the table. She was trying to be casual about it, but there was warmth and genuine curiosity behind her voice. A few months ago, I'd done everyone's hair and makeup for her wedding. Not because I was a professional. Not even because she asked. I'd offered.

And deep down, I'd hoped it would lead to something more. Maybe the right person would talk. Maybe the rumor mill would finally work in my favor for once, pushing my name through Tres Fuegos the same way it did everyone else's business.

"A little slow," I said, the words catching in my throat. The end of the sentence came out watery, and I swallowed hard. Admitting that out loud felt...too honest. Like a confession that I hadn't meant to say in front of this many people. "Actually," I added quickly, turning to face Jacinto, grasping for something steadier. "Marta stopped by the café the other day. She asked if I would be interested in providing the makeup service for the town play at the end of the year." My voice dipped low. "I haven't said yes yet."

Saying it aloud made it feel real—and terrifying.

Jacinto's head snapped toward me like I'd just announced I was moving to another country. His hand tightened around mine, firm and grounding. His other hand, which was resting against the back of my chair, shifted up to my shoulder in a slow, reassuring stroke. That was all it took. Just that tiny movement and I could feel my whole body fall toward his orbit again.

"What do you mean you haven't said yes?" he asked, voice sharp with disbelief. He wasn't playing the charming fake boyfriend card. He was dead serious. "Martu, that's huge."

I blinked at him, startled by the intensity in his tone.

"I don't know," I muttered. "It's just a small-town play. Not exactly the big screen."

"It doesn't matter, baby," Jacinto said, leaning closer. His body shifted in his chair, angling fully toward me like the rest of the table didn't exist. "You'd be doing something you actually want to do. That matters."

Victoria smiled softly from across the table. "He's right, you know."

"Yes, honey," Gabriela chimed in, dabbing the corner of her mouth with a napkin. "You did such a wonderful job at the wedding. And once Belén is back, you'll have more time to explore this."

Jacinto leaned in until his forehead nearly brushed mine. "You should do it," he said quietly, just for me. "Say yes, please."

I looked up, heart full to the point of aching. He wasn't saying it for show. He meant it. Like he believed in me more than I ever did.

"I think I'm going to do that podcast thing in the end," Jacinto said, looking at me and winking in the most perfectly placed comedic relief I ever saw. Charlie, who had been mostly quiet, lifted his eyes from his phone screen and grunted in disagreement, but his brown eyes shone with something I couldn't place. Like he was amused at yet another one of his brother's antics.

Santiago laughed mid-bite, and quickly covered his open mouth with his hand, a coughing fit following.

"I'm serious," Jacinto said, and his eyes never left my face. I turned slowly to him, a small, quick smile forming on my lips, because *how ridiculous.*

"Gato," I said, as he flashed me an absurd smile, something for just me.

"What?" he replied, lifting his hands in front of his body as if he were completely innocent, and we didn't just have an explosive fight outside of his parents' house, with potentially the whole town listening in on it. "It's fun. I'm naming it 'The Firekeeper's Archive.'"

"Who will ever listen to the oral history of Tres Fuegos,

Jacinto?" I asked, and a few people around the dinner table nodded and laughed in response. Charlie looked down at his phone once more, thumbs flying over the screen before adjusting in his seat. He paused for a second, then stood up and grabbed his plate.

"I'm leaving," he said, walking to the kitchen and most likely dropping his plate in the sink. Santiago turned to look at Jacinto and shrugged, probably some unspoken thing they'd witnessed before. Of all the Williams siblings, Charlie was by far the most reserved and set in his ways. He would come and go as he pleased and had very big boundaries in place. "See you all around," he called from the hallway, and the door slammed behind him.

Gabriela stood up, starting to clear the table, and I followed suit, but Jacinto pulled me down to my seat. "Stay," he said, his mouth hot on my ear. "We can wash the dishes later."

"Martina, honey," his mother said, "sit down, we've got it."

"See?" Jacinto said, that knowing smirk back on his mouth again. "They've got it."

————

The clink of cups and dishes and the soft hum of laughter and conversation from the living room filled the kitchen like the background noise I was used to at the café. I stacked some of the plates with one hand, the other grabbing the edge of the counter, trying not to think too hard about how natural this felt.

I had tried so hard to erase what had happened the night before, how I'd snuck out of Jacinto's house like something was on fire and running to the only safe space I'd ever known.

Jacinto stepped in beside me without a word, brushing his hand over mine as he took the stack of plates. A jolt shot straight through me, uninvited.

"You dry?" he asked, voice low enough that it felt like a secret.

I nodded, unable to say anything when my throat felt too tight. The sink filled with warm water, and he rolled up his sleeves without looking at me, but I caught the slight smirk on his lips like he knew exactly what he was doing.

We fell into a rhythm, the world slowly fading away around us. We worked together for a while in silence, and I avoided his gaze at all costs. It was dangerous to be close to him like this, with his scent enveloping me and reminding me of what could be.

My fake boyfriend stood behind me, effectively caging me in between the counter and his body. "Martina," he said slowly, dragging the last syllable like his life depended on it. "We're being watched."

I tensed instinctively, glancing over my shoulder just enough to catch Gabriela peeking in through the doorway before quickly pretending she was adjusting a picture frame.

I let out a slow breath. "Of course we are."

Jacinto chuckled under his breath, the sound vibrating against my back. "Guess we better make this convincing."

He nudged me gently, slipping one hand over my waist and pulling me a fraction closer. It wasn't scandalous. Barely a touch, But it felt dangerous in the most delicious way.

"You should say yes," he said, quieter now, lips brushing the spot just beneath my ear. "To the makeup thing."

I didn't respond right away, just kept drying the plate in my hands like it was the most interesting object in the world.

"Martu," he pressed, this time more seriously. "It's exactly what you said you wanted. Something yours."

"I know," I said, exhaling. It came out more dramatic than I intended, but I was sure Jacinto wouldn't notice. "But it's not that simple."

"Sure it is," he replied. "You say yes. You do it. You're amazing at it."

I turned slightly in his hold, enough to face him and see the sincerity behind his teasing smile. "And what do you know about makeup?"

He laughed and moved his hand, reaching up to tuck a strand of hair behind my ear. "Enough to know that you're really good."

"It's not just about me," I said. "Belén is coming back and the café will need someone to actually run it if my mom finally retires, and my sister has been out of the loop for years. She doesn't know the systems or the suppliers, or even how to manage the register properly anymore."

Jacinto's gaze softened, his thumb brushing against the curve of my waist. "And you think it has to be you who picks up all the pieces?"

I shrugged, eyes dropping to his chest. "It's always been me."

His hand found my chin, tilting my face back up until our eyes met. "You don't have to carry everything just because you can, baby."

I swallowed hard. "And if I let go of something, what if it all falls apart?"

"Then you'll figure it out," he said. "Or we will."

The words landed heavier than he probably meant them to. My chest tightened, and I felt like I was holding my breath in a room full of air. We stood in the moment for a beat too long, the dishes forgotten, his thumb tracing absent circles on my waist. The kind of moment that felt like it had been waiting for us, quietly, for years.

And then, just as the warmth crept up my neck again, he leaned down and kissed me.

Soft. Unhurried. Like he hoped we had all the time in the world. Like it wasn't pretend.

I kissed him back before I could think twice, my hands sliding up to the front of his shirt, curling into the fabric.

And just before I could forget where we were, he whispered, lips brushing mine, "Say yes, Martu. Say yes for you."

26

MARTINA

THE GLOBE LIGHTS were bouncing off the large windows in the café. The overheads inside weren't on, and I could see in the distance people moving about the square, finally returning home after a long workday.

Sometime last winter, Belén and I had strung strings of lights across the patio, back and forth from the lamp post that sat at the corner of the lot right to the middle of the café's courtyard. It was absolutely illegal, but as with most things, Jacinto had winked and smiled someone's way and next thing we knew, the electric company was up here hooking up the café lights in the correct way and completely authorized by the town.

My eyes drifted towards the bouquet of wildflowers at the end of the countertop by the register. Each and every flower was still fresh and pristine, as if they were still attached to the ground magically. Jacinto had stopped by earlier that morning to drop off today's flower, making it the fifteenth time he had stopped by with a bunch, just so that the vase was always filled. And even if the other night had been tense—us having a very private conversation about the little... mishap on the sidewalk, Jacinto pretended nothing had happened.

I had no idea where he was getting these flowers at this point in time—the majority of the fields were just now coming back to life as the days got warmer and longer.

Manuela emerged from her block in the distance, her hands clutching her coat closed at her throat. It had been unusually cold recently, the evenings dipping into lows we hadn't seen in a long time in Tres Fuegos in the spring. Victoria had cancelled last minute—something about a client emergency and a printer that refused to work—but she promised to stop by later to at least have a drink and say hello. I'd seen her at Jacinto's house for that family dinner, but, quite frankly, my attention had been elsewhere, so I was eager to catch up and hear all about her honeymoon.

"Martu," Valentina said from her seat. She was at a table towards the back of the store. Her fingers flew over her phone, and a small, secretive smile lit up her face. I hadn't seen her much since she came back early March—with Lucía leaving, she was probably busy trying to find a replacement doctor for the practice she worked at, and supporting her great uncle as he took over until they found the perfect person for the role. Whatever Valentina was typing made her smile, slow and private, the kind that anyone would try and hide but couldn't quite. "Bring over the glasses, I see Manuela heading over."

She turned back down to look at her screen, the text thread moving quickly with incoming messages, and her lips tilted slightly on one side.

"You're glowing," I said, dropping a bag of chips on the tabletop and setting the mismatched glasses right next to the wine bottle she had brought into the store earlier.

She glanced up and rolled her eyes, but the grin stayed. "Must be the lighting."

I laughed and sat down across from her, reaching automatically for the wine in the center of the table. Manuela showed up a few seconds later, dramatically shaking the chill from her coat like she'd just trekked across the mountain range instead of the mere six blocks that separated my home from hers.

"I swear to god every spring gets worse," she announced, shaking her hair as if it were covered in snow. Yes, Tres Fuegos springs were chilly, especially in the evenings, but it was getting better, and, as far as I could tell, there wasn't much wind tonight.

Valentina handed her a glass of wine. "Wait till you hear about New York winters."

Manuela slumped into the seat next to me, shivering dramatically. "Don't even get me started," she said, taking a long sip from her drink. "My mom cried again today when I left the house. We had the same conversation we've been having every day about how she must have done something *wrong* since I'm moving to the other side of the continent."

Valentina choked on her wine and laughed loudly. "Seriously, what is it with women and victim mentality in this town?"

"It'll be fine," I said, looking at Manuela.

She gave me a small smile and leaned her head on my shoulder. "I'm going to miss you, *amigas*."

That was all it took.

The tightness that had been building in my chest for weeks flared again. I wrapped an arm around her shoulders, trying not to show how much it hurt to hear that. Not just because she was leaving, but because everything with Jacinto was also up in the air. It was almost as if my only constant was also straddling the line and feeling flaky and fragile.

"Who am I going to call when there's new hot gossip?" I asked out loud, trying to lighten the mood. "You know how it is here."

"You won't need me anymore, girl. You have that hot boyfriend of yours," Manuela said. There was a knowing smirk there, and her eyes were shining with amusement. She absolutely loved this, and I wanted to groan and hide at her reaction every time she caught me looking out the window, hoping to get a glimpse of my *fake* boyfriend.

"Ohhhh, speaking of gossip," Valentina said after a beat, placing her phone screen down in front of her and grabbing her drink again. She was, indeed, glowing, and her eyes looked different—as if she were hiding a secret and was about to burst at the seams with it.

"Who are you texting?"

"Pff," she replied, glancing back at the buzzing phone nervously. I'd known her for years and I couldn't remember one single time she'd blushed like right now, just a slight red tint on her freckle-covered cheeks. "No one."

"Okay," Manuela replied as we exchanged a look. "Is it a hot new doctor? I might reconsider moving if I know a hot doc is coming to town."

"Yeah, how's that going?" I asked, actually curious to know more. I looked outside the window where a couple strolled by, hand in hand, their breaths visible in the cold night. The lights inside the law offices of the Williams family were still on, although I couldn't see from here if Jacinto was still in or not—his office was towards the corner of the structure, in the back. My eyes drifted again to the wildflowers in the vase, the pink petals shining bright even when it was dark in here. The conversation around me kept moving, something about the new physician and how they were seriously considering someone from San Clemente with a few years of experience.

But I couldn't hold a single thought, because everything kept taking me back to Jacinto. I couldn't stop replaying that night and the conversation that followed and how, inevitably, we would drift apart. Just like this group was doing.

Manuela leaving to follow her big dreams, Valentina

having secret conversations with someone. And I was stuck in this café—

"How *is* Jacinto?" someone asked. Both my friends' eyes were on me, watching me intently. I had no idea at what point the conversation had drifted to me and the hot topic of my *fake* relationship, but they were both expectant and ready for me to tell them more.

"Good," I said, lifting one shoulder casually and trying to convince them this wasn't all-consuming. "You know…"

"No, we don't know," Manuela said, leaning towards me and placing her chin on the palms of her hands. "You don't tell us anything."

"Well, you know how he is. I really don't have much more to tell you."

"Martu," Valentina said at the same time as her phone buzzed again. She silenced it with her finger and moved to put it inside her purse but took a quick look at the screen and half-smiled. "Please, give us details."

I tried to laugh it off. "What?"

Valentina smiled, and Manuela moved her eyebrows in quick succession, her expression more akin to something playful and casual.

"I don't know…" I blinked at them as they studied me. My eyes betrayed me yet again, moving on their own accord towards the vase with flowers at the front of the store. Those damn wildflowers. "It's weird. Right? Is it weird?"

"Why would it be weird?"

"I don't know," I whisper-hissed, burying my face in my

hands. I didn't know how to explain what was happening between me and Jacinto. It was perfect, the best thing that had happened to me in a while, yet it felt ephemeral. Like I was one of those projects he fluttered around, moving on to the next thing quickly. Like a tiny hummingbird flying from flower to flower once it's had its fill.

The looming deadline and the fact that this was fake didn't help matters at all.

"It's great."

"Of course it is," Manuela said quickly, looking back at my flowers. "You've known each other for decades."

"I mean, it's weird, right? That it's great?" I replied, eyeing my friends cautiously.

"Who would have thought, huh?" Manuela said with a giant smile on her face. "You guys have known each other for a long time! Of course it's great. And it makes sense that things are great. I won't be like the others in town and say it was inevitable because I personally didn't see it coming, but—"

The door opened and Victoria walked in, so put together it looked like she had had time to stop by her house to shower and style her hair before joining us for a drink. "*Perdón, perdón, perdón.* What did I miss?"

"Oh, just talking about your brother-in-law," Valentina said.

"Which one?" Victoria asked as she took the last empty seat. Valentina shifted in her seat, placing her purse on the floor with what I thought was mild discomfort. Manuela poured some wine in the last empty glass and slid it her way. "And what about him?"

"Just saying how great these two are together."

"Oh my god, I know," Victoria said, then took a long sip of her wine as she unbuttoned her blazer and removed it. "So freaking cute."

Manuela eyed me, ever so casually, then her gaze went straight to the flowers behind Victoria. I wanted to tell them that I was warming up to the idea of this—of him—but the moment I said it aloud, it would become real and I wasn't sure I was ready for it to be real just yet. But it was there, just permeating under the surface constantly…

27

JACINTO

"S̲ᴏʀʀʏ I'ᴍ ʟᴀᴛᴇ," I said as I slid open the door to Santiago's backyard. Charlie was sitting at the table, his right ankle propped on his knee exactly like my grandfather sat. Except that my brother was half a century younger and the pose made him look so serious. It fit him perfectly. "I was…"

I let the sentence drift into the air as I walked out of the house and onto the patio. My other brother, Santiago, was standing by the grill, poking the charcoal and moving it reverently under the cooking grate. He was very serious about how he liked his food, and this was almost a sacred ritual. "Where's Vee?"

I looked around for my sister-in-law and couldn't see her anywhere. Normally, she would be sitting with us, laughing and joking around until after the food was served, then she would take her plate inside and eat by the television, catching up on her shows while us brothers gossiped about.

Well, Santiago and I blathered away, and Charlie simply listened, sometimes intently, sometimes not as much. He didn't care at all about the town's comings and goings, really.

"Still at work," Santiago replied, turning from the fire to look at me. "You work her too hard."

I laughed loudly, sitting down on a chair and grabbing a piece of bread from the basket in the middle of the table. "Tell that to this guy," I said as I looked at Charlie, who was fumbling with his phone, scrolling through a long chain of text messages. "I'm a dream to work with."

"Yeah," my oldest brother said without even looking up from the screen, "a bad dream."

Santiago laughed loudly and bumped my shoulder with his closed fist.

"You jest," I said with a smile on my face to Charlie, who had finally looked up from his phone, "but who is the most requested attorney at the firm right now?"

"Sure," Charlie replied, turning the device screen down on the table and pushing it inwards, as if he were done with it. "Whatever helps you sleep at night."

Santiago laughed again and sat on the other side of me, pulling a drink from his beer bottle. It was cold outside, but he and Victoria had outfitted the back of the house to make it a winter paradise—they had outdoor heaters in the ceiling, and they were getting ready to close up the patio with big windows so that it was more like a sunroom and less of a patio. Perfect for every season in Tres Fuegos.

"How's Martina?" he asked, watching the food on the grill quickly before turning to me. He titled his head to the side, waiting for an answer.

"Why?" I asked quickly. "What have you heard?"

Charlie chuckled lightly, stretching from his stiff position at the head of the table and reaching for a tumbler with amber liquid and one single ice cube. "What is wrong with you?"

"Me?" I replied, suddenly nervous about this inquisition. "Nothing is wrong with me."

"I don't know, man," Charlie continued, his phone buzzing on the table. He eyed it swiftly before continuing. "She's your girlfriend."

"Right, yes, of course," I said, and Santiago tilted his head even more. He looked like a very confused puppy. "I'm still getting used to it, really."

And I was. That wasn't a complete lie. I was getting used to the idea of her just being a temporary tryst, momentary and meant to live in my memories after this fake dating situation was over. The days ticked by so quickly, one after the other, and it seemed like it was just yesterday we were agreeing to this ridiculous plot to get people off our backs.

"It's a lot, some days."

Now Charlie looked confused. His normally serious face had a mask of bewilderment that I'd hardly ever seen in my life. He was the sharpest person I knew, and nothing got past him.

"Too much attention from the town."

"But you love the attention," Santiago replied, standing up from his seat and removing the food from the grill. He set the steak on a cutting board and the foil-wrapped potatoes in a glass container, working fast to cut everything up so we could eat.

"Yeah, well, maybe I've evolved."

"You?" Charlie said with a sneaky smile forming on his lips. "I didn't believe this day would ever come."

"Oh, get fucked," I said, getting up to help Santiago with dinner. "We can't all be as boring and serious as you."

"Hey," he said, lifting his glass and taking a long sip, "I'm tons of fun."

"Yeah? Who will vouch for you, the town's librarian?" Charlie immediately looked at his phone and blinked. I cleared my throat, expectant. "What are you hiding over there?"

"*Boludo*," he said, then grabbed his phone and tucked it haphazardly in his pocket. "Let's eat."

"Sure," I replied, grabbing his plate and putting some food in it. He looked at me, studying my face with rapt attention, waiting for my next words. "But you know your secret will come out eventually, right?"

I looked at where his phone used to be and, in that moment, Victoria walked onto the patio, heading straight for her husband. Her hair looked slightly out of place, and her blazer was missing. "I'm back," she whispered into Santiago's ear, and he laughed in return.

"Were you drinking?" Santiago asked, his smile growing bigger on his already happy face. They'd been married for a few months now, but ever since they got together more than three years ago, Santiago's happiness had skyrocketed.

"I stopped at the café for a drink and to catch up with the girls before Manu leaves," she replied, looping her arms around Santiago's neck. He wrapped a hand around her waist and pulled her against him, kissing her softly on the mouth. "It was fun. We talked about you."

Charlie froze mid-bite, a small piece of potato falling off his fork.

"Me?" we both said at the same time. Except that my brother's voice was mumbled and sounded slightly panicked.

Victoria laughed at Charlie's expense. "Why, are you also in a relationship with someone and we'll hear about it from the town's rumor mill?"

I snapped my face to Charlie's, and he simply shrugged, the dread on his face long gone. He kept eating, so nonchalant that maybe I had imagined it all.

"What did you ladies say about me?" I asked, sitting down with the plate of food in front of me. Victoria eyed me cautiously, pulled at Santiago to sit at the table and promptly sat on his lap.

"Just how fucking cute you guys are," she replied, grabbing a small piece of beef from her husband's plate. "Did you know he drops off a single wildflower every couple of days so Martina's vase is always relatively fresh?"

"As a matter of fact," I said, lifting a finger, "it's every day."

Charlie grunted, his eyes still on the plate in front of him. I felt my cheeks flush, but I smiled and winked at my sister-in-law anyway, because yes, that was adorable. One of my smartest ideas, and something I had easily followed through with, because it was Martina.

It had always been Martina.

I had realized that while researching where in this town I could get the next flower.

"Where are you finding them?" Santiago asked from his seat. Victoria was blocking half his face, but he didn't seem to mind. "It's not wildflower season yet."

"Tell me about it," I replied, hoping they wouldn't notice how needy this woman was making me. So needy, in fact, that I now had three additional flower shops in two different towns on retainer, in case Valentina's first cousin, twice removed didn't work out. All the effort had paid off, because I had a fresh flower with an exorbitant price tag and a happy girlfriend.

I shrugged.

"I can get away with a lot in this town."

Victoria laughed again, nodding wildly at what I had just said.

"And I'd do anything for my girlfriend," I said with a cheesy smile, and I meant it.

"Aren't they adorable?" Victoria said to Santiago, and he laughed in return, his eyes shining with love and amusement and probably some secret things I didn't care to think about.

"All right," Charlie said, standing up and chugging the last of his drink. "I'm leaving. Food was good. Thank you."

His departure was abrupt, like everything Charlie did, but something about it landed heavier than usual. Santiago watched him go, his mouth pressed into a line, but he didn't stop him.

The front door creaked behind him as it shut, and then the night settled quietly around us. The remainder of the fire popped softly at the grill, the scent of woodsmoke drifting in the cool air.

"Charlie being Charlie," I said as I leaned back in my chair, staring up at the dark sky above the roofline. My beer was warm now, forgotten on the table after that conversation. "Think he's okay?" I asked, even though I already knew what Santiago would say. That yes, he was fine, he was just like that. Quiet and serious and sometimes a little...volatile.

Santiago shrugged. "Yeah, just Charlie being Charlie."

The silence stretched.

My foot tapped against the leg of the chair, restless. It should've been a good night—brothers hanging out, shooting the shit, sharing beers and bad advice and probably a few grunts from Charlie's direction. But now it just felt... unfinished.

My chest ached in that way it sometimes did when I

thought too hard. And tonight, I was thinking too hard. Well, not just tonight, if I was being honest with myself.

I should've kept my mouth shut. I should've never said it out loud.

"I think I'm in love with her."

Now it was Victoria and Santiago's turn to freeze. And they did.

The words echoed inside me, bouncing between my ribs like I wasn't sure if they were real or just something I said because the moment had turned soft enough to invite the truth, especially once Victoria had showed up.

But it was real. Oh, so real.

I'd known it for days—maybe longer.

Not just because of the sex. Not just because of the way her body folded into mine like we were always meant to fit. But because of the way she said my name when she was tired. The way she lived in this town like it was too small for her, yet she stayed anyway. The way she smiled at the regulars, even on her worst of days. The way she curled her fingers into the hem of her sweater when she was trying to pretend she wasn't nervous.

"Did you tell her that?" Victoria asked, turning to look at her husband as she finished the question. "I think she needs to know."

"It's complicated," I replied. But she was right.

I thought about her curled up on my couch or in my bed, or leaning against the coffee shop counter, phone in hand, watching yet another makeup video with so much attention that the world could end around her and she wouldn't even notice.

God, I wanted her to know it.

I wanted her to know that I saw her. That I was paying attention. That I didn't want someone easy—I wanted her. Her opinions and her silences and her coffee-stained fingers and her fire.

But how the hell was I supposed to say that to someone who was already pulling away?

No feelings.

How was I supposed to tell her that I could see her thinking ten steps ahead, planning our goodbye even while we were still mid-sentence?

Santiago's eyes cut sideways in my direction before they landed back on his wife's. They both smiled, curt and formal and pleasant, like I just said the most outrageous thing in the world. Either that or they were feeling sorry for me.

If I were a betting man, I would bet on the latter.

28

JACINTO

"Let me take you on a date."

"Can't."

"Please, Miranda," I whined like a little kid begging his mother for a piece of candy at the store.

"I have to work."

"But I'm so bored."

"Don't you have a job?" she asked while moving behind the counter and crouching down under the giant espresso machine to get something from the storage cabinet underneath.

"Meh," I said, lifting one shoulder as casually as I could.

I had strolled into the coffee shop dressed in my work clothes, slacks tightly pressed and a white shirt tucked neatly into the waistline. My usual, really. The tie had been left forgotten on my bed, and the suit jacket was hanging precariously from the top of my messenger bag, dropped somewhere in this shop. I looked like I had just come from court. I had a meeting with a client that had stretched longer than I wanted, making me late to pop into the café like I usually did in the mornings and missing my morning drive to the next town over to deliver the single wild stem. But we were also having an extremely slow week at work, and since we had a long weekend ahead with the peanut festivities, everything was delayed. The short week was both a relief and a death sentence, because that meant we were inching closer and closer to that deadline.

I knew she'd be here. She was always here.

Martina's eyes flicked toward me, mouth tugging slightly on one side, amusement dancing in her eyes.

From the corner of the room, Manuela made a sound in the back of her throat, something between a laugh and a gasp, and I startled at the noise because I hadn't even known she was there.

"Manu," I greeted, stepping up to the space between the chairs at the table she was sitting.

Manuela raised an eyebrow. "Williams."

"Second cup?" I asked, tilting my head to the side. Martina stood behind the counter, watching us with a neutral expression on her face. I couldn't figure out if she was surprised or amused or... what.

"First," Manuela said, crossing her legs and settling against the backrest. "But now I think I might stay for another."

I grinned, and Martina turned her body, her back facing

me now. She was keeping busy, constantly in motion when she was at work. I'd never seen her sitting still here—there was forever something to wipe, pick up, or refill.

Today was no different. She grabbed a tray loaded with fresh *medialunas* and turned, probably heading to the back of the store where a couple of locals gathered. I saw my chance.

I reached past her, fingers brushing her hip as I snatched a *medialuna* from the tray.

She stiffened. It was such a small thing. A thing I'd done a hundred times before.

"Come on," I said, stretching the moment as much as I could.

Manuela caught it. I saw the flicker in her expression, the way her gaze shifted between us, landing on Martina a second longer than usual—like she was seeing something unfold that neither of us had fully admitted yet.

Martina cleared her throat, plucking the pastry from my hand and putting it back on the plate where it belonged. "Pay for it first."

I let out a low laugh. "Didn't realize we were keeping track."

"We are now."

I leaned in slightly, just enough for the air between us to feel different. The faint scent of coffee clung to her hair, sweet and warm, and when I spoke, I lowered my voice just enough that only she could hear me.

"Alright, Miranda." I murmured, speaking directly in her

ear before she could walk away. "You'll let me know my tab, yeah?"

"I hate you," she mumbled as she turned on her heel to walk the order back to the waiting customers, but I reached out to stop her, fingers catching the knot of her apron at her back.

Martina's steps faltered, but that didn't stop me. I untied the knot like it was my own, letting the strings fall loose, and retied it with the right amount of tension so that she was comfortable.

"There," I said, stepping back like this hadn't set my entire nervous system on fire. "Always tie it too tight."

Manuela gawked.

"So, about that date?"

"Gato." She sighed as Manuela muffled a laugh behind her cup. "Begging doesn't look good on you."

"Meh," I said casually again, grabbing the coffee she'd prepared for me and walking away.

———

By five o'clock, she had given in. I had driven us out past the last expanse of Tres Fuegos, down the winding dirt roads that led to the wildflower fields. It was still too early for the whole fields to be in bloom, but I knew Martina loved this place anyway. It was quiet, open. The sky stretched above us, the fading streaks of orange still clinging to the horizon.

We didn't leave the car. Neither of us suggested it either.

Instead, I killed the engine and leaned back in my seat, the quiet settling over us like a warm blanket.

"I'm surprised you didn't insist on a big production," Martina said, her voice soft. "You know, a date with candles and wine and a full mariachi band serenading us with every instrument on the face of the earth."

I huffed out a laugh. "Didn't seem like your thing."

"It's not," she admitted, her fingers toying with the frayed edges of a rip in her jeans.

"You could've just said no if you didn't want to come out here with me."

Her eyes flicked toward me, a small smile curling at the corner of her mouth. "I didn't say I didn't want to come."

"You didn't say you did either."

She huffed a quiet laugh and shook her head. "You never really give people a chance to say no, Jacinto."

"That's because I'm very charming," I shot back, grinning.

This time, she laughed for real, and the sound settled something inside me. For a few minutes, we just sat there, listening to the quiet. Crickets chirped somewhere in the tall grass; a dog barked somewhere in the distance. The night was cold, creeping in through the cracks in the car window.

"I always thought I'd leave," she said suddenly, her voice quiet and with a small tremble around the edges. "I thought...I don't know. That I'd grow up, go to Buenos Aires or Rosario or maybe farther. But I didn't."

Martina shifted, angling her body toward me now. Her

knee knocked lightly against mine, but she didn't move away.

"You could still go," I said carefully. "If you wanted."

She let out a breathy laugh, one that held no humor. "No. I couldn't." Her fingers tapped lightly against her knee. "It's like... I blinked and suddenly I was still here. Still at the café, still doing the same thing. Everyone else kept moving forward. My sister... And I—"

"You're not stuck," I said quietly.

She looked at me then, really looked at me, her brown eyes softer than I'd ever seen them.

"I feel like I am," she said.

"But you're not, Martu," I said again, more firmly this time. "And things are starting to look up... I mean, look at the makeup gig for the town's play."

The quiet stretched again, heavier this time. I could feel the warmth of her knee against mine, the faint scent of her shampoo still lingering in the air.

"I don't know what I'm doing," she whispered, almost like she was afraid of the words once they were out in the open.

I turned to face her fully, shifting in my seat. "What do you mean?"

She shrugged, looking down at her hands and picking at the pink nail polish on her thumb. "Everyone else has it figured out. Manuela with her big job in New York, Lucía and her big job in Buenos Aires. Victoria—shit, Victoria looks so fucking presentable every time I see her. It's like everyone's—" Her voice dipped on the last word, like she hated the way it sounded.

"I don't know what I'm doing either," I said, but I didn't have to admit that to her. She knew exactly the person I was, fluttering from thing to thing with no end goal. "Most people just fake their way through it and hope nobody notices."

That made her smile again, barely there but still real.

The silence that followed wasn't uncomfortable, just heavy. Like that night hovering between us, waiting for one of us to bring it back to the surface.

I shifted closer, arm resting along the back of her seat.

"Martina," I said quietly, brushing a piece of hair behind her ear. It was the simplest thing, but her cheeks flushed and her breath caught slightly.

Her eyes met mine, wide and dark in the low light. My fingers lingered longer than they should have, grazing the side of her face.

My mouth was on hers in the blink of an eye, slow and steady, figuring it out as we went. She kissed me back just as softly, her fingers curling lightly against my arm. There was no rush to it, no frantic energy like before. Just warmth, steady and familiar, both falling into this glow we hadn't even realized was waiting for us.

When we finally pulled apart, Martina exhaled slowly, her eyes still half-closed. Her fingers lingered against my arm for a second longer before she let her hand drop to her lap.

"Yeah," she said quietly. "Maybe I am waiting for something I actually want."

We sat there a little longer, neither of us saying much. I didn't move my arm from behind her seat and she didn't ask me to. We just filled each other's empty spaces while we sat with the wildflowers.

29

The heavy office door squeaked when I pushed it open, one of those sharp, high-pitched sounds that seemed to cut through the quiet. I winced and paused, halfway inside, waiting to see if anyone noticed.

"Martina?"

I turned to see Victoria poking her head out of one of the side offices, her expression shifting from confusion to warmth.

"Oh hey, I didn't know anyone else was here," I said, like it wasn't obvious that she was standing in front of me. I stepped fully inside and walked in her direction, the box with warm food on the palm of my hand.

"Guilty," she quipped, adjusting the sleeve of her blazer. "Feels like I've been living here since we got home from visiting my brother."

I smiled, remembering her wedding—the loud music, the twinkling lights strung across the Williams' backyard, the way Santiago had looked at her like she was the only person in the world. "I haven't seen you around since the other night either."

"I've been drowning in paperwork," Victoria said with a sigh, tossing her blazer over the back of a chair at the front desk. "I took too much time off and now I'm paying for it. Worth it, though."

"I bet," I said with a smile.

Her gaze flicked to my hands. "Are those for Jacinto?"

I hesitated. "Yeah, figured he hadn't eaten."

Victoria's smile turned knowing. "Good call. He's been holed up in there for hours. Honestly, he's lucky you're around. Otherwise, he'd forget to eat half the time."

I wasn't sure what to say to that, so I just shrugged.

"Well," Victoria added, pulling her hair back into a loose bun, "if he gives you any trouble, just threaten to tell Granny he's skipping meals. That usually does the trick."

I grinned. "I'll keep that in mind."

Jacinto's office light glowed from beneath the door down the hallway. It was toward the back of the building, a converted house that had been home to the family's law offices since before we were even born. The large windows in his little corner faced what was once the backyard, now just a piece of land overflowing with plants in the most wonderful way. Probably Gabriela's doing.

I knocked twice before pushing the door slightly open.

"Come in."

I stepped inside to find him behind his desk, papers sprawled everywhere, a pen dangling from his fingers. His sleeves were rolled to his elbows as usual, his hair a mess, and—glasses.

I froze. Jacinto wore glasses.

And somehow, I didn't know that. After years of being his friend, of watching him take over rooms and charm his way through life, of peeling back layer after layer only to find more jokes and distractions—I hadn't known this. They were a thick, clear frame and made him look quieter, more grounded. Serious in a way I'd rarely seen him,

It hit me then, sharper than I expected, that I didn't know everything about him. Not really. I knew his habits, his humor, his easy affection. But the quiet parts? The parts no one else got to see—what made him retreat, what made him stay, what made him feel like he had to live life so casually in front of others?

I didn't really know that version of him.

And I wanted to.

God help me, I wanted to.

"I thought you had to work late today," he said. His voice, warm and familiar, cut sharply through my thoughts. Jacinto's eyes flicked to the box in my hand, "Are those for me?"

I held it up. "Don't get too excited. They're just *empanadas.*"

His smile was immediate. "You're my favorite person right now."

"Only right now?" I teased, stepping closer and hoping that my attempt at a lighthearted joke would cut the tension building between us.

After our vulnerable conversation in the wildflower fields, he'd walked me to my house, gave me a short peck on the cheek—in case of lingering eyes—and then crossed the town square and disappeared into the darkness of his street. No turning back to watch me, not a single word uttered.

Jacinto had stopped by every morning since with a single cut wildflower, tucked it neatly in the vase that was apparently now living on the counter permanently, then winked and walked away.

He hadn't even asked for coffee or lingered around the shop, dragging his feet before having to go to work.

"Let's see how good the empanadas are," he shot back.

I set the stuff on his desk and glanced at the chaos surrounding him—half-empty coffee mugs from who knew when, highlighted documents, a jacket tossed haphazardly over the back of his chair.

"You know," I said, pointing to his glasses, "I think this is the first time I've ever seen you wear those."

He pushed them up his nose like he'd forgotten they were even there. The move was so unlike him, almost shy. Such a different man to the one he was when he left the confines of these four walls. "Yeah, well... I only wear them when I'm exhausted."

"You should wear them more often," I said before I could stop myself.

Jacinto paused, his fingers still resting on the thick transparent frame. His eyes flicked to mine, slower this time. Softer.

"You think?"

I swallowed. "They make you look…less ridiculous."

He grinned wide, and on any other day, on any other normal occasion, the tension would have broken. Just melted off both of our shoulders, easily, like butter melting on a hot piece of toast on a cold morning.

"We should talk about it."

Jacinto looked up, caught mid-laugh. "About the glasses?"

"About the other night."

The smile slipped from his face, just slightly. Enough that I caught it. And the silence that followed felt thick and buzzing, like the air in the seconds before a summer storm. His fingers tapped on what looked like the only empty space on his desk, a sound that was rhythmic and soothing.

"Oh," he said.

I hated that the word landed like a stone in my stomach.

I hesitated. "I just think we need to clear the air. Those kisses…" I trailed off, unsure where I was even going with it. "The lines are starting to blur, and I-I don't want that to ruin anything."

His brows pulled together, but he didn't interrupt.

"We're friends, Jacinto. You're my friend. One of my best

ones." I forced a shaky breath. "And everything is already shifting so fast. With Manuela leaving, and I'm barely holding it together as it is. And Valentina..." My throat tightened. "She's pulling away, too. I can feel it." I looked at him then. At his soft expression behind those glasses. "I can't lose you, too."

Jacinto's jaw flexed, but he didn't move from where he was. He simply sat there, still and quiet and listening to me ramble on and on about why this couldn't happen.

"I don't regret the kisses or the sex," I said quickly. "It wasn't that. It's—god. It's amazing. It was...it meant something. Which is kind of the problem, don't you agree?"

He exhaled, leaning forward slightly, resting his elbows on his desk. "You think if we keep doing this, whatever this is..." He gestured with his hands. "We won't come back from it."

I nodded enthusiastically. "Exactly. And I don't want to mess this up. Us. You're—" My voice faltered. "You've been my constant. Through a lot."

His eyes softened. And maybe that's why this felt so dangerous.

Because deep down, in the part of me that rarely spoke up, I didn't just fear losing him—I feared that he'd leave first. That I would open myself up and he'd get bored. Like he had with the mural project and the podcast and the garden behind his parents' house that he abandoned halfway through building.

What if I was just another one of those things? A phase.

Something to throw himself into, full force, until something shinier and better came along?

I wasn't built for that kind of heartbreak. I'd seen it in my mother when our dad left us. And I didn't know how to casually recover from someone like Jacinto. Because this—us—had always meant more to me than I was allowed to admit.

So I stayed quiet.

Jacinto was quiet for a beat, then two. "You don't have to do anything with it, Martu. We were caught up in the moment. We've been pretending a lot. Maybe we crossed a line, and maybe that's all it was." He sat back on his desk chair and eyed the empanadas again. "Anyway," he said, voice lighter now, "you're still my favorite person who brings me food and insults my face."

We sat on the floor to eat, using one of his legal documents as a makeshift placemat. Jacinto leaned back against the bookshelf, long legs stretched out in front of him, one foot lazily knocking against my ankle like we were still those teenagers sneaking beers at the edge of a bonfire years ago.

"You know," he said between bites, "I'm starting to think you just wanted an excuse to see me again."

I snorted, mouth full. "Yeah, right."

"It's okay," he teased, tapping my ankle with the toe of his dress shoe again. "You can admit it. I'm irresistible."

"You're impossible, is what you are," I muttered, taking another bite. But, *yes*, I wanted to scream. When did this happen? That I started to look at him under a different light?

At the core of it, we were still *us*, nothing had really changed, except for the fact that we'd seen each other naked.

"You keep saying that," he drawled, "and you keep showing up."

I glanced at him then, half-expecting his usual smug grin. But there was something else. A softness in his eyes, like he was only half-joking.

For a second, I wanted to tell him the truth.

That every time he looked at me like that, like I mattered and was more than the coffee shop girl, it scared the hell out of me.

That I didn't know how to stop myself from falling, even though I knew—in my bones—that he'd leave me, just like everyone else always did.

And when he did, I wouldn't just be hurt. I'd be gutted.

Instead, I reached for another empanada.

"You're just lucky I'm too tired to cook for myself," I said, taking a deliberately large bite.

He laughed, low and warm. "Yeah," he said, almost to himself. "Lucky."

As we cleaned up, our hands brushed.

It was such a small thing, barely a second, but I felt it everywhere. The warmth of his skin against mine, the way he paused just a beat too long before pulling away.

I grabbed the crinkled paper bag and turned quickly toward the trash, desperate to ground myself.

"I should go," I said, my voice too light and casual.

"Martina."

I froze, my back still to him.

"Thanks for dinner," he said softly.

When I turned back, he was watching me. Studying me, really, like he wasn't sure what to say next but wanted me to know he'd thought about it.

"Yeah," I said, feeling too warm, too seen. "Anytime."

30

MARTINA

"*Mamá*," I called from the dining room. I could hear her moving upstairs, probably changing her clothes one last time before sitting down for lunch. It was just the three of us around a too-full table, but it felt like childhood and memories. "*¿Dónde están las servilletas?*"

Our house always looked like this for the National Festival of the Peanut holiday, with the long table pulled away from the wall in the dining area and the good silverware—yellowing and dented from years of use—laid out like we were hosting someone important. The smells were familiar too—the sauce recipe she'd taught me and Belén how to make when we were teenagers, the salty water boiling and ready for the ricotta ravioli we got from the bakery earlier that morning before the town shut down for the festivities.

It was as ridiculous and as quirky as the town itself,

because we didn't even do something to honor *peanuts* but did have an excuse to take a few days off to rest and recharge before the tourist season started again and the heat came in with full force. It was also an excuse to expect everyone who lived in the city to come back to visit, enjoy the warmer weather and spend some quality time before the end of the year got crazy.

Belén dipped a piece of stolen bread into the sauce in the pot, the edge of her sleeve brushing against the rim and getting slightly covered with the tomato mix.

"Do you have any idea where she puts the cloth napkins?" I asked as I turned on my heels, trying to figure out where my mother had decided to stash the thing I was looking for. I'd lived in this house for my whole life, but sometimes I felt like I had just moved in... She had a knack for reorganizing her kitchen every few months, and it absolutely made no sense to me.

"I don't know," she mumbled, mouth full, and shrugged her shoulders in a disinterested way. Her phone pinged on the counter and she lifted it, a smile immediately on her face. Belén had gotten into town late on Wednesday, using the excuse of a low load at work to visit Tres Fuegos. She was finishing up her last semester of school and worked part-time at a large multinational company doing things I didn't understand, so she'd hardly visited over the summer, choosing instead to stay in Buenos Aires while she was on school break so that she could earn a few extra *pesos* and increase her hours.

The water hissed on the stove, droplets falling onto the iron grid and evaporating in an instant with an angry sound. I should have added the *ravioles* a while ago, but the table wasn't fully set yet and I wanted it to be perfect.

"So," Belén said, glancing between me and the stairs, maybe waiting for our mother to come back down for lunch. "Guess who got a call from the internship supervisor last week?"

I glanced over my shoulder, ladle hovering above the sauce pot. "Good news?"

Belén nodded, chewing thoughtfully. She looked out of place in this kitchen. She always had since she started spending more time in the city. Her normally long, dirty blonde hair was bright white and short, with an edgy cut that I doubted anyone could get at our small-town hairdresser's. Her hands were covered in rings in all shapes, different colors and stones adorning her fingers. Even her voice was louder now, less shy and diluted. "She asked if I'd consider staying on full-time after I defend my thesis."

My hand froze over the pot. I set the ladle down, the metal clinking against the ceramic gravy boat we were using to serve.

"Wait, like...staying in Buenos Aires?"

She looked at me, her expression as unreadable as ever. "Yeah. Like, they want me to interview for a full-time job. If I get it, I'll stay on with full benefits and double the salary." She paused. "It's not for sure yet, obviously. I still have to finish school and they have to offer me the job."

The upstairs floor creaked—our mother was coming back down—but the silence in the kitchen was deafening. I felt like I had stepped into a room I didn't know how to be in anymore.

"That's great," I said finally, reaching for the saltshaker just to do something with my hands. "They must really like you."

Belén shrugged, so fucking nonchalant and city-like. "I guess so."

I guess so. The most non-committal answer one could get. So easily uttered from her mouth, yet it felt like my whole world was crumbling down.

Our mother walked into the kitchen, outfit changed and hair down, ready for lunch. "*¿Qué pasa?*" she asked, catching the shift in the air immediately.

"Belén might be staying in Buenos Aires," I said without looking up as I walked to the table to arrange the silverware again. I felt my heart beating in my throat, and the urge to walk away was strong.

My mother's expression flickered. "For how long?"

"Um," Belén said, and looked at me, maybe trying to figure out a gentle way of laying it on her. "Permanently? I still have to interview for the job, but it would be full-time, after I defend my thesis, obviously."

My mother hummed, walking over to check on the ravioli that had yet to go into the boiling water. "Sounds like a big opportunity," she said, dropping the first sheet into the water gently. Her tone was even, but I could tell she wasn't surprised.

"I was going to tell you both later," Belén added. "But it felt right now that we're all here."

I nodded, chewing on the inside of my cheek. "Makes sense."

Actually, it didn't make sense at all, and I wanted to scream at her, at my mom, at this fucking town that had the uncanny ability to wear people down until the only thing that made actual fucking sense was leaving.

We stood in silence for a few moments while our mom dropped the pasta into the water, then turned down the heat. She moved like she always did—brisk, focused, without wasting energy—but there was a tightness to her shoulder that hadn't been there before.

Once we were sitting at the table with a hearty plate of pasta in front of each of us, I cleared my throat, trying to sound casual. "I got hired to do the makeup for the play."

Both my mother and Belén turned to me in unison, eyes wide—not with shock, but something close to surprise that quickly gave way to warmth.

"For the summer production," I added quickly. "They're doing an adaptation of *La Sirenita*. A small cast, and frankly, I'm a little scared of what it could turn out to be." I laughed lightly, trying to mask the nerves bubbling up again now that I'd said it out loud.

Belén's expression shifted instantly. "Wait, seriously? That's so cool."

My mother smiled—soft, proud, like she'd been waiting for me to bring it up. "That's wonderful," she said, and handed me the ladle.

I grinned, because, yes, it had felt wonderful when the community center director approached me on a rare dull moment at the coffee shop. I'd swung by the community center earlier this week to say yes, half expecting for them to change their mind the second I walked through the door. But they didn't. Marta was thrilled, clapped her hands together and immediately started listing cast members and costume ideas like we were already knee-deep in production. I'd stood there nodding, trying to keep up, wondering if that was what real momentum felt like.

"Well," my mother added after a beat, her tone more practical than hesitant, "just make sure you balance it well with your hours at the café."

It wasn't criticism. It was a reminder. A nudge.

"*Mamá*," I started saying, but Belén stared at me for a moment, blinking her eyes as if she were trying to give me a silent message.

She reached for her glass of water. "I love that for you. You're so good at it, Martu."

"Thanks," I said to my little sister, my chest tightening in a way that wasn't unpleasant. It felt like hope, almost. Or something close to it. Perhaps this was the thing Jacinto kept mentioning—the one thing I was unconsciously waiting for.

My sister tapped the edge of her plate with her fork.

"Maybe it's a sign that you're meant to be doing more of that. The things you actually care about."

I didn't reply, not with my mother's sharp eye on me. I busied myself with ladling sauce on my plate and covering the delicious pasta with parmesan cheese, just the way I liked it, trying to keep the heat from rising to my cheeks.

How could Belén be so casual about all of this? I was meant to be at the café, the coffee shop girl, working there almost every day of the week, week after week. Because that was what our mother had worked for our whole lives.

As we ate, the table felt warm with the weight of what hadn't been said. We were still three girls—three women—at the table, the same way we'd been for years. And something had shifted.

And even if we didn't say it outright, we all felt it.

31

MARTINA

THE BELL above the door jingled, a sound I'd heard a thousand times before, but tonight it rang louder somehow, cutting through the quiet of the empty café. I didn't look up right away. My focus was on the stubborn pile of coffee grounds that had smeared and dried across the counter, and I scrubbed harder than necessary. The place had been closed for nearly an hour, and I just wanted to finish cleaning so I could go home and sleep.

I looked up when I heard the door again. Someone was trying to come in even when we were closed. Jacinto's grin stretched wide, one arm raised over his head, the other at the doorknob trying to get inside.

And he was wearing the goddamn glasses.

The clear frames he, allegedly, only ever wore at work, the ones I'd said offhandedly made him look good. They sat perfectly on the bridge of his nose, making him look annoyingly handsome in that effortless, knock-the-air-out-of-you kind of way.

"*¿Comiste?*" Jacinto called from behind the door, his voice that same warm, teasing drawl I knew by heart. "Brought dinner."

I looked up to see him holding a large paper bag from Santiago's restaurant, the unmistakable aroma of *milanesas* and maybe some sort of pasta dish trailing behind him. His hair was slightly messy, his shirt sleeves rolled up to his elbows like usual, the town's golden boy not caring about his appearance. He looked like he belonged here in this spot, even more than I did sometimes.

"I didn't ask for dinner," I said, though my stomach betrayed me with a quiet growl.

He grinned, sauntering over to the counter and plopping the bag down beside me. "Didn't say you had to."

He said it like it was the most normal thing in the world, like showing up with food and those damn glasses wasn't going to completely derail my night.

Jacinto pulled something from out of the bag, presenting it to me with a flourish. He winked, then turned half his body dramatically to tuck that one single stem into its vase. Today, it felt like this had stopped being for show and it was just for us, a long-standing joke between us that only we understood.

I sighed, dropping the rag into the sink with a heavy

splash and washing it in the soapy water. "I'm not in the mood to socialize with people right now, Gato."

The truth was, I felt raw. My head still buzzed from the night before, and my brain wouldn't stop replaying every moment of that conversation I had with Belén. Not the part about her maybe staying in Buenos Aires or even about my makeup gig. But the quiet shift under all of it—the slow but certain way people were moving on, making plans, building lives that didn't revolve around Tres Fuegos.

And what was I doing?

Hiding behind a coffee shop. Stuck in this fake relationship that was starting to feel a little too real. Waiting for the other shoe to drop.

"Good thing I'm not people," he shot back with a crooked smile. "I'm a public service."

Despite myself, a small laugh escaped. I turned back to the counter and started wiping down the espresso machine. "You're a menace."

"I'm a charming menace." He grabbed two plates from the shelf above the counter without asking and began dishing out food like he belonged here. "Eat with me."

I stared at him for a beat too long, but he didn't seem to notice. Or maybe he did and just didn't say anything. I sighed again, but softer this time, and pulled off my apron.

"Fine. But you're cleaning up afterward."

He grinned wider, that full-bodied smile that lit up his entire face. "Deal."

We ended up eating on opposite sides of one of the

tables by the window, the chairs tucked a little too close for comfort. The town square outside was quiet, only the faint glow of streetlights catching in the windows of parked cars along the curb. Occasionally, someone walked by, their silhouette stretching long across the rough cobblestones. But mostly, it was still. The kind of quiet you only got at the end of a long day, when everything finally exhaled. Especially as winter approached.

"You good?" Jacinto asked between bites, watching me like he was actually waiting for an answer.

I shrugged. "Yeah. *Cansada*."

He didn't buy it. He never did.

"You've been tired a lot lately," he said.

"Yeah, well." I twirled my fork in my noodles, avoiding his gaze. "There's been a lot going on."

Jacinto leaned forward, resting his arms on the table. "Are you still thinking about Manuela leaving?"

I blinked, caught off guard. I hadn't expected him to go there.

"No, actually," I said after a moment. "I mean... yeah, a little. But not in a bad way."

He looked at me like he didn't quite believe that.

I twisted my fork through my noodles again in hopes I could continue to avoid him, then set it down and wiped my hands on my napkin. "I accepted the makeup gig, by the way. For the play."

Jacinto's head snapped up so fast, I thought he might

knock over his drink. For a second, he just blinked at me, like he was making sure he'd heard me right.

Then his whole face lit up.

"That's my girl."

It hit me like a wave in slow motion, heat blooming in my chest and rising straight to my face. The words weren't flirtatious. They weren't teasing. They were full of something steadier, warmer, deeper. Pride. Belief. Like he'd seen something in me I hadn't even let myself hope for.

I looked down, suddenly shy in a way I wasn't used to feeling around him. "It's not a big deal," I mumbled, twisting my napkin in my lap.

"It's a fucking huge deal, baby," he replied, his voice softer, just for me, even though we were the only ones here. "You said yes. That's everything."

I smiled, small at first, then bigger. "My days are probably going to get longer, especially as we get closer to the performance. But I figured I could practice a few looks on myself to build a plan, maybe even document it in case someone takes over next year."

He nudged my foot gently under the table. "You can practice on me," he said casually. "I would be honored to be your model."

I laughed, shaking my head. "You are ridiculous."

"Ridiculously supportive." He grinned, going back to his food with that perfect smile on his face.

I didn't say anything, but I didn't need to. The warmth in my chest was enough.

We ate in a quiet lull after that, the kind that didn't need filling. But then Jacinto set his fork down and looked over at me again, something more serious tugging at the edges of his features.

"I didn't stay away when I could have," he said suddenly. "Did I ever tell you that?"

I looked back at him, startled. "What do you mean?"

He dragged a hand through his hair, messing it up even more. "I was supposed to. After I finished law school. Had a job lined up in Buenos Aires. But..." He let out a breath that sounded half like a laugh, half like something heavier. "I couldn't. Didn't feel right. I told myself I was coming back for my family, for my parents, my grandparents and the firm, but..." His voice faded, and he shook his head. "I don't know. Maybe I was just scared."

I stared at him. The flickering street lights outside threw shadows across his face. I'd never heard this before—never knew he'd even considered not coming back. It was a given for all the Williams siblings: go to university, maybe work a few years in the city, get some experience, then move back, where they had jobs and responsibilities waiting for them. And somehow, knowing that made everything feel... different.

"You're not scared of anything," I said quietly.

"Yeah, well." He gave me a small, crooked smile. "Turns out I'm better at faking things than you think."

I didn't know what to say to that. So I didn't say anything at all.

Instead, I reached across the table and took a slice of bread from his plate, tearing off a piece for myself. He arched an eyebrow but didn't say anything, and the quiet between us stretched again.

"I'll wash up," he said eventually, standing and grabbing both our plates.

"I'll dry," I offered, following him into the kitchen.

32

JACINTO

My house felt hot when I woke up.

It was the first sign that I'd forgotten to turn on the fans, something that happened to me every year around this time.

But also, it was something else. It was the impending feeling that summer was coming and this whole thing with Martina would be over before it even started.

The morning light barely reached through the thin curtains, slanting across the worn arm of the couch. The pillow beside me carried the faintest scent of Martina's shampoo, like honey and wildflowers. I stared at it longer than I should have, running my fingers along the crease where her head had once rested.

It felt like eons ago.

It *was* eons ago. More evidence that this had an end date and I needed to figure this out even more.

Beto stretched lazily in his spot at the foot of my bed, yawning wide before curling into himself again. I groaned, pushing myself upright.

"Yeah," I muttered to the cat. "I know. I'm getting up."

My body protested the movement—too many restless hours of half-sleep, too many dreams I couldn't piece together but woke up from with her name lingering just at the edge of them.

I swung my legs over the side of the bed, letting them hit the cool floor, and reached for the first shirt I could find on the dresser chair. It smelled like sleep and something familiar. Hers? No, just my imagination playing tricks on me.

Jeans followed. Socks. The hoodie with the loose cuff. My movements were on autopilot at this point, especially as we headed into the tourist season in our town.

I reached for the instant coffee on the counter, opened the lid and cursed. Empty. Of course. I stared into the jar for a second longer than I needed to, like something would magically materialize if I waited. Like maybe today, the universe would give me a break. It didn't.

With a groan, I rubbed my hand down my face, the pads of my fingers pressing into tired eyes and a jaw that felt too tight. The ache in my neck had nothing to do with sleep and everything to do with waking up alone in a house that still smelled like Martina, even though the last time she'd been here was weeks ago.

The café would have been quicker. Logically, it made sense—she'd probably have a fresh pot going by now and a crowd of locals waiting for the next public display of our relationship.

But logic wasn't winning today.

I didn't want to see her. Not when the end felt so close, like I could just about touch it with my fingertips. The past few weeks had been wonderful—getting together a few nights a week, either enjoying dinner out or hanging out at the café, way past closing time. Then I would walk back home or drop her off and that was that. No touching, no kissing. No anything else except lingering looks and a warmth that ran through my blood like never before.

And the flowers. Every day, it was the flowers.

So, I turned in the opposite direction and headed to my parents' place, letting the warm air settle around me like armor. The streets were mostly empty, coated in that early morning feel that made this town look like it was out of a movie set.

I pulled into the driveway and let myself into the house, quietly and like I'd done a million times before when I would come back at dawn after sneaking out the night before. Familiarity tugged at my chest.

It seemed like today was just one of those days I would have my parents all to myself. The kitchen smelled like coffee and toast, and the warmth from the fireplace in the family room filled the air. My dad was at the table, his usual spot, the newspaper stretched wide in front of him like a wall. His glasses sliding halfway down his nose, the bottom of his coffee cup resting too close to the edge.

It was such a familiar scene, so deeply tied to my childhood that I could almost hear the clatter of dishes and the low hum of conversation that seemed to hover in the air even when the room was empty. This place always felt full, warm, like the walls remembered every holiday, every birthday, every argument, and every late-night cup of tea shared at this table.

"Mom out?" I asked.

My father nodded without looking up. "Nursery run. She's reorganizing the planter boxes inside the community center courtyard and needed a few extra plants to complete her designs."

"Of course she is."

My dad chuckled, setting the newspaper down. "Good morning to you, too."

I bit back a smile and grabbed a mug from the same cabinet they'd always been in. The scrape of my cup against the countertop made my father look at me. He stared for a second too long, then shook his head like he'd figured something out.

"You look tired," he said, and it wasn't just a casual observation. His voice was careful and measured, and I could feel like he wasn't so sure about what to expect. "Didn't think I'd see you before noon." His eyes were back on the newspaper now as he flipped the page.

"I have to go to work," I answered, lifting my mug to hide my face. "And I didn't have any coffee."

"Martina keeping you up?"

I nearly choked on my coffee. "What?"

My dad lifted his coffee mug, watching me over the rim. "You heard me."

"It's not like that," I said quickly, but my dad's smile widened, cutting me off.

"Sure," he said, voice too casual to be genuine. "When I met your mother, I thought she was too good for me. Too serious, too smart. I figured if she said yes to one single date, I'd already won the lottery."

"And look at you now," I muttered.

"Look at me now," he repeated, grinning.

He didn't say anything else for a while, just let the quiet stretch between us. The ceiling fan turned overhead, stirring the warm air, and I stared down into my coffee like it held some kind of answer I wasn't entirely ready to hear.

"You know," my dad finally said, a soft voice that I remembered from his gentle parenting when we were growing up, "when we were dating, your mother told me something I've never forgotten. She said there's a difference between wanting something and being afraid to lose it."

My chest tightened.

"She said when you're really in it, you stop thinking about what you want. You just... you can't imagine your life without them in it."

And if he was talking about Martina, then it was absolutely true. But it had never been false. Because, even before this whole fake dating fiasco, I couldn't imagine my life without her.

"I'm just saying," my dad continued, taking a sip of his warm drink, "if you're spending all this time convincing yourself you're not falling for her... you might want to ask yourself why you're trying so hard."

I didn't answer. I couldn't. I wasn't sure what I was afraid of—wanting her or knowing I wouldn't be the same if I lost her.

"I should go," I said abruptly, pointing towards the door with my thumb, setting my mug down and pushing back from the table. "To work."

"Sure," my dad said, watching me stand. He didn't say anything else, but I felt his gaze follow me all the way from the kitchen to the entry before he spoke again. "And Jacinto?" I turned on my heel, watching him study me from his seat at the head of the table. "You look like someone who's about to get in his own way."

"I have no idea what you're talking about," I said, too fast.

"Okay," he said again. He settled his hands on his belly and waited, newspaper long forgotten. I was itching to run, to get out of this big house and into the humid air that would snap me awake from this torture.

"Whatever it is," my dad added, voice soft and quiet because he didn't want to startle me, "maybe stop running from it for once."

I didn't answer. Just stared at his hands, his wedding ring shining in the overhead light of our kitchen.

"I'm not running," I said, and the furrow in my brows

gave me away. I didn't sound convincing, not even to myself. And I'd been lying to myself for most of my life. "But I don't know if I can give her what she wants."

"And how do you know that?" he questioned, delicate and warm.

"She needs stability, and I'm not that."

My dad was quiet for a second. Then, softly, "Is that what you think of yourself? That you're not stable or reliable?"

I shrugged, but it was stiff and defensive. "I think that's what I've shown, yeah. I jump from thing to thing and I don't follow through. You've said it before."

"I've said you're restless," he replied, his voice steady. "That's not the same thing."

I glanced at him, surprised.

"You've never let us down," he added. "And when it matters—when it really matters—you're the first one who shows up. That's more than a lot of people can say."

I didn't answer. My throat felt too tight.

My dad didn't push. He just gave me a small nod, like he knew there was nothing left to say, and stood, grabbing his mug and taking it to the sink.

The humid air hit me as I stepped outside, but it didn't clear my head like I hoped it would. The streets were quiet, and for a second I thought about heading home, making a grocery list like a responsible adult instead of pacing my house like a lunatic.

But my feet didn't take me home. They took me to the

town square instead, my gaze flicking automatically to the window of the café where I knew Martina would be moving behind the counter, always busy, always half in her own head.

I stood like that for a long time, watching her, like seeing her would somehow make everything make sense. But all it did was make my chest tighten.

I was afraid of wanting her and not being able to have her.

33

MARTINA

"Martu, we need to talk," Jacinto muttered behind me, his warm body crowding me against the coffee shop door. The street lights flicked on as I locked it, key dangling in my hand. The day had been long—one where every customer seemed to want something complicated and no one knew how to count their change properly. I exhaled deeply, leaning my forehead against the closed door for just a second before turning to face him.

"Martina." Jacinto reiterated my name. I turned and found him leaning lazily against the building like he'd been waiting there for hours. He was wearing his signature look, relaxed, like he belonged in that moment. Like he'd been made for it.

"Shit, that's never a good sign," I replied, stuffing my keys into my bag.

He grinned, taking a step in my direction with that easy swagger of his. "I know, but I need you to do me a favor."

I gave him a look. "I'm not lending you money."

"I'm hurt," he said, hand to his chest. "Truly, I am. But no. It's much worse than that."

"Oh, no," I deadpanned. "What could possibly be worse than lending you money?"

He glanced dramatically down the street, his voice dropping to a whisper. "The town. Watching us. Judging us. Expecting us to do... couple things that we haven't done in a while." He wiggled his eyebrows, and I snorted despite myself.

"You're impossible."

"Exactly. So for the sake of Tres Fuegos' most beloved fake couple"—he grinned—"come have dinner with me. For appearances."

"For appearances?" I repeated dryly.

"Purely for optics."

I sighed, but my lips betrayed me by curling into a smile. "Fine. But you're paying."

"Wouldn't dream of letting you pay, *mi amor*," Jacinto said, stepping back and gesturing dramatically toward the street. "Right this way, Miranda."

———

Jacinto's house felt different at night. I'd always thought that. It was quieter, and the clutter of his living room—

shoes kicked off by the door, an open book facedown on the armrest of the couch, Beto curled up like a loaf on Jacinto's sweatshirt in the armchair—all made the space feel oddly intimate.

"I have no idea how you survive living like this," I teased, stepping inside and kicking off my shoes. The floor was cool beneath my feet, the kind of chill that reminded me winter was still trying to hold on for dear life.

Jacinto closed the door behind me. "With style," he said with mock arrogance, tossing his keys onto the table with a loud clang.

"Please," I shot back. "You're the least stylish person I know."

"Rude," he said, but his grin widened. He moved to the kitchen, fiddling with his phone until soft music played from a speaker somewhere. Something new—a reggaeton song I couldn't place.

"Ambiance," he announced proudly, moving to the living room and lighting a candle that was placed right in the middle of the coffee table.

I snorted. "*Ay, dios.*"

"It's called having style, Miranda," he shot back, spinning toward me. Before I could step away, his hand was on my waist.

"Oh, no," I warned, already laughing.

"Yes." He grinned, spinning me in a slow, lazy circle. "Just one dance. For appearances."

"No one's watching, Gato," I reminded him with a laugh,

but I didn't stop moving. His hand stayed warm against my waist, fingers curling slightly in the fabric of my shirt. My hand rested lightly against his shoulder, and when I felt him draw me just a little closer, I didn't resist.

The music was fast, the kind of song that made you want to move your body to its rhythm, no matter what. The lyrics said something about two friends being out of sync with their timing for a romantic relationship. It was catchy and angsty, the woman's voice really hoping for a chance.

Our steps slowed, until we were barely moving at all. Jacinto's hand shifted from my waist to my back, his other palm resting firm and steady just above my hip. I felt his breath near my temple, warm against my skin.

"I could stay like this forever," he murmured, so soft I wasn't sure he meant to say it out loud.

My breath hitched, and I shut my eyes for a second longer than I should have. His scent, his warmth—it was all too much. I wanted to say something clever, something that would ease whatever this feeling was building in my chest. But no words came.

Instead, I stayed where I was, letting the moment linger. Letting it feel real.

The soft hum of music hung in the air, faint and fading like a memory. The kitchen smelled warm and familiar now, traces of olive oil and garlic hanging in the air, mingling with the barely-there scent of Jacinto's cologne that seemed to cling to everything in his house. The heat from the stove had given the space a cozy, hazy warmth that wrapped around me like a blanket.

I leaned back on the couch, stretching my legs out in front of me. My toes grazed the edge of the coffee table, the solid wood grounding me in place. Jacinto sat beside me, one arm stretched across my legs, fingers idly playing with the frayed hem of the blanket I'd pulled across my lap.

The air between us felt easy, and it was only a matter of time until this had to be named, for the sake of my sanity, at least.

"Your cat's judging me," I murmured, glancing at Beto, who was curled up in Jacinto's armchair, his narrowed eyes locked firmly on me.

Jacinto huffed out a soft laugh. "He's been plotting your downfall since the first time you didn't give him a piece of your *medialuna*."

"Smart cat," I said, shifting slightly so I could look at him.

He was still smiling, but it was softer now—lazy and easy and... warm. His fingers moved absently along my arm, fingertips brushing my skin in slow, barely-there movements. It wasn't intentional. At least, I didn't think it was. But it made something tighten low in my stomach anyway.

I should have moved. I should have shifted away, made some excuse about needing to get home or being too tired or... something.

But I didn't.

Instead, I let myself relax into the warmth of his side, let my head tip slightly against his shoulder. His arm shifted to accommodate the movement, curling more securely around me, like it was the most natural thing in the world.

"I don't think I've been this full in weeks," I muttered, my voice softer than I intended.

Jacinto made a noise of agreement, and I felt the faint vibration of his laugh against my temple. "Yeah," he said, his voice warm and low. "We did good."

I didn't mean to close my eyes. I was just tired. That perfect, heavy kind of tiredness that came after a long day when your body finally let go of everything you'd been holding on to. The warmth of the room, Jacinto's arm, the sound of his steady breathing—it all pulled me under before I could stop it.

I woke up some time later, groggy and disoriented. The room was dark now, and only the faint glow of the stove light illuminated the space.

Jacinto's arm was still around me.

I blinked hard, trying to shake the fog from my head. His breathing was soft and steady against my hair, the weight of his arm warm and solid across my waist. My fingers were still curled loosely around his wrist, as if I'd fallen asleep holding on to him.

I should have moved. I knew I should have.

Instead, I closed my eyes again and let myself stay. Just for a little longer.

His hand shifted slightly, fingers twitching like he was half-dreaming. The tips of them pressed faintly against my ribs, the touch so soft it almost tickled. But it didn't—it just felt warm. Safe.

I told myself that was all this was. Comfort. A quiet moment where I could forget about everything else—the gossip, the expectations, how things had been shifting between us in ways I wasn't sure I could control.

34

MARTINA

The morning seemed to drag on more than any other Wednesday in recent history. I didn't know what it was—if possibly the fact that spring was finally settling, the morning was covered in that clear dew that lingered for a few hours before it fully dried. Or the gnawing panic that had been clinging to my chest for days and refused to leave.

The drink carrier balanced easily against my hand, the way it always did when the morning rush slowed down and there were deliveries to be made. Gladys at the pharmacy had called for a mid-morning pick-me-up, so I was about to make my way out of the shop and across the square to her building with an extra hot coffee and one lone *vigilante* pushed neatly against the warm drink, wrapped in a small paper bag.

I tucked my face deeper into my coat to avoid the rain

drops falling on my face and stepped outside, the door swinging shut behind me with a soft thud.

For the past few weeks, everything had been normal—as normal as Tres Fuegos ever allowed it to be. Almost enough to trick me into thinking today would stay quiet, predictable.

Safe.

Almost enough to forget how Belén's news had been looping in my head for days or how Manuela's departure crept closer. Even whatever was happening with Jacinto was hanging over me like a ticking clock I couldn't stop. We had said no feelings, we had talked about how this complicated things, but...

The coffee cup shifted lightly, and I tightened my grip, adjusting the weight on my arm as a group of people walked by laughing.

Somewhere behind the London plane trees that shaded the benches in the square, I heard the low ripple of conversation. Familiar voices. The kind that carried even when you didn't want them to.

"She's sweet," one of the women said, a slice of fondness in her tone that didn't quite reach kindness. "Always has been. But following him around for years... *pobrecita*."

My steps faltered.

Another voice, lighter, sharper, answered, laughing low. "Well, he finally noticed. I guess that's what he likes. Someone available and someone who won't leave. It makes it so much easier for him, doesn't it?"

The words hit like a slap I hadn't seen coming.

Were they talking about me?

I knew the answer before I even finished the thought.

"And what does it matter?" a third voice chimed in, almost carelessly. For a second, I thought it sounded like Elisa. "They're cute, but it won't last. He'll get bored of her. She's just the coffee shop girl."

The blood drained from my face, my breath lodging itself somewhere between my ribs. I froze behind a lamp-post, my heart slamming against my chest, the drink carrier trembling precariously in my hand.

Pobrecita.

Easy.

Won't last.

"And you're just mad he didn't look at you twice," a different voice teased.

"Oh, please," Elisa snapped. "I'm seeing someone."

Someone else laughed, sharp and cruel.

"Running into Emiliano at a bar in San Clemente once doesn't count as seeing someone."

There was a collective gasp from the group, and then I heard some rustling. I was frozen in place by the previous words that were uttered by the group, the ones that confirmed they were about me.

"You bitch," Elisa said, standing up and moving in my direction. "Who is jealous now?"

I needed to keep walking, so I took a step back, my heart

slamming so hard against my ribs it drowned the rest of the conversation out.

I didn't wait to hear more. My legs moved before the rest of me caught up, weaving between the benches and hurrying through the footpath towards the corner where the pharmacy stood.

Pobrecita.

Someone easy.

It won't last.

Of course it won't last, I wanted to scream. It's fucking fake!

But it didn't feel fake anymore, not in the ways that mattered.

And that realization cut even deeper.

————

The kitchen door creaked as I slipped inside, the comforting sound of the coffee grinder replaced by a suffocating silence. I shoved my apron onto a pile of stuff in the corner, although the move didn't bring any of the satisfaction it usually did.

Everything felt airless. Stagnant.

My hands trembled as I wiped them down my pants, but I couldn't shake it off. Couldn't blink away the way their voices clung to me like a second skin.

I always knew people talked about me around town. Hell, I heard the way they talked about every single person in the town day after day at the café. But I'd never had confirmation, of course. This town had gossip built into its fabric, but the one thing they would never do was say it to someone's face.

I caught my reflection in the scratched mirror above the storage lockers.

Hair pulled back into a limp bun. Coffee-stained long-sleeved shirt. Tired eyes.

Ordinary.

Forgettable.

Exactly what they saw.

Exactly what he would see, too, eventually.

The breath I dragged in shook with the effort. *Don't cry here. Don't let it show.*

I sank down against the wall, my back hitting the cool plaster, pulling my knees up and pressing my forehead to them, trying to fold myself into something smaller.

Trying to disappear.

The words echoed again.

Pobrecita.

Won't last.

He'll get bored.

I didn't know how long I stayed there, counting the cracks in the floor tiles, pretending my heart wasn't splintering into pieces that might never fit back together. I wanted to scream. Mostly, I just wanted to be someone else. Someone they didn't talk about in half-pitying, half-predictable tones.

The coffee shop girl who never left.

By the time my shift ended, I didn't even remember half of it. I floated through the closing routine like a ghost, answering customers in half-smiles, moving dishes and wiping tables that didn't need cleaning.

The walk home felt like a lifetime, the streets too quiet, the wind too sharp against my cheeks in the short passageway between the shop and my actual house. My body was heavy with everything I hadn't said.

Inside my room, I collapsed onto the bed without even changing, staring up at the cracked ceiling of the same place I'd slept for the past twenty-eight years.

And I laid there for hours, just staring up into nothing, my thoughts moving at warp speed in my brain.

The clock blinked in the dark. 4:11 a.m.

I turned onto my side, curled so tightly into myself it felt like maybe this time I could disappear.

One thought circled, relentless and mean, sharp and broken: *Just a coffee shop girl,* pobrecita.

35

MARTINA

I couldn't sleep. I tried curling under my blankets and counting the soft ticks of my vintage bedside clock. I tried listening to the low hum of the fridge down the hall from my bedroom. But nothing helped. My thoughts kept spinning, looping through the same exhausting reel.

Manuela was leaving tomorrow, and my sister was supposed to come back around this time, but wasn't. And the café stayed the same, day after day, the same routine and the same customers telling the same stories as if no one evolved.

And Jacinto... Jacinto, somewhere in the middle of all of this, snuck into my thoughts even when I didn't want him to. Being the most constant person I could have asked for, even through the insanity of this fake relationship and the impending deadline and everything else that had happened.

I kicked the blanket off and stared at the ceiling again,

feeling restless and boxed in. It was stupid and everything was fine. But that was the problem, wasn't it? Everything was *always* fine. Predictable and familiar and safe.

I wanted to scream.

I swung my legs off the bed and padded quietly toward the bathroom. The light flickered on, buzzing faintly like it had always done. My reflection stared back and me—tired eyes, tangled hair, my shirt slipping off one shoulder. I didn't even know what I was looking for.

I leaned over the sink, gripping the cool porcelain edges. Was my life changing before my eyes?

I should have been grateful. I had a family who loved me, a steady job that I was very good at. And people who cared.

But I didn't feel grateful. I felt stuck.

Before I knew what I was doing, I grabbed my phone from my bedside table and started scrolling. I wasn't even sure what I was looking for until I found it—a photo of an influencer I didn't know, smiling wide with a head full of bubblegum pink hair.

I stared at the picture for what felt like hours, and suddenly, the sun was slowly creeping through my blinds, a thin streak of sunshine reflecting back on the bathroom door.

It was stupid and reckless and possibly ammunition for more small-town talk.

Without letting myself hesitate for even a second, I pulled on a sweatshirt, grabbed my keys, and left the house.

The pharmacy smelled of stale air and cleaning products, and the cramped aisles were too bright and too empty this early in the morning. My shoes squeaked against the floor as I moved past rows of vitamins and cough syrup, finding the hair dye section tucked in the corner. My hand hovered over the boxes—copper, dark chocolate, jet black—before landing on pink.

I turned the box over in my hand, skimming instructions I didn't really need to read. I knew what I was doing. I'd dyed my hair before, a lifetime ago when we were in high school and Manuela had convinced me to try red streaks for no reason other than boredom. It had been messy and chaotic and fun, and when it washed out weeks later, I barely recognized myself.

I wanted that feeling again, of being someone else for a while. Someone who wasn't stuck in the same place, in the same life, day after day. Someone who wasn't...me.

Gladys barely looked up from her seat behind the counter as I approached, her reading glasses perched halfway down her nose as she was reading a text on her phone. She blinked at the box in my hand, and the corner of her lip curled ever so slightly. "Well," she said, her voice raspy as if these were the first words she'd utter this morning, "that's a bold choice for seven in the morning."

I gave a noncommittal hum, placing the box on the counter.

She scanned it slowly and then glanced up at me with a too-curious glint in her eye. "Feeling adventurous or heartbroken? Because those are the only two moments that really warrant a drastic decision like this," she said, her tone far too casual for the personal invasion. She was sizing me up for sure, trying to see what I could divulge so that she could immediately feed gossip to the fodder.

"Just trying something new for the summer," I replied, trying to sound breezy and careless. My voice came out dry.

Gladys pursed her lips like she didn't buy it. She tapped at the register screen multiple times with her middle finger, then looked at me again. "Did you hear about Elisa and Emiliano?"

I shook my head. "No."

"Mmm." She leaned back slightly, preparing to deliver, even though my whole body was screaming that I didn't care. "Well, she's been seen sneaking out at night. Twice this week. And someone said they saw them having drinks in San Clemente. And you know what youths go to do in San Clemente, so... Draw your own conclusions."

I blinked. "With all due respect, Gladys, why should I care?" I was so tired. The words tasted bitter coming out of my mouth, and once I'd uttered them, I couldn't stop. My pulse was pounding in my ears. I was seething—exhausted in a way that had nothing to do with the sleepless night. Tired of the way this town clung to every scrap of gossip like they were their own personal lifelines. Tired of the way women were picked apart, dissected, judged for simply existing a little louder than someone thought appropriate.

Pobrecita.

"They are free to do whatever the hell they want with whoever they want to." My voice trembled, but I didn't stop. I couldn't. I was too full of it now—frustration, grief, the bone-deep ache of feeling stuck and unseen. My hands were shaking inside the pocket of my hoodie. "Why are you talking about them like this?"

And what I meant was: Why do you talk about *me* like this, too?

Why does everyone?

Gladys's mouth opened slightly, clearly not expecting any pushback from this *sweet coffee shop girl*. "*Bueno*," she said after a beat, her voice wobbling between indignant and offended, "no need to get defensive, Martina. I was just making conversation."

"Except it's not. It's not *just* conversation." I grabbed the box off the counter and handed her a bill. "You say things like that and call it harmless, but it's not. It never is. It makes people feel small and insignificant."

Gladys blinked at me, stunned into silence, the first time in my almost thirty years I'd ever seen her without something to say.

"And feel free to tell this to your friends."

I didn't wait for her to recover or to give me my change back.

I pushed the door open, the bell jingling behind me like it had something to say, too, and stepped out into the brisk morning. The air smelled like eucalyptus and pavement, and the sun hadn't even cleared the rooftops yet, but everything indicated it was going to be a hot day. A fluffy cat darted across the road, heading in the direction of the inn. My footsteps echoed as I moved, fast and deliberate, past shuttered shops and ivy-covered walls.

By the time I reached the house again, the sky had brightened completely and I could hear the gentle sounds of my mother moving around in the kitchen, getting ready to open the café.

I moved quietly, trying to tiptoe past her, but the wooden floor betrayed me with a loud creak.

"Martina?" her voice called, muffled behind the kitchen door.

"Just grabbing something from the bathroom," I said quickly, not stopping. "I'm still off this morning, remember?"

A pause. Then: "I remember."

I hesitated at the end of the hall, one hand on the bathroom door.

"*¿Está todo bien?*" she asked. Her voice wasn't prying—purely soft and maternal. She had poked her head out of the kitchen and had her hair up in a ponytail, a sign that she wasn't quite ready to leave the house.

I turned slightly, offering a small, tired smile. "Yeah. Just couldn't sleep." *And this fucking town has me riled up to the max*, I wanted to add.

Her eyes narrowed like she didn't fully believe me, but she didn't push. "There's hot water on the stove if you want to make some coffee."

"*Gracias, Ma.*"

She nodded once and turned back to whatever she was doing. I walked into the bathroom and locked the door, the box still tucked in my pocket.

I twisted my hair into sections, coating strand after strand in that deep pink color that came out of the bottle. The air filled with the sharp, chemical scent of peroxide, and my scalp tingled faintly.

It felt good. Amazing. A push forward in a direction that felt both foreign and momentous at the same time.

I stood over the sink, fingers sticky in the too-big plastic gloves, and watched as the color deepened. The bright pink strands clung to my temples, already staining the skin there.

An hour later, I stared at my reflection again. My hair was damp, curling softly at the ends. The pink looked vivid—not bubblegum or neon—but a mix, like flower petals pressed into pages of a book, of wildflowers that were just blooming and had been caught at the right time.

I didn't know if I liked it. But at least it was different.

I turned off the bathroom light and crawled back into bed, my damp hair sticking to my shoulders and making the pillowcase wet. My chest still felt tight, but at least I'd done *something*. For one, I hadn't just sat there waiting for things to happen to me. I'd made a choice, albeit a reckless one that would definitely have the town talking.

I closed my eyes, and finally slept.

36

I saw her before she saw me.

The café window framed her like a painting, Martina moving behind the counter with her back to the door. Her hair—*her hair*—was impossible to miss.

It wasn't just pink; it was a bright, vibrant streak of wild rebellion that hit me square in the chest. The kind of pink that caught everyone's attention and turned heads.

Something told me this decision to change her hair wasn't as soft as the pink strands falling over her shoulders in waves. Something told me it was personal, more of a challenge. Maybe even a *fuck you* to this town and its people.

I stood on the sidewalk longer than I meant to, my hand frozen on the door handle. My pulse thudded, too fast for something as simple as hair. But it wasn't just the hair. It was *her*. The curve of her neck when she turned her head, the way the pink caught in the light, shifting like one of the petals of the numerous flowers I'd brought her over the months we'd been faking this, curling at the ends. The way she tucked a strand behind her ear, casual and unconscious, like she didn't know what it was doing to me.

I swallowed hard.

It was reckless. It was impulsive. It wasn't like Martina.

But it was, somehow.

Like she'd peeled back a layer she kept hidden from everyone else, and for the first time, she wasn't hiding at all.

And god help me, it made me want to go inside, wrap my hands around her new pink strands, and kiss her until neither of us remembered what the hell we were even doing.

I exhaled sharply and pushed the door open. The bell jingled overhead, and Martina looked up. Her eyes widened for a fraction of a second before she schooled her expression back to something neutral.

"Gato," she greeted, turning back to the espresso machine. "Thought you were working."

"I was." I slid onto a stool at the counter, still watching her. "Got distracted."

"By what?"

I grinned, leaning my elbows against the wood. "By you, apparently."

She snorted under her breath, still fiddling with the machine's levers like she could avoid looking at me altogether.

I pulled the single flower from inside my coat pocket and placed it neatly in its vase. They were still going strong, even so many weeks after this had started. Martina would clean up the flowers that were wilting, and I would replace them immediately with a new one. We worked like a team even without discussing it. And it was such a big parallel to our actual lives...

"Looks good," I said, and meant it. "The hair, I mean."

Her hands stilled, fingers resting against the edge of the counter, but she didn't turn around. "Yeah?"

"Yeah." I paused, my eyes moving over the shape of her shoulders, the curve of her spine. "You finally lost it?"

That got me a laugh, quiet but genuine. It was warm and familiar, the kind that always made me want to say something else just to hear it again.

"It felt like the right time," she said.

"It's bold." I tilted my head, letting my grin widen. "But you've always been bold."

She turned then, setting a mug in front of me. And that was when it hit me.

Up close, the pink was even brighter, fading into her natural blonde at the roots, messy waves all down her ponytail. It wasn't perfect—some strands brighter than others, the color uneven where she'd clearly done it herself—but it didn't matter.

It *worked*. Because it was her. A little chaotic, a little stubborn. Impossible to look away from.

"It's stupid," she said flatly. "I'm almost thirty. I shouldn't be doing this."

"*¿Quién dice?*"

Martina shrugged, wiping her hands on a rag and tossing it onto the counter. She pushed a tiny cup of espresso across to me, adjusting it just so while avoiding my gaze. "Just doesn't feel like something someone my age should be doing."

"You're twenty-eight, not eighty," I shot back. "And besides, the town's already—"

"About that," Martina said, cutting me off as she bit her bottom lip and looked up at me with that cautious, almost guilty expression I knew way too well. She looked soft. Hesitant. Like she wasn't sure if she was about to get in trouble or praised. "I might have..."

I narrowed my eyes, setting my coffee down. "Martu. What did you do?"

She inhaled and winced. "I told Gladys off this morning."

I blinked. "Gladys? Like *Gladys* Gladys? Pharmacy Gladys?"

She gave me a minuscule nod, like she was confessing to a crime.

And I lost it.

A laugh burst out of me so loud it echoed off the walls. I actually *whooped*, loud and sharp and impossible to contain. I couldn't help it. I needed to touch her. I needed to move.

I jogged around the counter and reached her in three steps, sweeping her off her feet before she could even protest. Her squeal hit my ear as I spun her around in a full circle, my hands gripping her tightly, like I never wanted to let go.

I set her down just enough to look at her-—cheeks flushed, hair bouncing, eyes wide with surprise—and I couldn't stop the grin that took over my whole fucking face.

"That's my girl," I said, breathless and stunned and ridiculously proud.

And then I kissed her.

Right in the middle of the café. Not for an audience. Not because it was a performance, Just the two of us and this spark between us that refused to die out.

She melted into it, hand clutching my shirt, mouth soft and warm and familiar in a way that made my whole chest ache. It didn't feel like pretending. It didn't feel like a moment we'd have to take back later. It just *was*.

When I finally pulled away, I didn't go far. Her forehead rested against mine, her breath brushing my lips. We were still tangled, still close and real and...

"I just..." she whispered after a second. "I needed something to feel different. Even if it's just this."

Her hand rose, fingers winding through her hair again, and I couldn't stop watching—couldn't stop *wanting*. The way her fingers dragged through the pink, making the strands shift and shine, it was like she'd grabbed every part of herself I hadn't seen before and brought it up to me. Something bolder, braver. Something *hotter*.

I watched her closely. "And does it?" I asked, keeping my voice even.

"What?"

"Feel different."

She let her hand fall back to the counter and studied my face. "Yes."

She said it quietly, and I immediately knew she wasn't just talking about her hair.

I wanted to tell her that she *was* different. That I'd felt it the second I stepped inside. That I couldn't stop thinking about the way she felt when she leaned into me the other night or the way my fingers had accidentally brushed her hip when I'd reached for that stupid pastry.

But before I could say anything, the café door opened again, and someone called her name—a regular from across the square. She muttered something about needing to refill the sugar bowls and disappeared into the back before I could say anything else.

I stood there a while longer, finishing my coffee, watching the door she'd disappeared behind. The pink stayed with me, blazing and impossible to ignore, like something I hadn't realized I'd been waiting for.

37

MARTINA

"HELLO, MY LADY," Jacinto said from the archway that led to the café's patio. The evening was perfect—one of those late spring days that were cool enough to be outside, but rarely happened anymore—and every single window and door at the coffee shop had been open, letting in the fresh, dry air.

It had been a few days since my pink hair moment, as I'd come to call it privately, and while the shock had faded, the whispers hadn't. People still looked and stared. Still tilted their heads like I was a new version of myself they hadn't figured out yet. But not a single person had said anything directly to my face, which I appreciated.

I was dragging the tables back inside when his voice cut through the quiet.

"How many more nicknames are you going to try?"

"However many it takes for me to find the one that sticks," he replied, and when he stepped beside me, the warm brush of his arm against mine sent a shiver up my spine.

He was too close. He always was. It was maddening how easily he slipped into my space—how my body didn't know to feel neutral around him anymore. It was always charged. The scent of him, clean and citrusy, just a touch of his cologne, slid under my skin like the secret we were hiding.

I shifted away from him in the direction of the stack of chairs, needing space, but he moved with me. His knee bumped mine, a slow, deliberate knock that felt like a question, like he couldn't quite help it and was getting my approval to do so.

Beside me, he reached for one of the tables. His forearm flexed as he lifted it, the movement casual and unhurried, like he was doing this for the view he knew I was getting. And I was looking. Of course I was. The veins on his hand, the tan at his wrist where a watch used to be, probably forgotten in a drawer in his house. The slight lift of his shirt where it caught against his back as he leaned over. I was painfully aware of every single detail.

I told myself it was for the performance. For the town. But it didn't feel like a performance anymore.

Out in the town square, Carmen was perched on her usual bench, whispering to Estela with her face lit up like she was sharing something scandalous. Across the street, the sounds coming from Santiago's patio restaurant were filling the air. The whole town was lingering, watching.

I caught Jacinto's gaze flick toward them—a glance that

paused for a second too long—before he turned back to me. He knew they were watching, too.

"We should go," I muttered. My voice sounded off, weaker and thinner than I meant it to be.

His eyes slid from my mouth back to mine. "Why?"

"Because..." I gestured vaguely at Carmen and the others, all heads tuning like sunflowers when we so much as breathed in the same direction. "Because of them."

"They'll get bored eventually," Jacinto said, voice low and calm as usual, but his eyes held that undeniable spark that had always been there right before he did something funny or dramatic.

"I don't think they will." I shifted again, the heel of my shoe scraping against the pavement. My chest felt tight, my pulse too loud in my ears. "I mean, they haven't yet."

"You always think too much," he said, and there was no teasing in it now. Just that steady look, the one that saw too much of me.

I locked the door, and we started walking toward the end of the sidewalk, away from the café and from the town's sharp eyes. The shadows stretched longer along the streets, and the air cooled slightly. It was quieter here, just us two, but the weight of their eyes felt oppressive.

"Jacinto," someone called from behind, far too loud and smug for my liking. Jacinto's hand found mine, lacing his fingers and tugging me tightly towards him, anchoring us. Holding me like a statement.

He didn't move. Didn't turn to face whoever was calling him or prepared to crack a joke. Didn't roll his eyes like he would normally do. He was motionless and watching me, his expression unreadable.

"Jacin," I said quietly, either to urge him to respond or to keep walking, just the two of us in this town of nosy people that were way too involved in each others' lives.

"Show her some love!" the voice, who I now recognized as Emiliano, said. My stomach flipped. I wanted to roll my eyes at him, because he had no business spending time with the gossips.

I opened my mouth to brush it off—a laugh, maybe a wave as a redirection to get them off our backs—when Jacinto shifted, one of his hands going to the back of my neck. His eyes dropped to my mouth, and my breath caught.

Like everything that had been going on with him, this was unexpected but so very much welcome. He leaned in, no warning, no devious smirk. Just his warm hand anchoring me to the moment, to him.

"*¿Todo bien?*" he murmured, voice barely a breath.

I didn't know if I nodded or if I simply didn't stop him. But then his mouth was on mine, and it was slower than expected. The kind of slow that felt deliberate and intentional, and allowed me to control the situation. Giving me enough time to pull away and put a stop to this.

I didn't.

His hand moved to my jaw and curled tight against it,

his fingers sweeping higher until it caught in my hair. I felt the warmth of his palm pressing close behind my ear, the sure weight of him grounding me and holding me tight before I slipped away.

I kissed him back before I had a moment to think better of it. My fingers knotted in his shirt, pulling him closer, harder. And for a moment——a single moment suspended in time—I forgot everything else. The town, the fake dating and its looming deadline, the fact that this was supposed to be for show only.

I forgot I was supposed to be pretending. Because kissing this man was the only thing I wanted to be doing at that moment.

Someone wolf-whistled, sharp and loud. Carmen laughed, loud and victorious and almost as if this whole scheme she'd put on was finally paying off. None of that felt real, final. It all felt like a show *they* were putting on, egging us on deeper into this hole that only seemed to have one simple way out.

In that moment, the only thing that felt real was him— the way he angled his head, the warm slide of his hand moving down to the small of my back. The way he kissed me like he meant it.

We broke apart only when someone shouted something crude from the grocer across the street. I didn't hear the words, only felt the way Jacinto's shoulders stiffened beneath my hands, his breathing unsteady against my cheek.

I stepped back first. My hand fell from his shirt, but the fabric stayed wrinkled, crumpled where I'd held on too tightly. I stared at it, my breath still coming too fast.

"That," Jacinto said slowly, "was for them."

I swallowed hard. "Yeah."

"Sure."

"Yeah."

His thumb brushed my wrist before he let go completely. A flick of skin against skin, barely there.

"You good?" he asked again, quieter this time.

I wasn't. I wasn't remotely close to being any sort of good in any combination of anything. But I nodded anyway.

"Yeah," I said. "All good."

He didn't look convinced. But he didn't push. Instead, he slid his hand into the pocket of his slacks like he hadn't just kissed me like his life depended on it.

"We should go," he said after a beat, his voice rougher than before. "Before Carmen starts printing wedding invitations."

I huffed out a breath that might have been a laugh if I weren't still dizzy and my knees weren't about to give out. "Good idea."

We walked away together, side by side. His hand found the small of my back, fingers resting lightly against my spine. Enough to remind me he was still there, just enough to make my skin burn beneath my clothes.

It was for them. That's what I told myself. That's what he'd said.

But the way my heart raced in my chest told me something else entirely. Even if we only had a few weeks together, like this.

38

We walked slowly, hand in hand, in the direction of my house. My keys jingled in my pocket as we crossed the street, from the corner of the community center all the way across the square and to my house. My car was parked right outside, slightly separated from the curb and at a weird angle since I'd parked it carelessly this morning, running late to get Martina's flower from the shop in the other town.

"Where are we going?" Martina asked, almost as if she didn't recognize the way to my house. She looked a little dazed, and I didn't blame her. Every time we were in such close proximity, my heart beat faster, my thoughts clouded, and I couldn't think straight.

She was absolutely all-consuming.

"Let's go for a drive," I replied, reaching for my keys and opening the car door for her. "It's really nice out."

"Yes," she said, a small smile on her lips. She looked up

at me before getting in the car, and for a second, neither of us moved. Her eyes were wide, pink hair curled around her cheeks from the humidity, her mouth slightly parted like she wanted to ask me something.

Once she was seated, I rounded the car and took a deep breath. All day, I'd been on edge. The play was only two days away, so that meant this was the end.

"How are the play rehearsals going?" I asked as I turned right on the road that exited our town. We had driven through the middle of Tres Fuegos in a silence that felt taut and frayed at the edges. Almost final.

Martina rested her arm against the window, fingers tucked beneath her chin. Her body angled slightly away from me, but her eyes drifted in my direction once I spoke.

"They're fine," she said, almost too casually. "The kids are chaotic, but it'll be fine. I just need to survive the glitter explosions and make sure I don't stab anyone with eyeliner."

I smiled faintly, but the ache in my chest didn't ease. The road ahead stretched in long, familiar lines—dust and summer light, the smell of blooming wildflowers drifting in through the cracked window. I felt the weight of time pressing in from all sides. Two days. Two days, and the curtain would close and this thing between us—whatever it was—would have to fade out with it.

"You'll do more than survive, Martu," I said quietly, trying to be encouraging. "You're good at it."

She didn't respond at first. Just stared out the window,

her fingers fidgeting with the loose threads on her shorts. Finally, she said, "It's weird. Knowing it's almost over."

I tightened my grip on the steering wheel. "Yeah."

I didn't ask what she meant exactly. If she was talking about the play or her sister coming home or us or Manuela leaving or something else entirely. I didn't want her to have to lie to me. And I didn't think I could take the truth either.

The silence settled between us again.

When we reached the edge of the fields, Martina gasped. The grass had grown wild again, green and gold stretching towards the hills, dotted with purple and pink and orange blooms everywhere. The sun was beginning to dip low, bathing everything in an amber glow.

She stepped out before I could even circle the car. Her arms crossed over her chest, like she was holding on to the last remnants of this. Of us.

"I didn't know if you'd still want to do this," I said, walking up beside her. "Go on a date with me."

Martina scoffed and turned to face me. Her features were illuminated by the dipping sun, and her pink hair shone differently out here. With more defiance. Or perhaps it was just the way the breeze caught it, like the world was daring her to keep pretending this didn't matter.

"Why not?" she asked, a small shrug accompanying her words. "We're still friends, aren't we?"

"Yeah," I said after a beat, forcing my voice steady. "But the play is this week."

"Gato," she interrupted gently, like she already knew

where I was headed. Her voice wasn't harsh or dismissive—it was soft, like she was trying to save us both from the truth. "We said we'd make it until then. And we did."

I stared at her, at the way her arms crossed over her chest like she was holding herself together, like if she didn't, she'd shatter right there in front of me.

"But this doesn't feel like the end to me," I said quietly.

She didn't look away, but her eyes softened in that way that always knocked the wind out of me.

"It's not the end," she said. "It's just... not more."

My throat tightened as I stepped closer, and there was only a sliver of space between us among the wildflowers. I wanted to pull her in, to tell her I'd wait until she could be ready for me. I wanted to promise her that I would never leave. But the words felt like too much and too late.

We sat on the blanket as the last of the daylight dipped behind the mountains. The wind rustled through the grass, carrying the distant hum of insects and the faint scent of jasmine blooming nearby. A few fireflies blinked in the meadow, and somewhere nearby, a cicada started its evening chant.

"Why did you bring me to an insect-infested field, Gato?" she asked, but there was a new smile on her face, like finally the fog had lifted and she was letting go. "You know how I feel about the outdoors."

"It's called ambiance, actually."

She laughed, and it was real. It was sharp and bright and spilled right into my chest. I'd missed that sound more than

I wanted to admit, even if I'd heard it just a few days ago at the café, when she told me she'd finally stood up to Gladys.

We leaned back, shoulder to shoulder, our hands almost brushing in the middle of the blanket. Almost. I felt her pinky graze mine once, then again, like she was testing something.

"What?" she asked eventually, catching me staring.

"Nothing." I paused. "You look like a wildflower. That's all."

Her nose scrunched adorably. "A wildflower?"

"Yeah," I said, bumping her knee with mine. "Bright, unpredictable, kind of stubborn. The best kind."

She rolled her eyes but didn't argue.

I reached over and tucked a piece of hair behind her ear. She went still.

"Is this part of the fake dating plan?" she asked, voice lower now.

"Nope," I said. "Not even a little."

She leaned in, and I didn't wait this time. I kissed her, and she kissed me back like we'd been doing this for years. There was nothing slow or unsure about it now. Just heat and promise, and a thousand repressed moments exploding at once.

She pulled back just barely. "Okay," she said breathlessly. "So, I guess we're doing this."

"You sound surprised."

"I mean, I know you like to make a scene, but literally *anyone* can see!"

I laughed against her mouth. "At least I brought a blanket."

"And wildflowers," she added.

"Exactly. I'm a romantic."

I kissed her again before she could argue further. My hands slid under the hem of her shirt, fingertips brushing along her ribs, and her breath hitched just a little. She shifted closer, legs tangled with mine, her hands finding my jaw, my shoulders, my back.

"Don't look so smug," she whispered as I trailed kisses down her neck.

"You sure?" I asked against her mouth, hoping this wasn't a dream.

She nodded, eyes blazing. "I'm sure."

We undressed each other in pieces—her shirt lifted carefully over her head, my fingers fumbling at the buttons of my jeans. Every moment was laced in quiet laughter and soft gasps. She reached for me with both hands, like she needed the reassurance of skin and heat and closeness.

"Martu." Her name came out much quieter than I meant to, like the secret I was hiding between us. "Tell me to stop."

She didn't.

Instead, she shifted, lifting her leg over my lap until she was straddling me, knees pressing into the edge of the picnic blanket, one hand braced on my shoulder. Her other hand tugged gently on the back of my hair, pulling my mouth back to hers.

There wasn't any hesitation this time. No second-guessing, no overthinking. Her lips were soft but sure, moving against mine because she'd already decided.

When I finally sank into her, it was with a low, guttural sound—one that came from somewhere raw and unguarded. She clutched my shoulders, a sigh caught on her lips, and her name on mine.

And there was nothing but her. Her mouth, her sighs, her quiet gasps, and the way her fingers clutched at my skin like she was afraid I might disappear, like we might lose this moment with the wildflowers around us, blooming and bearing witness.

39

JACINTO

THE FOLDING CHAIRS weren't cooperating one bit. Like everyone else in town the day before the play. Each one was stiff at the hinges, their metal legs scraping against the floor with a sharp screech that set my teeth on edge. I wrestled another one into place, only to watch it wobble slightly when I stepped back. I pushed my palm down against the seat, testing the balance. Still unsteady.

"That back row is going to collapse before they even finish the first scene," I muttered.

Martina was a few rows ahead, arranging programs on each chair. She barely glanced up. "Then maybe don't leave your half crooked."

"My half?" I shot her a look. "I'm doing all the heavy lifting here."

"Please," she said, flipping another program open with one hand while tucking her pink hair behind her ear with the other. "You've been playing engineer with that same row for ten minutes."

I leaned against the crooked chair and crossed my arms. "I'm just giving the town something to talk about. Dramatic scenes? Unexpected plot twists? People love that stuff. And I bet you they'll love it more than *The Little Mermaid*."

That almost got a smile out of her—almost. Her mouth twitched, but then she pressed her lips together, face slipping back into something more careful. The warmth behind her eyes dimmed. I felt it happen, like someone pulling a curtain across a window.

"Hey," I said, quieter this time. "What's going on in that pretty mind of yours?"

She didn't look up right away. Just kept moving down the row, smoothing out each program like it mattered. "I'm fine. Just tired."

"Yeah, I replied. "Me too."

The lie sat so heavy on my tongue. I wasn't tired—not in the way we were both saying out loud. I was restless. Had been since... well... since two nights ago with the wildflowers. Since the way her hand twisted in my hair like she was afraid to let go. Since her breath had hitched right before I kissed her for the last time.

"I'll finish the programs," I said, stepping closer. "Sit for a minute."

"*Estoy bien*," she said again, so quickly and harshly I doubted she even believed the words that came out of her mouth.

"Martina." I touched her arm lightly, and she stopped. She didn't turn right away, didn't look at me. But she didn't pull away either.

"Just sit," I said again. "I'll fix the crooked row. You can take the credit after."

That earned me a small yet tired smile—a real one this time. "Jacinto, you're impossible."

"Yeah," I said, feeling something tight in my chest loosen just a little. "I've heard that before."

She let out a breath, then walked over to a seat by the wall and sat down, curling one arm around her waist like she was holding herself together. I went back to straightening the chairs, feeling her eyes flick toward me now and then.

———

The walk back to her place dragged longer than usual. The community center sat almost in the middle of the town with the café on the same block and only a few buildings down. But we took the long way, around the corner and through the actual entry instead of the side path that connected the shop to her family's home.

The air had warmed plenty, leaving a damp layer on everything it touched. The streets were mostly empty, save for the faint flicker of light behind drawn curtains and the muffled sound of a TV spilling out from an open window. It smelled of flowers and trees, the scent curling low against the cobblestones.

Martina walked beside me, her hand sliding into mine as if it belonged there. Her fingers wrapped easily around mine, her palm warm against my skin. This wasn't the way someone grabbed on because they were cold—it was something else entirely. She wasn't guarding herself; she simply seemed... far away. As though her thoughts were drifting somewhere I couldn't follow.

"Are you going to tell me what's on your mind, *girlfriend*, or are we playing the guessing game tonight?" I asked, breaking the silence.

She huffed out a small breath, barely a laugh. "There's nothing to guess."

"Yeah? Could've fooled me."

She didn't answer, and instead kept walking, her pace a little slower than normal. The cobblestones were uneven here, and her shoes scuffed against the ground like she wasn't really paying attention to where she was going.

"That back row really is going to fall apart," I said after a minute, reaching for anything to break the quiet. "Bet we don't even make it through the second act."

"Mm," she hummed, her eyes fixed on the ground. "That'd be a shame. The whole town has been waiting for that performance."

"Exactly." I shoved my free hand into my pocket. "I can't believe they let me be part of the setup. I'm a liability."

This time, she did laugh, a quick and sharp sound. "They should have put you on cleaning duty."

"Too late for regrets now."

I smiled, but she went quiet again, her fingers tightening around my hand. I should have left it alone, let her sit in whatever thoughts were buzzing in her head, but the silence felt so heavy, pressing against my ribs.

"Martina," I started, but the end of her name got caught in my throat. It came out quiet and hesitant, insecure.

Her steps faltered, and she stopped walking, finally raising her head and looking at me.

"What's next?" I bit my lip in a cautious way.

"What do you mean?"

"I mean..." I shrugged, forcing my voice to stay light. "The town's greatest relationship is ending."

She smiled at that—a quick flash that was gone in an instant. "Fake relationship, Gato. After the play, I guess. That's what we said, right?"

I swallowed hard, trying to mask the way her words hit me. "Yeah, yeah," I said. "Yes, that's what we said. That makes total sense. Tomorrow."

"Yeah," she echoed quietly, her voice thinner now. She shifted her gaze toward the street ahead, her face unreadable. "It's probably for the best."

I opened my mouth to say something, but every single word I'd ever known got stuck in my throat. The words felt too big, impossible to get out. The last thing I wanted was for this to end, but if she wanted out... What was I supposed to do? Ask her to keep pretending with me so I didn't have to admit I wanted her for real?

We kept walking, turning the corner towards her house, only a few feet away. Her steps felt smaller, slower. I wondered if she felt it, too, the weight of something slipping through our fingers. Something amazing slipping us by with no chance to ever catch it again.

The iron gate to her house creaked when she pushed it open, loud enough to make her flinch. She paused there, one hand on the cold metal, the other still wrapped around mine. Her fingers flexed once, and I was afraid she was going to let go. She didn't.

"I guess this is it," she said quietly.

The words punched through my chest. I knew she was only talking about the night and the walk back home, about ending another day, but it felt beyond that. I shifted my weight, holding her hand and relishing the last few minutes of her warmth against my palm.

"I—" I cleared my throat.

"Yeah?" she replied, leaning back against the gate, her fingers sliding from mine. Slow enough that I almost convinced myself she didn't really mean to do it.

Her brown eyes were studying me, following a path down my face, lingering on my lips in a way that made my heart beat so fast I could barely take it.

I almost told her then. The words were right there, crowding my chest, pressing against the back of my teeth. I almost said I didn't want this to end. That I couldn't imagine waking up in a world where she wasn't part of it—where she wasn't slipping her hand into mine like it belonged there.

But her gaze flicked back to my eyes, and I saw it, how tired she really looked, the way her smile barely held. She was already letting this go, walking away from the best thing that had happened to me in years.

The only thing I'd ever wanted to finish.

I let the words die in my throat.

"Good night, Martina."

She smiled, but it was thin, a pale shadow of the real thing. "Night."

She turned, her keys jingling faintly as she climbed the few steps to the front door. It clicked shut behind her, and I stood there long after she disappeared inside, watching the light in her window flick on.

I'd missed the chance to say it, to tell her I wasn't ready to let this end.

And I ruined the one thing I was ready to commit to.

40

I DROPPED ANOTHER MUG. It hit the counter hard, the dull clatter ringing out too loud in the quiet space. My hands hadn't stopped shaking since last night, and I couldn't seem to hold on to anything. The mug didn't break, but I nearly did, breath catching, throat tightening. Because today—

I turned too fast and knocked over the sugar caddy, sending packets skidding across the counter. I grabbed for them, fingers fumbling. The napkin holder rattled dangerously, but I caught it just in time.

My mother walked in just as I was gathering everything up, fanning her face with her hands and lifting her hair so it would give her some reprieve from the suffocating heat outside. She paused when she saw me, her face tightening with concern.

"Martu," she called softly. "Take a break."

"I'm fine," I said, shoving the sugar packets back into their holder. My fingers refused to stay steady.

"Martina." My mom's voice was quiet but firm.

"I'm just tired," I mumbled. I bent down to pick up the last of the sugar packets and realized my hands were still shaking.

She exhaled quietly, stepping closer. "You've been like this all morning." She set her keys down on the counter. "Did something happen?"

"I haven't been sleeping well," I muttered. It wasn't a lie, but it wasn't the truth either. I turned back to the espresso machine, pretending I needed to clean the wand again. My fingers slipped, and I nearly scalded myself with the steam. "I can't seem to get anything right today. And I need to leave soon to prep for the play, and-—"

"Martina," she said gently and then cleared her throat. "I spoke to Belén last night."

She paused, like she wasn't sure how to say it. "She's..." My mother cleared her throat again. "She got the job."

I stared at her, my hands suddenly cold against the counter. "She's... *¿qué?*" The words barely made it out. My voice felt distant, thin, like it didn't belong to me.

My mom shifted her weight, a nervous habit when she was having difficult conversations. "I know you were hoping she'd come back..."

"She said she would," I cut in, my voice sharper now. "She said..." I trailed off, breath unsteady.

I turned to the espresso machine, flipping the switch

just for something to do. The low hum of it filled the silence, but it didn't drown out the knot curling tighter in my chest.

"*Mamá*, she said she'd come back," I said again, quieter this time. "She promised."

My mother stepped closer, hands working to tie her apron around her waist. "I think she wanted to, but then this opportunity came up and..."

"And what?" My voice cracked. "And she decided I wasn't worth telling?" I felt my breath hitch, and I turned away, blinking hard. My hand clenched around the edge of the counter. "I'm always the one getting left behind."

"Martina," she said with a small sigh. "You don't have to be fine. It's okay to want things to be different."

"Is it, though?" I paused, breath shaking in my chest. "No one ever asked what I wanted, *Mamá*," I said, voice rising. "I just... stayed. I stayed because I thought I was supposed to. Because I thought I was needed here. And now I look around and everyone's moving on, and I'm still right fucking here. Still in this café, still serving the same people, still... still just me."

I pressed my fingers against my temples. "I'm almost thirty, and this is my life? I'm the sweet girl who works at the corner café and follows the town's golden boy around? This is my legacy?"

I laughed bitterly, tears pooling in my eyes. I turned away from her, staring hard at the row of mugs on the shelf. "I don't even like it here, *Mamá*." The thought finally verbalized. Something I'd been thinking for years but never dared to utter out loud, not even to myself. "And I know that hurts you because this is what *you* chose. And you made it work, you built something." I widened my arms and turned in a circle. "But I never wanted this."

I paused, dragging in a shaky breath. My mother stood before me, blinking in my direction, probably trying to wrap around the fact that the sweet girl was no longer here. "I just stayed because I thought I had to. And it's really on me because it was easier than figuring out what I actually wanted. I don't know how to leave or where I'd even go."

The bell above the café door jingled, and I barely had time to turn before Manuela strode in. She took one look at me—red-faced, breath shaky, and tears streaming down my cheeks—and didn't hesitate.

"Come on," she said, grabbing my arm.

"What are you—"

"You need a break," she cut in sympathetically. "Let's go."

"I can't just leave," I said, glancing back at my mom. "I have to set up for the play."

"I'll close up," my mom said quietly. Her face was still drawn tight, but she nodded. "Go."

Before I could think of an argument, Manuela was tugging me outside, the warm air clinging to my skin. I didn't know where we were going. I just let her pull me down the street, then toward her mother's car, parked right in front of their house.

"Get in," she said.

I slid into the passenger seat, the air inside still cool. Manuela didn't say anything for a while, just drove—out past the edge of town, past the familiar residential streets, until the roads narrowed and the landscape opened wide.

We stopped near the wildflower field. The blooms were still there, still bright and blinding just like two nights ago, and the space stretched wide and quiet. Manuela turned off the car and leaned back against her seat with a sigh.

"Okay," she said, turning to me. "Now tell me what's going on."

I didn't answer. My fingers dug into the fabric of my skirt, twisting and pulling until my knuckles ached. The silence stretched out, so, so heavy. Manuela didn't push. She never did. She just waited, eyes on the windshield, hands loose in her lap.

I swallowed hard and stared out the window. The sun baked the field, golden and dry where wildflowers now bloomed in wild, tangled bursts. I wanted to say something, but my throat wouldn't cooperate.

"Martina," Manuela said quietly, "I'm not going anywhere until you talk to me."

"I don't know what I'm doing." My voice faltered. "This whole thing with Jacinto... I thought it was supposed to be simple. Just a way to shake things up, something to make me feel different. Less stuck." I paused, staring down at my hands, dry and worn from endless days behind the counter. "But now it's ending, and I can't even tell what's real and what's not anymore."

Manuela's face softened. "Martina…"

"And now Belén is staying in Buenos Aires. She told me, when she came home for the Peanut Festival, that she was going to apply for the job," I said, my words spilling out faster. "She didn't even call me to tell me because she probably thought I couldn't handle it. Like I'm some… fragile person who can't handle change and is stuck to this routine."

"That's not true."

"Isn't it?" I let out a shaky breath. "Everyone's moving forward. You're leaving. My sister… and me. I'm here. At the café. Just me."

"Just you?" Manuela's brow lifted. "Martina, you're one of the bravest people I know. You take care of this place, your family… You hold so much together." She shook her head. "You fucking held it together when your father left, and we were, what… thirteen? You know what you remind me of? Those wildflowers." She gestured out the window at the shimmering field. "They don't even try to stand out—they just *are*. Bold, bright, impossible to ignore. You're like that. You grow through anything, whether people are paying attention or not."

"Wildflowers," I said flatly. "You're comparing me to a bunch of weeds?"

"Hey," she shot back with a wobbly smile. "Wildflowers survive the winter, Martu. They find a way to grow back stronger, brighter. They're strong and stand tall, just like you."

I nodded, her words lodging deep in my chest and wrapping around it tightly.

"You're not stuck," she said softly. "You're holding steady until you know what comes next."

"What if I never know?"

"I think you already know," she said simply. "It's time to let it come to you."

41

I WASN'T TRYING to overhear anything. I was just cutting across the square, minding my own business on the way to the community center to check on things before the play. The sun was starting to set, slanting gold across the cobblestones. Shops were closing up, their windows glowing warm as people drifted home or gathered at the inn's restaurant for an early dinner.

I wasn't paying much attention until I heard Carmen's voice, sharp and smug, the kind that carried even when she was trying to whisper.

"...decided to stay," she said. "Didn't even tell Martina until the last minute. Poor girl... First Manuela leaving, now her sister's not coming back. Imagine how that must feel."

"At least she has that boy," someone replied, but the statement felt muddled.

I slowed down, my steps dragging on instinct. I couldn't

see them, but I knew they were tucked into their usual corner on the last bench before the tree line ended. I kept walking, hoping that if I moved fast enough, I wouldn't hear the rest.

"She'll be fine," a third person chimed in. "She's strong."

"Sure," Carmen muttered. "But it's got to be lonely."

Lonely.

The word hit me square in the chest. I continued my stroll, but slower now, like I was moving through mud. I didn't want to hear any more, but the words kept looping in my head.

Lonely.

I thought about Martina's face last night—the way she barely smiled when I walked her home, the way her hand slipped from mine like she was already there, not here. I thought about how she'd been quiet lately, quieter than usual. And now I knew why.

I stopped in front of the community center steps, staring up at the dark windows. I should've gone inside, checked on the rows of chairs or made sure the props were still where they were supposed to be. Instead, I stood there, hands tucked in my pockets, Carmen's voice still buzzing in my head.

Lonely.

Yeah. I knew what that felt like.

I turned away from the steps and kept walking, shoes scraping against the cobblestones. My breath disappeared into the heat, swallowed whole by the heavy summer air. I took a lap around the square before finally heading back to my house to get ready for the final event.

———

I showed up at Martina's house fifteen minutes early. I didn't know why—maybe because I couldn't stand still anymore. Maybe because the thought of her hurting made me feel like my ribs were too tight around my lungs.

The light to her room was on, and I waited by the gate, shoving my hands deep into my pockets while pacing back and forth. It was excruciatingly hot, and I knew I should've just knocked and went inside, but something kept me from doing it.

My thoughts ran Carmen's words on a loop—about how Martina was the only one who hadn't changed and she was being left behind.

And now? She was about to lose me, too. This had been the one thing steady in her life these past few months, and that was ending tonight. The thought twisted something sharp and mean in my chest.

We wouldn't recover from this. There was no going back.

The door opened, and she stepped out onto the porch.

I forgot how to breathe.

Her hair, almost always tied back at the café, hung loose now, falling in soft waves over her shoulders. Her dress— dark green, with a neckline that dipped low enough to make my thoughts stumble—clung to her body in all the right places. She wasn't trying to look stunning. She just... was.

"Hey," she said, draping a thin coat on her forearm.

"Hey," I echoed, and my voice felt wrong. Too hushed and rough, like gravel had taken up residence in my throat. "You look..."

I couldn't even finish the sentence. My brain kept scrambling for the right words and coming up with nothing.

"I what?" she asked, her lips tugging upward just a little, but her eyes were dim.

"You look...nice," I said. Nice. *Nice?*

She laughed under her breath, soft and small, but it still curled warm against my ribs. "You okay?"

"Yeah," I lied. "Fine."

"*¿Seguro?*" she asked, her gaze sharper now. "Because you look like you're about to jump out of your skin."

"I'm good," I said too quickly. "Just... long day."

We started walking together, her arm brushing against mine now and then as we moved down the quiet streets. The town felt different today. Most of the shops were closed, the windows dark. The only real light came from the string of lanterns lining the square, flickering like little fireflies in the deep of summer.

I wanted to reach for her hand, to hold it like we had done a dozen times in the past few weeks, but I didn't. Ending this—walking away before either of us got too tangled up to escape—was probably the smartest move. The *kind* move.

"How was the setup?" I asked, looking at her profile, studying her reaction. Her face lit up for a second before turning to me and stopping.

"It was crazy," she said, blinking rapidly. "The kids were so antsy, but luckily we finished everyone on time."

"I'm so proud of you, baby," I said honestly.

And I meant it more than I'd meant almost anything in my life. Watching her now, glowing from the chaos, it hit me all over again. She'd wanted something to feel different, to feel hers. And somehow, in the middle of everything, she'd found it.

The kind of thing worth waiting for.

She was shining in a way that had absolutely nothing to do with me—just her and her talent, and the way people had started to finally see her for something other than the girl from the café.

The community center was already filling up when we walked in. The crowd was buzzing, families fanning themselves with folded programs, kids tugging at parents' hands, and neighbors greeting each other in low, happy murmurs. Martina and I moved quietly through the room, smiling and nodding at familiar faces. It felt... normal, like nothing between us was ending at all.

She slipped her arm through mine without a word when we found our seats near the back. Her fingers curled lightly against my sleeve, and I didn't dare move an inch. I told myself it was part of the act—one last performance for the town—but I knew better.

During the first act, she leaned in close to whisper something—a joke about Gervasio forgetting his lines—and I couldn't stop myself. I smiled and leaned in, too, brushing my lips against her temple. She didn't pull away. She simply stayed close, her head resting against my shoulder like it belonged there.

I knew better than to hope she meant it, but for the remainder of the play, I pretended she did.

On stage, the lights flickered softly over a cardboard castle that was lightly painted and hung crooked in the background, and Ursula's wig was definitely slipping to one side. Gervasio had been cast as Sebastian and was singing half a beat behind the music while waving his clawed hands in the air. His face was not all red, like one would expect from someone playing a crab, but instead his cheeks were highlighted with glitter and his eyes looked like they were three times their normal size. The entire front row was made up of small children in glittery mermaid tails and spectacular eye makeup, clapping and moving along to the songs.

"His makeup is amazing," I whispered to Martina. She smiled softly but didn't look away, instead following the cast for the entire duration. "Everyone looks spectacular, baby. Great job."

When the show was over, we lingered with the rest of the crowd, stepping outside into the hot night air. People spilled out onto the steps, laughing and congratulating the cast and crew. Martina kept her arm linked through mine, and I continued to tell myself it was just part of this fake relationship we were in for the sake of the town. But when her fingers tightened slightly against my sleeve, something in me twisted painfully.

"*¿Listo?*" she asked softly when the crowd started thinning out. Her voice had that careful stretched quality—unsure of what she hoped I would say.

We walked to her house quietly, her steps slower than ever. I kept waiting for her to say something—anything—but she didn't. Her arms stayed folded tightly against her chest, her face unreadable. She didn't even glance my way.

When we reached her front door, she stopped but didn't open it right away. She stood there, fingers wrapped around her keys, staring down at her shoes like she was gathering her thoughts.

I waited, barely breathing, hoping she'd say something that would make it easier to leave. But she didn't. She just let out a quiet breath, pushed the door open, and stepped inside.

The door clicked shut, and I stood there, staring at the empty space where she'd been.

I wanted her so much. So badly. But she deserved better than someone who didn't know how to stick around. Someone who kept convincing himself that leaving was safer than staying.

42

MARTINA

I DIDN'T REALIZE where I was going until I was halfway there. My mind kept spinning in loops, replaying every moment from the past few weeks. The way Jacinto had walked me home like it was nothing, how his hand had hovered at the small of my back as though he couldn't let go. The way he kissed my temple at the play, soft and simple, but enough to crack something open inside me. I kept thinking about how he'd smiled less lately, how he'd looked at me like he was holding something back.

I told myself I wasn't going to cry, but my breath was already catching in my chest and tears stung my eyes. I rubbed at my face with my fingers as I turned the corner, wiping the tears off my cheeks as I went.

There was no plan, no perfect speech or rehearsed words, only a knot in my stomach and a heart that wouldn't stop pounding. My dress shoes slapped against the cobblestones and the strap of the dress I'd worn just for him kept slipping down my shoulder. The heat stung my face, the humid air sharp in my lungs, but I didn't slow down. I couldn't. If I stopped moving, I'd lose my nerve.

I caught sight of him just as he was walking up the steps to his house. His shoulders were hunched, one hand digging in his pocket for his keys. He looked exhausted. Like he'd spent the entire night carrying something too heavy to put down.

"Jacinto!" I called, my voice breaking the mountain stillness.

He froze, keys halfway to the lock. When he turned, his face twisted in surprise.

"Martina?" He stepped down from the porch, meeting me halfway. "What are you—"

"I have to say this," I cut in, breathless. "Please, before I chicken out."

His expression shifted, cautious now. Guarded. "Okay," he said simply.

I swallowed hard, chest rising and falling too fast. I shifted from one foot to the other, unsure what to do with my hands. I nearly shoved them in my dress pockets before deciding against it. I didn't want it to look like I was holding anything back—not tonight.

"I should have said something sooner," I continued, my voice quieter now. "But I kept talking myself out of it. I told myself you didn't really want this, that you'd be relieved when we ended things. I thought...maybe you were just waiting for an easy way out." My hands refused to stay still, curling and uncurling at my sides. "I thought this"—I gestured between us—"this whole thing—us—was just a way to break out of the same boring routine. Something easy and natural to shake things up, to make me feel like I was actually moving forward."

His face didn't change, but I saw the way his shoulders tensed.

"And it worked," I said quietly. "But not in the way I thought it would."

I dragged in a breath, forcing myself to meet his eyes. "I was scared." The words came out shaky, almost too quiet to hear. "I've been scared for a long time, not just about you. About everything. About staying here forever, about never figuring out what I actually want.

"Scared that if I wanted more, I'd just end up disappointed. Everyone else was leaving—my sister, Manuela—and I convinced myself that if I stayed small, if I didn't ask for anything... no one could let me down."

"Martina..." His voice was cautious and rough.

"But I'm done with that," I pushed on, feeling my chest tighten. "I don't want to be scared anymore. I don't want to keep pretending this hasn't been the best thing that's happened to me in years. Because it has." I took a shaky step closer. "*Te amo*," I said, the words tumbling out before I could stop them. "I love you."

My breath hitched. "And I don't mean it in the *I care about you* or *I'm glad we did this* way. I mean... I'm in love with you. The kind of love that makes my chest hurt when I think about walking away. And if you don't feel the same way... that's okay. I get it. But I can't keep pretending I'm fine letting you go. I'm not."

His face broke—a flicker of what looked so much like pain. He shook his head, and my stomach dropped.

"I know," I said quickly. "I know I'm probably too late, and maybe I'm just making a fool of myself, but I had to tell you." My voice cracked again, and two silent tears streamed down my face. "I'm tired of being scared. I'm tired of waiting for things to happen to me. If you don't want me, that's okay. I need to leave, to find something else. Something that's all mine."

I took a deep breath that shook all the way down my body. "I can't keep waiting around, hoping someone else will decide what my life is supposed to look like." The words were stumbling out, wobbly but there. I didn't stop. "I want to decide that for myself—even if I mess it up, even if I fall flat on my face." I laughed weakly, the sound breaking. "And if I do... Then at least I'll know I tried."

He stepped forward then, so fast I barely saw him move. His hands cupped my face, warm and steady. Before I could say anything else, his mouth was on mine—fierce and desperate, like he was terrified I'd disappear if he didn't hold me there.

I kissed him back just as hard, My fingers clawed into his shirt, holding him close, afraid to let go. There was no caution now, no pretending. Just him and every emotion we hadn't dared name until it spilled out between us.

When he finally broke away, he pressed his forehead to mine. We were both breathing hard, our chests rising and falling in sync, like we were trying to calm the same heartbeat.

"You think I don't want you?" he asked, his voice unrecognizable. Rough, raw. "I've been losing my mind trying to let you go. Trying to convince myself you'd be better off without me."

"Then why—" I started, but he shook his head, cutting me off.

"Because I've never been good at sticking around, Martina," he whispered, his voice cracking. "I ruin things. I get restless and I leave, you know this. You've seen it. The garden, the library project, the fucking podcast." He paused, blinking fast. "I wanted to believe I'd changed, but I couldn't risk hurting you."

"You don't get to decide that for me," I said, the words sharp but steady. "I deserve someone who loves me. Someone who actually wants to be with me."

"I do," he breathed. "God, I love you so much. And it terrifies me, because this—what we have—it's real. You're not just someone I want. You're home. You're... the first thing I haven't wanted to run from."

He kissed me again, slower this time. Like he was memorizing every inch of me all over again. Like he was asking for a second chance without saying a word. Saying I love you with his whole body and soul.

Heat radiated from our skin, the summer night pressing in around us. My dress clung to the back of my legs, his palm was still on my jaw, and everything in me ached with the need to believe him.

When we finally came up for air, his arms didn't let go right away. He held me there, forehead resting against mine, breathing unevenly. His fingers trailed down my arm, lacing with mine like he was afraid I'd slip away again.

"I'm here," he said quietly. "I'm not going anywhere."

I looked up at him, at those deep green eyes that held so many memories between us. The humidity curled the hair at his temples, and his shirt was wrinkled from where I'd grabbed him. His eyes were glassy, like he was still trying to believe I was real.

My voice was barely a whisper. "Promise?"

He didn't smile. He didn't joke. He just nodded once.

Something cracked wide open in my chest. I blinked fast, but I was still crying—though I wasn't sure if it was from sadness anymore. It felt more like relief.

This time, when his arms curled around me, I held on just as tightly, knowing neither of us was going anywhere.

43

We barely made it inside.

The second the door clicked shut behind us, Jacinto pressed me against it like he was starved for me and wanted to waste no time. His mouth found mine with a kind of hunger that made my knees threaten to buckle, his hands sliding under the hem of my dress like a man on a mission.

"Tell me this is real," he murmured between kisses, his breath hot against my cheek. "Tell me I didn't just imagine you showing up like that, all furious and stunning and saying you love me."

I laughed, a shaky sound that dissolved into a sigh when his hand found bare skin. "You didn't imagine it. I'm right here."

"Good," he said, lips brushing my neck. "Because I'm about to do unforgivable things to you, and I need to know I have your enthusiastic consent."

"You have it," I said breathlessly, "with all my enthusiasm."

He groaned, low and desperate, and then he was kissing me again—without restraint and because he was allowed to.

Eventually, we managed to stumble to the bedroom, clothes falling like breadcrumbs behind us. My dress got caught over my head, and he helped me tug it off, only to toss it onto a chair like it had personally offended him.

"God, look at you," he said, eyes roaming my almost naked body. "You're going to ruin me."

I arched a brow. "I haven't already?"

"Martina," he growled, stepping in close again. "I've been obsessed with you since you laughed so hard at one of my jokes in tenth grade that soda came out of your nose."

"Oh my god," I mumbled, covering my face with one hand and shoving at his chest with the other. "Don't bring up that moment while I'm half-naked."

"Too late. I think that was the moment I knew."

I pulled him into a kiss before I could come up with a witty comeback, partly because my brain wasn't working anymore and partly because the way he looked at me made me feel invincible. Like I was some rare, magical creature that only he could see clearly.

When his mouth moved lower, trailing hot, open-mouthed kisses down my neck, between my breasts, over my stomach, my hands curled into themselves like I needed to anchor myself to this room or I would float away. Every brush of his lips felt like a promise—a worship of every part of me he'd only gotten to admire from afar.

He knelt between my legs and kissed the inside of my thigh, just above the bend of my knee. My breath stuttered, and I arched into the sensation.

"Martina," he said, his voice low and reverent. He removed my underwear, inch by inch in painful slow motion. "I've dreamed about this."

I held onto his hair, tugging lightly to bring his eyes up to mine. "Yeah?" I sounded breathless and needy, and I loved what it was doing to him.

Jacinto looked up at me from his position, eyes blazing. "It's been torture. About how you taste. About how you sounded when I had you like this."

My stomach flipped, heat licking up my spine.

"I used to imagine it at night and then feel guilty as hell in the morning."

"You should've told me," I said, swallowing hard.

His lips curled in a wicked grin. "Would you have let me?"

"Probably."

That earned me a sinful smile before he buried his face between my thighs, and everything after that was heat and pressure and the kind of pleasure that made me forget every single bad thing that had ever happened to me. I forgot the café, the play, the fact that the whole town was probably still talking about my hair. There was only Jacinto —his fucking mouth on my clit, his hands, the way he made me feel like I was the only thing that ever made sense to him.

He pushed me slightly, using one of his large hands to sit me on his undone bed, and crawled over me, hair crazy from how tightly I had been holding on to him.

"You know what?" he said once he reached the hollow of my neck. He nipped at it playfully, pulling a surprised laugh from me. "We wasted so much time pretending we were friends."

"I agree," I said as I ran my fingers through his hair again, pulling him in for a kiss. Jacinto's hands settled at my waist, his grip easy, like he couldn't quite believe we were there, on his bed. No audience, no pretending. He laughed low in his throat, the sound vibrating against my mouth as he kissed me again—slow and hungry, a starving man with me as the only thing that could satisfy him.

"Do you have any idea how hard it's been for me?" he asked, moving his hips against mine. His hard erection pressed against me, and he sighed, deep and needy and guttural.

"Oh my god," I said, laughing even as my entire body flushed. "You're obsessed with me."

"*Absolutamente*," he said, dragging his mouth across my collarbone, his voice dark and gleaming with amusement. "If only Gladys and Carmen knew..."

"Jacinto, I swear to god."

He laughed, and both our bodies shook. "Ask me how many times I've dreamed about your pussy."

"You need help."

"I need you," he said, and just like that, I wasn't laughing anymore.

I stared at him, all the air gone from my lungs. But before I could come up with something even remotely clever to say, he shifted, rolling so I was on top. My knees braced on either side of his hips, my palms flat on his chest.

"Your turn," he said, eyes locked on mine. "Take what you want."

And maybe I should have teased him again, maybe I should have made him work for it. But I was probably as desperate as he was, my core aching with the need he so desperately showed. I didn't want to be anywhere but here, touching him, moving against him, feeling the way his hands tightened and his breath caught every time I rolled my hips just right.

He sat up slightly, one hand on my waist, the other threading into my hair to keep me close as I sank onto him, slow and deep. My mouth fell open, the stretch, the pressure, the heat of it all making me gasp.

"Fuck," he said, forehead pressed to mine. His back was against the headboard and his whole body was tense. "You feel like heaven."

A laugh stuttered out of me, shaky and uneven. "You're not so bad yourself."

We moved like that, slow and heady, every roll of my hips sending little sparks down my spine and deep into my belly. His hands roamed restlessly, impossible to decide if he wanted to hold me tighter or figure out what every inch of me felt like. His eyes never left mine.

"You drive me insane," he said, breathless, as I leaned down to kiss him. "Completely unhinged."

"Good," I whispered, biting his lips gently before pulling back. "The feeling is mutual."

That made him laugh, a real one, his body shaking again beneath mine. "We were so fucking dumb."

"The dumbest."

The rhythm shifted, deepened. My hands curled into his shoulders, nails digging in as the heat between us grew sharp and insistent. His mouth found my nipple, teeth scraping just enough to make me gasp. I felt him everywhere —his breath, his hands, the hard curve of his smile when I moaned his name.

I came first, fast and hard and blinding. And when he came, it was with a gasp of my name, his hands clutching at my hips, unable to let go.

I collapsed against him, my skin slick with sweat and my breath uneven, his chest still rising and falling fast beneath mine. Neither of us spoke for a long time.

"So," I said eventually, my voice quiet. Not teasing, not light. Just tired. "We're definitely not pretending anymore."

Jacinto let out a dry huff of breath, more sigh than laugh. "Definitely not."

44

JACINTO

I woke up to the weight of Martina's leg draped over mine and the faint sound of a cat meowing somewhere in the house.

For a second, I simply lay there. Let the morning light filter in through the blinds, golden and soft. Let myself take in the sight of Martina in my bed, still asleep, her pink hair a messy halo on my pillow. Her mouth was parted slightly, and one hand was curled against my chest, claiming me.

Mine. The word hit me with a force that nearly knocked the breath out of my lungs.

Another meow. A louder one.

"Do not let him on here," Martina mumbled without opening her eyes. "I'm naked and I don't trust him.

I laughed. "What are you talking about? He's your biggest fan."

"He's been plotting my death for months."

Beto yowled again.

"All right," I whispered, groaning as I peeled myself from the bed, regretting every second I wasn't plastered on to her already. "I'm coming, you little drama king."

"Takes after his dad," Martina said with a chuckle, moving under the covers and nestling in deeper. Beto hopped off the bed with a satisfied chirp, tail high in the air like he owned the place.

I tugged on a pair of basketball shorts and padded barefoot into the kitchen to feed him. The floor was cool underfoot, the summer air already thick and warm. Outside the window, the mountains were soft with early light, and the wildflowers in my backyard had exploded almost overnight —yellows and oranges and purple patches that made it look like the hills were on fire.

It felt like Tres Fuegos had finally cracked open. Like the season had shifted without asking.

The kettle whistled for a second before I took it off the stove, pouring hot water into two mugs with a spoonful of instant coffee on the bottom. I was no barista, but this felt like home. I pulled down one of the *alfajores* I kept hidden from Beto behind the rice and opened it, setting it on a plate.

Beto scarfed his food like he hadn't eaten in weeks and promptly jumped on the counter to sniff at my girl's breakfast.

"No, *amigo*," I said, pushing him slightly to get him to move. "*Estás equivocado.*"

Behind me, I heard footsteps and a soft chuckle.

"Good morning," I said, openly staring. Martina was wearing one of my t-shirts and nothing else. Her hair was a mess, lips swollen, the tiniest smug smile tugging at the corner of her mouth when she saw me staring.

She blinked at the coffee. "Are we pretending last night didn't happen or are we going full domestic?"

"Full domestic," I said without hesitation. "Starting now."

She padded over, stole a bite of the *alfajor* on the plate, and kissed me—quick and sweet, like she'd been doing it forever.

"Can I borrow your shorts?" she asked between chews. "We're not walking Beto naked."

I paused. "Wait, we're walking Beto?"

She grinned. "He needs fresh air."

"You're going to make me leash-walk our cat through town?"

"You said full domestic."

She laughed and headed back to the room, opening and closing drawers by the sound of it. I followed her and stood at the door, watching her move so naturally in my most intimate space.

Martina turned her head and blinked. "How do you even live like this?" she asked, eyes returning to the dresser where everything was stored into the drawers with no rhyme or reason. "You're lucky I love you."

I smiled and took a step in her direction, kissing the

corner of her mouth like I'd dreamed of a million times. "I know."

———

We made it two blocks before someone shouted about how cute Beto looked with his pink harness on. He strutted like a show pony between us, leash clinking and his name tag moving side to side as he walked with his tail high. Martina had my shirt knotted at the waist and the borrowed shorts rolled at the top, her legs on full display. I was trying very hard not to think about last night. Or how I'd barely kept it together when she'd said my name like it meant something holy.

Beto walked ahead, pausing every few steps to sniff a weed in the sidewalk or peer suspiciously at Carmen, who was sitting on the last bench of the square, hands on her lap, trying to look innocent. He had the self-importance that only a cat on a leash could manage.

Martina laughed under her breath every time someone stopped to coo at him.

"He's a local celebrity," I muttered.

She looked over at me, her eyes crinkling at the corners and her hand sliding right into mine. "Wonder who he takes after."

"Smartass," I said, pulling her in for a kiss just because I could. And because she was *mine*.

Tres Fuegos was small and soft around the edges this

time of year, right before the tourist season started, with sunlight pouring through the jacaranda trees and the scent of jasmine and peaches heavy in the air. We walked slowly by the bakery and then by the inn. We were nearly at the café when Martina slowed a little. Her hand tightened around mine.

"What is it?" I asked, voice low and just for her.

Martina glanced inside the coffee shop, where her mother was moving inside with a huge smile on her face.

"Sorry about the scene last night," she said, her eyes fixed on her mom inside the café. "This whole thing with Belén and... This changes things, you know?"

My chest squeezed. I stopped walking and tugged her gently until she faced me. "It doesn't have to."

I reached my hand up and gently swiped my thumb over her cheek. Her hair was wild today, the pink strands all over the place with the humidity and the wind. I tucked an errant lock behind her ear, and she leaned into my hand, searching for my touch. "Did you talk to your mom?"

She shook her head no and looked inside the café. Her mother was standing behind the counter staring at us, eyes fixed on the image right outside her shop. She looked a little sullen, maybe because Belén wasn't coming back, maybe because Martina was finally blooming. But whatever it was, I would support this girl to the end.

"Do you want to go talk to her?"

"I probably should, right?"

"Yeah," I whispered against her mouth, kissing her simply because I could. Again. "I'll see you at home?"

"Okay," she replied as she walked into the café where her mother was waiting.

Beto and I stood outside for a minute, taking it all in. This town, its quirks and what made it so unique.

Carmen materialized almost out of thin air, clearing her throat in front of me with her ever-present tote bags hanging from each of her hands.

"Jacinto, *querido*," she said, looking from me back inside to the café. She was wearing something I could only define as an oversized floral dress, something I'd never seen her wear in all the years I'd roamed the streets of Tres Fuegos in the summer.

Beto meowed as if to alert me of her presence or maybe to encourage me to reply to her. Or maybe he wanted to stay far, far away from her.

"Carmen," I said with a polite smile. "How are you today?"

"Oh, just fine. You know, my knee still hurts occasionally, especially when rain is coming." She turned her head upwards to look at the clear blue sky, not a cloud in sight. "Maybe tonight we'll have our first summer storm. God knows we need the rain."

"Yes," I said casually. "Everything is looking a little dry, isn't it?"

"Yes, yes," Carmen repeated, looking back into the café.

"Let me ask you, young man, do you think your girlfriend would give me a few makeup lessons?"

"Tsk, tsk, tsk, Carmen," I said, letting Beto twine between my legs like he was echoing my disapproval. "Don't you have plenty of granddaughters who could help you with that?"

"Yes, well." She pursed her lips and blinked a few times. "Martina is very talented, and you know those granddaughters of mine are..." She let the thought trail off, dangling it between us like live bait.

I didn't take it.

But I did know exactly how they were.

She glanced again toward the café windows. I could almost see the gears turning behind her smile, the careful calculation being her sudden friendliness. This wasn't about makeup lessons. Not really.

"So, what do you think?" she pressed.

I shrugged, keeping my voice even. "I think you should ask her yourself."

Her mouth tightened.

"You recognized her talent," I continued, not letting her off the hook. "Tell her that. Don't make it about favors or appearances. Just be honest. Maybe even start with an apology."

Carmen blinked again, slower this time.

"An apology?" she asked, tone clipped.

"You know what people in this town said. What they still say." I kept my voice calm, but Beto's tail flicked sharply between us, like he could feel the shift in tone. "Martina doesn't forget things like that. She just doesn't always say them out loud."

Carmen lifted her chin slightly, her grip tightening on the handles of her tote bags.

"She's more than the girl who serves your coffee. And I think you know that now."

We stood there in silence for a beat, the summer heat settling heavy between us. Across the square, someone honked, and there was a holler in response. Carmen exhaled, long and slow, as if she was deflating.

Then she turned toward the café, adjusting her dress and smoothing her hair awkwardly while still holding on to her canvas bag. "Such a shame Elisa was never interested in you," she said, almost absently. "I think you would have made a great pair."

I smiled without warmth. "I'm sure, Carmen. I'm sure."

And just like that, she disappeared through the café door, the scent of summer flowers trailing behind her, like the conversation hadn't happened at all.

EPILOGUE

MARTINA

"Gato," I said over the loud sound of the gravel under the car tires. The windows were down, the warm breeze filtering in and creating a nice little current as I drove down the backroads of Tres Fuegos. The wildflower fields were showing off today—the pinks as bright as I'd ever seen them, dancing lazily against the crisp blue of our characteristic summer sky. "Are you sure this is the right way?"

He hummed through the car speakers, and I heard a door shut on the other end of the call. "What's wrong, baby?" It was Thursday midday, and I was on my way to a wedding. It was an out-of-town bride that had hired me almost exactly a year ago after business started to pick up as a result of the town's play. She had seen some of my stage makeup on a mutual friend and called me to see if I was free.

Of course, Jacinto pushed me to accept, and I dreaded meeting her all year.

But she ended up being extremely easy-going, and our trial a few days ago was perfect. Now I was driving to the venue to work on her and some of her bridal party for her evening ceremony and reception. "Are you sure you put the right address in my GPS?"

"What? What do you mean?"

"I'm on some back road and I don't recognize much of anything."

"I don't know. I put in the coordinates you gave me."

"Well, I think something is wrong."

"Is there a chance you're still going there? Like maybe the event is, in fact, on some back road?"

Five days ago, I had gone to the house where the bride and her family were staying for the duration of the festivities. It had been a straight shot down the mountain to a huge vacation home a few towns over. The drive had been clean and aesthetic, the mountains turning to hills, then to fields that absolutely looked like a hashtag waiting to happen.

This… was not.

The road beneath the car's wheels crackled with every bump, and the canopy of the trees had thickened so much, I could barely see the sky. I slowed slightly, one hand tightening on the wheel. "I swear, if I end up in some compound where they talk about *vibrations* and *manifesting,* I'm never letting you touch my phone again."

Jacinto laughed in my ear, that low, lazy sound that still did something to me, even after all these months. "Baby, I double-checked it. Maybe your GPS is being dramatic."

"Excuse you, *yo estoy siendo dramática*," I corrected. "The GPS is probably trying to save my life."

There was a pause, then the sound of rustling. "Do you want me to come get you?"

"No," I sighed, glancing at the time. I'd made a habit of showing up to any job between one hour to forty five minutes early, always, so that would give me a buffer in case of any delays, and the brides would always be relaxed in case we needed extra time. "I don't have time to turn around. I'll just keep going a little farther and see where it leads."

"You're going to be great, you know," he said. "You always are."

I bit down on a smile. "You're only saying that because you got laid this morning."

"My god, Martina, that mouth." He gasped dramatically, then chuckled to himself. I could picture him, sitting lazily somewhere in our living room, the cat watching him from his perch on that ancient chair he refused to get rid of. "I'm glowing with post-lunch, post-orgasm optimism."

"You're disgusting."

"'You love me."

"Tragically," I muttered.

Another pause. "Martina?"

"Yeah?"

"I'm really proud of you. Look at what you've built from scratch."

I blinked fast at the road ahead, heart giving a little twist. From day one, he had been my biggest cheerleader, liking and sharing all my posts on social media with what I'd done to add to my portfolio. "I had help."

Just then, the trees began to thin, and I saw a familiar curve up ahead—a wide hilltop clearing, the vacation home just behind it, dressed up with fairy lights and white tents.

Relief flooded my chest.

"Never mind," I said. "I'm here."

"Told you."

I rolled my eyes, but I couldn't stop smiling. "Thank you. I'll see you in a few hours."

———

I'd gone the whole afternoon without texting him, as I usually did when I was working. Jacinto still texted me constantly. He was usually bored to death, so as soon as I got back in my car, I would catch up with his day, reading text after text of a play-by-play summary of his activities.

I stepped out onto the balcony just as the sun was setting. I heard the processional music, excited about how the day had turned out with the stunning bride. This was my favorite part of my job, seeing brides on what was the happiest day of their lives, just looking and feeling their best.

The golden light hit just right through the trees; low, warm, and catching the edge of the beaded veil pinned to the bride's hair as she stood at the end of the aisle, waiting for her cue. I smiled to myself and returned inside to pack my kit, slipping each brush into its holder with practiced ease. It had been a perfect day, and for the first time since this side-now-turned-main-job started, I felt like I'd actually been part of it and not just an observer or a vendor.

I swung my heavy bag over my shoulder and walked down the gravel drive toward the car, mentally already halfway home. My fingers itched to text Jacinto, but he hadn't messaged since we spoke hours earlier. No *bored*, no *please come back*, no pictures of Beto doing something completely normal like napping on his chair. Radio silence.

One thing was abundantly clear at that precise moment: Jacinto was hiding a secret. It was extremely suspicious of him to be radio silent for more than forty-five minutes at a time, especially since he didn't have court or any long meetings on his agenda for the day.

As I reached the car, I paused. There was a figure standing by the tree line, partially tucked in the shadows. The sun had almost dipped behind the hills, and the wildflower-covered slope was glowing, every pink and gold bloom lit up like it was part of some painting.

I squinted.

Tall. Lean. Absolutely perfect.

Of course it was Jacinto. I could see the sneaky smirk from where I stood by the car and the reflection of the house's lights on his reading glasses. I pressed my lips together, trying not to grin like an idiot. "Okay, what the hell are you up to?"

The figure didn't move. Just stood there for a minute. Watching me as I loaded my things inside the trunk of the tiny yellow car I now used more than its original owner.

"If this turns out to be a horror movie prank, I swear to god, I'm breaking up with you and then telling your grandmother."

Jacinto laughed loudly from his spot but didn't take any steps in my direction. Instead, I locked the car and found myself walking toward him.

"Jacinto," I called out, then louder: "Gato!"

And then he moved. Fast. I yelped when he darted out of the shadows and bent at the knees, folding me over his shoulder and wrapping one hand around my thighs.

"Jacinto!" I yelled, hitting his back so he would let me go. "Put me down."

"Come with me," he said, breathless, like he'd just ran a mile instead of standing in the shadows being a creep.

"What? Wait, where are we goi— Put me down!" I said as he started jogging back towards the trees and through a narrow worn path between the tall trunks.

"You'll see."

He pulled me through the field behind the venue. The sun now hit the peak of golden hour, turning everything soft and unreal. In the year since we'd been officially dating, everything had changed. I finally saw Tres Fuegos for what it was: a town that was soft and blurry at the edges, where people cared deeply for others, even if it had a very clumsy way of showing it. My relationship with my mother was stronger than ever. My friends were all thriving, and Manuela had, indeed, been back a number of times to visit.

My sister was still in Buenos Aires, but I could see the writing on the wall and was sure she would be back soon—finally seeking that slower pace that this town had to offer.

And Jacinto… We had wasted so much time pretending we were friends, and this was exactly what we should have been from the beginning.

The tall grass tickled my calves, the wind tossing my hair around my face. I had kept it pink ever since, and I thought it really suited me. I felt freer, like all I had to do was get a little push and all of this would present to me in due time. Like it had been waiting for me all along.

Jacinto set me down and in that moment, I saw it. The field. A perfect, chaotic, breathtaking stretch of wildflowers, extending into the distance, the colors riotous and uncontained.

Like us.

"You found some," I breathed.

His hand squeezed mine.

He led me right to the center, turned to face me, and pulled something from his back pocket.

"You know what they say," he said, pushing up his glasses with his index finger like he did every day. His eyes were shining, the green stronger than ever now that we stood in the middle of an explosion of color. "A wildflower a day keeps the saddies away."

I laughed, my whole body shaking, and he followed, grabbing my hand and squeezing again. "Is that so?"

"Yeah, baby," he whispered. He took a step in my direction and rested his forehead on mine. The ever-present flutters in my belly quickened. "That's what they say."

Jacinto dropped to one knee.

No words. No speech.

Just that crooked, nervous smile I loved more than anything in the world and a simple, sparkly ring held up between us.

I laughed, the sound caught somewhere between disbelief and complete awe. I didn't expect this at all, but I wasn't entirely surprised. "Are you serious?"

He nodded once. "Martina González. Miranda. Love of my fucking life. Say yes."

I didn't realize I was crying until he looked up, eyes moving over my face like he was cataloguing everything. He stood and tucked the ring back in his pocket, then reached for my face. His thumbs swiped at my tears, and his face grew concerned for a moment.

I launched myself at him. "Of course I'm saying yes, you idiot."

He caught me at the waist, lifting me up into the air and spinning us in the middle of the field. I kissed him, hard and fast and messy, and I didn't stop even when we both stumbled slowly down into the grass.

We lay in the middle of the field, the pink sky fading above us, wildflowers brushing our skin, and our breaths synced like we'd always known how to find our way back to each other.

Maybe this was always meant to be. Us, here, with the wildflowers.

FIN

———

Thank you so much for reading With the Wildflowers! If you liked this book, please review wherever you are able to. Reviews help indie authors like me reach more readers like you, and it would mean the world.

WHAT'S NEXT?

Manuela's book is coming this fall... ••

You can preorder **The No-Pressure Pact**, a no strings vacation fling set partly in New York City, and partly in the Swiss Alps.

ACKNOWLEDGMENTS

With the Wildflowers is a book that started with a completely different premise. Yes, it was always meant to be friends to lovers and fake dating, but everything else snuck up on me.

I joke that I write romance for the stuck girlie™ because all my characters are, at some point or another in their story, stuck with something that they feel defines them. Martina is the most obvious one yet—a girl whose world is moving around her and she's rooted to the same spot—but somehow this boy who can't commit sneaks into her heart and gives her enough momentum to move forward.

This particular story carries a lot of me. The messy parts. The loud parts. The parts I was afraid to put on the page. But here it is: soft and blooming anyway.

To every reader who picked this up—thank you. Whether you've been with me since the beginning or you've found me because of this book, I'm endlessly grateful you're here. Thank you for loving this small town and my characters. I hope Jacinto and Martina and the whole Tres Fuegos crew stay with you long after the last page.

To Katie and Bobbi: thank you for always, always rooting for me, even through the rough drafts and the messy bits and the endless em dashes (I admit I went a little overboard this time around.)

Bekah and Kait: Thank you for your sharp eye, honest notes, and the kind of guidance that doesn't just improve this book, but also makes me a better writer. And for putting up with me. Sorry I'm so needy.

To the Hottest, Menaces and Presidential Erections: This wouldn't exist if you hadn't pushed me —softly and with kind words—to be consistent and write! You've celebrated every win like it was your own and I'll never stop being grateful for that.

To my family and friends: thank you for the patience and the moments of quiet when I needed to write, especially towards the end. It's something that brings me so much joy and I'm grateful I'm allowed the space to fulfill this part of my life.

And finally, to the version of me who once believed she had to stay small and invisible to be safe: look at us now (who would have thought!) Still growing. Still blooming.

ALSO BY MARIA RIGOU

TRES FUEGOS SERIES

After the Fire: An Enemies to Lovers Small Town Romance

Before the Storm: A Second Chance Small Town Romance

With the Wildflowers: A Fake Dating Small Town Romance

LOVE IN LAYOVERS

Misbooked for Love: A Valentine's Day Novella

ABOUT THE AUTHOR

Maria Rigou is a US-based author hailing from Argentina. She writes love stories full of longing, tenderness, and the exact amount of ache right before the HEA.

She lives in South Florida with her husband and two daughters and loves to read.

With the Wildflowers is her fourth book.

———

CONNECT ONLINE

www.mariarigou.com

@mariarigouauthor